HIS OTHER WOMAN

VALERIE KEOGH

Boldwood

First published in Great Britain in 2025 by Boldwood Books Ltd.

Copyright © Valerie Keogh, 2025

Cover Design by Head Design Ltd.

Cover Images: iStock

The moral right of Valerie Keogh to be identified as the author of this work has been asserted in accordance with the Copyright, Designs and Patents Act 1988.

All rights reserved. No part of this book may be reproduced in any form or by any electronic or mechanical means, including information storage and retrieval systems, without written permission from the author, except for the use of brief quotations in a book review. This book is a work of fiction and, except in the case of historical fact, any resemblance to actual persons, living or dead, is purely coincidental.

Every effort has been made to obtain the necessary permissions with reference to copyright material, both illustrative and quoted. We apologise for any omissions in this respect and will be pleased to make the appropriate acknowledgements in any future edition.

A CIP catalogue record for this book is available from the British Library.

Paperback ISBN 978-1-83617-847-7

Large Print ISBN 978-1-83617-846-0

Hardback ISBN 978-1-83617-845-3

Trade Paperback ISBN 978-1-80656-047-9

Ebook ISBN 978-1-83617-848-4

Kindle ISBN 978-1-83617-849-1

Audio CD ISBN 978-1-83617-840-8

MP3 CD ISBN 978-1-83617-841-5

Digital audio download ISBN 978-1-83617-844-6

This book is printed on certified sustainable paper. Boldwood Books is dedicated to putting sustainability at the heart of our business. For more information please visit https://www.boldwoodbooks.com/about-us/sustainability/

Boldwood Books Ltd, 23 Bowerdean Street, London, SW6 3TN

www.boldwoodbooks.com

For David Purkiss

1

LYDIA

It was still dark when I opened my eyes so I wasn't sure how long I'd been unconscious. My cheek was pressed into the thick pile of the carpet, and my head felt like it had been cracked open. I tried to sit up but the pain was excruciating, making me cry out and give up the attempt. Without moving, I could see where Rich lay on the floor a few feet away. He was looking in my direction, his arm extended, his hand close enough that I was able to reach for it. I wrapped my fingers around his and squeezed gently.

'Rich? You okay?'

He didn't answer. Nor did his fingers return the pressure on my hand. Worst of all – what made my eyes fill and a lump appear in my throat so that I swallowed convulsively – he didn't blink.

I was a crime fiction fan. TV or books, it didn't matter, I devoured them all. I particularly liked true-crime documentaries with their detailed explanation of the misdeed and the hunt for the perpetrator. Like a sponge, I'd absorbed knowledge along the way. So even in my shock, with my face still pressed to the floor and pain radiating from the back of my skull to blur my vision, I knew why he wasn't blinking. I recognised the nauseating stink that curled into my nostrils for what it was.

Rich was dead.

There was something else. It was hovering at the back of my mind, something important I was supposed to do... something... but whatever it was, it kept bouncing out of my grasp.

Gritting my teeth, I raised myself enough to look around the spacious hotel room. I'd spent hours on the website assessing the various options before choosing it. It was the wrong time to wish I'd made a different choice, that I'd chosen a compact room instead, one where a shout might be heard in the room next door or in the corridor outside. One where the phone wasn't taunting me from the console on the far side of the room.

A tentative effort to get to my feet, even to sit, failed. The pain made my head swim, my vision blurring even further. Raising a hand, I felt a warm, wet mass tangling my hair. It explained the pain, the confusion, and my inability to remember what it was I was supposed to do, because I was suddenly certain there had been something... but whatever it was, it was lost in my injuries.

I was hurt, but I was alive. A grim determination to ensure I stayed that way made me inch forward towards the phone.

Every movement sent my head swimming. I pushed Rich's arm out of the way and shuffled a few inches forward. As I came level with him, I stopped, ignored the pain and rose on my forearms to gaze into his face. Perhaps I'd been wrong. Perhaps it was the air-conditioning that had made his body stiff and cold. 'Rich?' I rested a hand against his cheek. 'Rich?' I slapped him, gently at first, then harder, the sound of flesh on flesh loud in the quiet. Tears blurred my vision even more.

I collapsed onto his shoulder and pressed my face into the curve of his neck. It would have been nice to think of happier times when I'd done the same, of days lying on the beach or in the fields after a picnic, but my imagination had never been that good. I'd always been the prosaic type, the doer and organiser, the facts person, not the dreamer.

Rich was dead. I was hurt – how badly, I wasn't sure. Perhaps I could simply stay there resting on him until housekeeping came in to service the room mid-morning. They'd get me help then. My eyes closed and I felt myself drift away. Head injuries could be fatal. It didn't need a vivid imagination to picture housekeeping turning up to find our dead bodies. But I'd gone through too much to give up now. Had worked way too hard to lose everything at this stage. The thought galvanised me.

The quickest way across to the phone was blocked by Rich. In death, as in life, he was a big man. Six-foot two of solid muscle, impossible to move. I rose onto my elbows, ignoring the instant dart of pain, and looked down at his face. A strong face. Handsome in a rugged, masculine way. There was always a twinkle in his eye, as if he was secretly laughing at you. I'd found it incredibly sexy. Until somewhere in the last few years, and I'm not sure when, that twinkle seemed to have died. Instead, when he looked at me, there had been something else lurking in his eyes, a certain hardness, almost a resignation that this was it: he was stuck with me. And somewhere in those same years, I seemed to have given up and become just the kind of woman I'd never wanted to be: pathetic, drab, and boring.

It was a bad time and way too late to have regrets, but I had them all the same. If only we'd sat down and talked when we'd first started to fall apart, perhaps we wouldn't have done. I rested my hand against Rich's face. Perhaps if he'd told me everything when we'd first met, things would be different. But he hadn't, so they weren't. He was dead; I might be dying.

The phone was tantalisingly close, but so far away. If I could have stood, I'd have stepped over Rich's body, but even propping myself on an elbow was taking its toll. When black dots shimmered across my vision, I knew I was going to faint. I lowered myself to the carpet but it took several seconds for the sensation to fade. I couldn't stand to step over my dead husband, and even if his body didn't look like an insurmountable mountain, I couldn't have brought myself to crawl over him.

Instead, I began to make my way around him. Inch by agonising inch. The carpet was against me, its thick pile slowing my progress as I pulled myself forward on my elbows, shutting my eyes against the pain. Blood trickled from the wound in my head, through my hair and down my forehead. I wiped it from my eyes and licked it from my lips and tried not to be too concerned when it kept coming.

They'd have to replace the carpet. The random thought brought me to a halt and I lowered myself to the floor once again, my forehead sinking into the soft pile. What did it say about me that I was lying inches away from my dead husband with an injury that might prove fatal, and my first thought was for the state of the carpet?

How terribly banal I was.

My eyes were heavy. According to all those crime series and documentaries I'd watched, it was a bad sign when someone became sleepy after a head injury. A bad sign... but I couldn't help it... Maybe, after all, it was better this way... Maybe, this was a better end than the one I'd planned... Maybe...

When the next blow came, it was almost a relief.

2

EIGHT WEEKS EARLIER

'I swear, I didn't know—'

'Well, now you do. Every detail of what I went through because of you. So you know how much you owe me, don't you?'

'I—'

'Don't!' Anger made the word vibrate. 'Don't you dare insult me by making excuses. This is the only thing I'm ever going to ask of you. Do it, then you'll never hear from me again.'

'Right.' A loud sigh followed. 'It's not going to be easy—'

'No, but you'll do it, yes?'

'Yes, I will.' Another sigh, longer, filled with guilt and regret. 'I owe you.'

3

FIONA

Fiona Carlton swirled her gin and tonic, making the ice cubes tinkle and the slice of lemon fight to stay afloat. 'Never wanted to be that girl,' she said, staring into the glass.

'Sounds like a line from a song,' her friend Jocelyn said.

'It is. Well, the title of a song, to be accurate. A Carly Pearse one. It could have been written about me.' So much so that Fiona had played the song on repeat when she'd discovered the man she was seeing – a man she was already falling in love with – was married. It didn't matter that she'd always known. Perhaps not from their first encounter, but certainly from that first evening.

Never wanted to be that girl.

The other woman. She'd thought she was so clever, that she could always spot those married men who were looking for a bit of fun. Sometimes, it was blindingly obvious: the indent on the ring finger where a wedding band normally sat, a certain reticence in sharing details, a caginess about where they lived. So many giveaways.

Perhaps if she'd met Rich in the usual way. In one of the wine bars she frequented, or through one of the many dating apps she'd tried when her friends told her she had to join the twenty-first century. They'd insisted it was the only way, the modern way, and totally acceptable. But she hadn't met him that way. She'd met him by accident. Literally. She'd been rushing to a meeting with a client, later than she'd hoped, and was desperately trying to read her notes as she speed-walked along the street.

Her head down as she rounded the corner, she'd crashed straight into a man coming the opposite direction. With a cry of alarm, her carefully collated notes had flown one direction and she went the other. A nearby wall had saved her from falling to the pavement. She'd hit it with a grunt, immediately bending to scrabble around her feet for the pages that had come unstuck and were in danger of being swept away. Unfortunately, she'd leant down at the same time as the man she'd walked into, and they'd knocked heads.

'Ouch, fuck.' She straightened and put a hand to her forehead.

'I'm so sorry,' he said, bending again to collect her paperwork and hand it to her. 'It was getting a bit Laurel and Hardy there, wasn't it?'

She'd have said *Fawlty Towers* herself, but maybe it was an age thing. She took the folder he'd handed her, shuffled the pages back inside the cover and hoped she'd have time to get them in order before her appointment.

'I think you have it all,' he said, bringing her eyes to him.

She was good at assessing people quickly. A smart coat over a sharp suit, crisp, white shirt, elegant tie – silk, she guessed – dark hair, greying at the temples. *Distinguished* was the word she'd have used if she'd been asked to describe him. She'd have said *handsome* too, and as she noticed the twinkle in the grey eyes, she added *sexy*.

'Yes,' she said.

He smiled then. Not just a polite upward tilt of his lips, but a full, teeth-baring, face-splitting smile. 'Yes, you'll have a drink with me?'

Colour crept over her cheeks. She considered herself immune to every chat-up line she'd ever heard – and she'd heard many – but there was something about this man. She didn't believe in love at first sight, but lust, that was a different matter and she was old enough, wise enough, to acknowledge exactly what it was that had flared between them. Unadulterated lust.

'That's not possible—'

He held the smile, tilting his head a little. 'Because you can't, or because you don't want to?'

Because you're way too sure of yourself. Because you might just as well have dangerous *tattooed across your forehead. Because I'm old enough to know better.*

'I have an appointment.' She tilted her wrist to check the gold watch that circled it. 'In five minutes, to be exact.'

'And after?'

He was persistent. With no dimming of his smile, or in the pronounced twinkle in his eyes. She glanced at his left hand. He was wearing gloves so she couldn't check to see if he was wearing a ring.

'A coffee, or a glass of wine? I'll leave the choice to you.' His smile faded, the light in his eyes dimming a little as he waited for her reply. 'To make up for almost knocking you over.'

Almost knocking her over. Weakening her defences. Making her say, 'Yes, okay, a glass of wine would be nice,' when she really, really should have laughed, shaken her head and moved on.

His smile returned. Full-on. He pointed to the street ahead. 'Do you know Dexters?'

It was a wine bar she knew well. Lots of polished wood,

small, comfortable booths, flattering lighting. It was a perfect assignation spot and she instantly had a change of heart.

'Maybe this isn't such a good idea.' There was no *maybe* about it. It was a very bad idea. This kind of man, so confident in his skin, so damn sexy, brimming with charisma, he was the type of man she should run from. She was definitely old enough to know better, but also, stupidly, old enough to think she could handle this. Later, she'd wonder if that had been her first mistake.

He reached out, tapped her arm gently with a hand. 'It's just a glass of wine. Don't overthink it.'

He was right. Of course he was. It was just a glass of wine. A welcome drink after what had been one of those days when anything that could possibly have gone wrong had done. She made one last attempt to put him off, one more attempt to save herself. 'I won't be free for at least an hour.'

'An hour?' He flicked the cuff of his shirt back and frowned at his watch. 'Actually, that works perfectly.' The smile returned. 'Dexters in an hour. I'll be waiting.'

He was gone before Fiona could change her mind. Because she was about to. She shook her head, glanced quickly at the contents of the folder she'd dropped, reshuffled some pages, then resumed her journey. She'd get through this meeting, then catch a taxi home. Have a bath, get cosy, have a glass of wine and watch something mindless on TV.

That was what she'd do.

It was what she should have done.

Instead, she'd gone to Dexters. When she went inside, he was there, sitting on a stool, his eyes fixed on the door, a smile spreading when he saw her. He got to his feet and walked towards her, closing in to kiss her on both cheeks, as naturally as if they'd known each other for a long time. She caught the scent of him, clean, earthy, masculine, and felt a jolt of desire. She had enough self-awareness to recognise the sensation for what it was. Nothing wrong with it. She was thirty-eight, in the full of her health. Desire was a natural reaction to a handsome, sexy man.

It was what you did with the sensation that mattered.

And she wasn't planning on doing anything.

* * *

She thought back to that first encounter and swirled the ice cubes around in her glass again as she felt Jocelyn's eyes on her. There'd be sympathy in them. Perhaps even pity. They'd been friends for a long time, had shared tears over disastrous relationships: men who had broken Fiona's heart, women who'd broken Jocelyn's.

Fiona stopped playing with her drink and swallowed half in a couple of mouthfuls. 'It was just supposed to be a glass of wine. His apology for almost knocking me over.'

* * *

One drink had led to another, and another, he laughing that they should have bought a bottle, she wondering where her willpower had parked itself. Dexters did food, but nothing either of them fancied, so he suggested they go to a restaurant he knew. 'It's not far; we could walk,' he'd said.

'It's Friday night; we won't get a table.'

'Of course we will,' he'd said, with a certainty she quickly came to understand was the way he approached everything. As if the world wouldn't dare to let him down.

A part of her wanted him to be proved wrong, for them to be turned away when they walked through the door of a very upmarket restaurant. But not only were they offered a table, but the maître d' had greeted him by name and with a deferential manner that only came from knowledge – and from money.

More wine, excellent food, stimulating conversation. By the time his expression took on a serious slant, when he'd stared into his wine glass and said, 'There's something I should tell you,' it was already too late. None so blind as those who don't want to see, and she hadn't wanted to. The instant attraction she'd felt when they'd literally bumped into each other, the jolt of desire when she'd walked into Dexters, they were nothing to what she felt now. Not love – she wasn't that naïve – more a powerful attraction that grabbed her and knocked sense out of the window.

Live in the moment, she told herself as she held a hand up to stop whatever it was he was going to say. Anyway, he didn't need to say anything. He hadn't been wearing his gloves in Dexters; she'd seen the truth. 'Why don't we keep it simple. It's just tonight. A lovely evening. No strings. No promises.' She'd meant it. She didn't need complications, and she'd known from their first encounter, from the way he'd looked at her with such intensity, as if he was looking at her soul, that this man had them in spades.

* * *

'He should have told you he was married before it went any further,' Jocelyn said.

'He tried to. That first night, he'd said there was something he wanted to tell me and I stopped him, so you can't blame him. It didn't matter anyway; by then, I'd seen his wedding ring. I knew he was married.'

Jocelyn sniffed. 'He didn't strike me as a man who could be stopped from doing anything he wanted to do.'

'You only met him once.' At an exhibition in the art gallery Jocelyn's wife owned. It had been Rich and Fiona's third date. They hadn't slept together as yet, and that was going to be the night they did. Both knew it and she supposed they'd made it clear with their constant touching, the knowing smiles, the sexual chemistry that could have powered the rather overwhelming lighting that the artist had insisted on using for his exhibition. They'd moved from one gigantic painting to the next, from the over-lit areas to the darker corners where they'd kissed, where his hands had shimmied over the slip dress she'd worn. The heat of his fingers had seared her skin, making her forget herself, forget where they were.

She remembered Jocelyn had been less than impressed, shooting them quelling looks that only made Fiona giggle and Rich shrug his shoulders before pulling her into a clinch.

'Once was enough,' Jocelyn said. 'Honestly, you behaved abominably, as if all the filters of normal behaviour had been wiped away. I still think you were both high on something.' She held a hand up quickly. 'And please, don't say you were high on each other unless you want me to puke!'

'I wasn't going to say that.' Embarrassingly, Fiona was about to say just that, because it was exactly how she'd felt. After dinner that first night, they'd gone for a walk along the Thames, holding hands, lost in conversation, deaf and blind to the traffic. By the end, before he'd left her at the door of her apartment block, she knew three things:

That he was married.

That she didn't care.

And, for the first time, she thought maybe... just maybe... she could have it all.

4

FIONA

Fiona wasn't lying to her friend. Or to herself either. She had never wanted to be that girl. And she hated herself for being in a situation she'd always sworn to avoid. The problem was that she loved Rich more.

Jocelyn lifted a hand to catch the bartender's attention; once she had it, she lifted her glass, wagged it, and held up two fingers. 'So what are you going to do?' she said, bringing her attention back to Fiona.

'Do?' As if it was that simple. As if she could do something to make everything okay. Wave a magic wand. Cast a spell. Turn back the clock to the day she'd met Rich, choose a different path to travel to that meeting, leave the office a minute earlier, a minute later, avoid that twist of fate that had her bump into him. 'I'm not sure.'

Two fresh drinks arrived on the bar before them. Jocelyn emptied the last of her drink into the new one. Lifting the brimming glass carefully, she took a sip. 'I suppose it's only been two months,' she said putting the glass down.

Fiona resisted using the perennial cry of the misunderstood, the childish *you don't understand*. She was a mature, intelligent, university-educated, successful woman. And Jocelyn was right. It *had* only been two months. But she was also wrong. There were no shades of grey in Jocelyn's world. She saw things in uncomplicated black and white. Perhaps because for her, things aways had been – she'd started working in the gallery when she finished an art's degree in university. Ten years later, she and the gallery owner married on a beach in Mexico. Fiona wasn't sure if everything worked out for Jocelyn because she was so black and white, or because she was so black and white, everything worked out for her. It was the old chicken-and-egg conundrum.

But she was wrong to think that two months was too short a time to change someone's life. How could a woman who'd married the first person she'd fallen crazily in love with, and to whom she was still happily married after all these years, possibly understand Fiona's situation? Especially as she wasn't sure she completely understood it herself.

Since that first evening, a day hadn't gone by that she didn't speak to Rich. Not just messages. Proper old-fashioned phone calls squeezed into minutes between rushing from appointment to appointment, phone pressed to her ear as she hurried along the street. She'd speak to him in a hushed voice while sitting on the toilet, giggling like a school child when she told him where she was. They chatted on the Tube, in a taxi. Anywhere. Everywhere. It quickly became an addiction. An obsession. She simply couldn't get enough of him.

Normally careful, fully focused on her career, wise to men and their shenanigans, she sometimes felt as if he'd cast a spell over her. Bewitched her.

Feeling Jocelyn's eyes on her, she huffed a laugh and picked up her drink.

'Seriously,' Jocelyn said quietly. 'I think you need to forget about this guy.'

Again with the stupid advice. Making everything seem so fucking simple. It was so damn easy for her. She had it all: a successful business, a woman who loved her. Was it wrong that Fiona was just a tiny bit envious of what her friend had, and wanted it for herself? Maybe Rich had cast a spell over her, because despite being married, he struck her as being perfect.

'I can't forget about him. It's not so easy to detach myself from my emotions!'

It was Jocelyn's turn to huff a laugh, and she did so, loudly, shaking her head as if it was the funniest thing she'd heard. 'Come on, Fiona, you're not an eighteen-year-old filled with hormones and angst. You're thirty-eight, supposedly sophisticated, worldly-wise. You're a kick-ass businesswoman, with more balls than most men I know, so of course you can. What you need is more introspection. Socrates says—'

Fiona chopped a hand in the air between them, startling her friend into silence. Jocelyn's expression quickly changed from supportive to aggrieved. It put Fiona on the back foot, making her once more the guilty party. 'I'm sorry,' she said. And she was, she didn't mean to offend her friend but God almighty, every bloody time she had a problem, Jocelyn came out with the same blasted quotation. *The unexamined life is not worth living.* Fiona wasn't sure if it simply happened to fit whatever predicament she'd found herself in, or whether it was the only quotation Jocelyn knew. Did she think that quoting Socrates made her sound profound? It would take a lot more than that to make the rather superficial woman approach any level of profundity.

Fiona sighed as the bitchy thought sizzled through her head. Her friend deserved better. 'I really am sorry, and you're right. I need to put Rich from my head and my life.'

Luckily, although Jocelyn was easily offended, she was also easily appeased, and Fiona's apology resulted in almost immediate relaxation in the tension between them. Before more advice she'd no intention of following was offered, Fiona hurried to change the subject. 'Enough about my love life – tell me about this next exhibition you're arranging.'

It was the perfect distraction; Jocelyn was always more than happy to have the conversation turned towards her beloved gallery. Her enthusiasm was both entertaining and infectious and usually Fiona, who was genuinely interested in the workings of the gallery, was happy to listen. And she did, for a few minutes, until her thoughts drifted back to Rich and when she was going to see him again.

'...on the fifteenth. Do you think you'll be free to come?'

Fiona tuned back in. She assumed Jocelyn was still speaking about the upcoming exhibition and nodded emphatically. 'I wouldn't miss it.'

'Brilliant. I wasn't sure it'd be your thing, although it's such a good cause, isn't it?'

A good cause? Maybe she hadn't been talking about the exhibition at all. Shit. What had Fiona just agreed to?

'Yes, yes, it is, an excellent cause.'

'Fancy dress is optional, of course, but I think most people will get into the spirit of the thing since it's so close to Christmas.'

Close to Christmas? So the fifteenth of December, not November. But double shit! Fancy fucking dress. She'd have to confess and tell Jocelyn that she hadn't been listening. While she was being honest, perhaps she should confess that she'd no intention of putting Rich out of her head or her life. That she was consumed by him. Jocelyn would raise her eyebrows, shake her head, and she might even try to quote Socrates again.

No, perhaps confessing wasn't a good idea. It was a better

option to try to prise the information from her without having to admit she hadn't been listening. 'What are you and Kate planning to go as?'

That drew a devilish laugh from Jocelyn. 'Kate wanted us to go and Mrs and Mrs Claus but I nixed that. Too twee for words. So we're going as the little drummer boy. I'm wearing a rather sexy little military-style suit and Kate is—'

'Going dressed as a drum?' Fiona couldn't help it; she laughed. 'I don't know how she puts up with you. So you are going to look fab, and she's going to be sweltering inside some big drum costume?'

'I did say that I'd wear the drum costume, but she insisted she wanted to, so what's a girl to do?'

They had been married ten years, and Kate was still absolutely smitten. If, sometimes, Fiona shook her head at how lovey-dovey they were, at the way Kate obviously adored Jocelyn, and if she sometimes sneered at the whole exclusiveness of their love, mostly she envied it.

Now, with Rich, she didn't have to. He looked at her the way Kate looked at Jocelyn. There he was again, intruding into her thoughts. She shut him away and concentrated on the conversation. 'You could have gone as two Christmas fairies, then both of you would have looked amazing.'

'Way too much of a cliché,' Jocelyn said with a smile. 'You could get away with it. I'd like to see you as a fairy.'

'Not my scene at all, my friend. But I'll think of something.'

'Well, you'd better look into it soon. The fifteenth of December will be here before you can blink and it's a busy time for costume-rental companies. Plus, if you're going to stay over, you'd better book a room if the hotel isn't already booked out.'

Stay over? Triple shit. Why hadn't she put Rich out of her head for just a few minutes and listened to what Jocelyn had been saying? How long had Fiona been lost in her thoughts that it had gone from talk about an exhibition to whatever the hell this was? 'Perhaps I'd better try them now. Do you have their number to hand?'

Jocelyn reached for her handbag, pulled it open and rummaged inside. She pulled out her mobile, tapped for a few seconds, then handed it over. 'There you go.'

Fiona took it and read quickly.

Cranford Castle is delighted to host the Art United Christmas Charity Ball.

She didn't read any further. Art United. The words were flashing, neon bright, making her blink and reach up to squeeze the corners of her eyes with her thumb and first finger, careful not to smudge her eye make-up, refusing to descend to panda-eyed misery.

'You okay?' Jocelyn's voice, full of quick sympathy.

Fiona took her fingers away and blinked rapidly. 'New mascara, it seems to be irritating my eyes a little.'

It was the perfect excuse to offer the make-up-obsessed Jocelyn, who launched into a detailed monologue on the dubious ingredients some companies added to their products.

Once again, Fiona wasn't listening. The Art United charity. Rich had mentioned it; she thought he might be a patron. So he was bound to be at the ball.

With his wife.

If she was still around.

December the fifteenth was six weeks away.

Anything could happen between now and then.

Fiona pictured herself walking into the charity ball with Rich. They'd go as themselves. A dynamic duo. And heads would turn to look at them and people would whisper that they were obviously so in love.

She had six weeks. It was plenty of time for secrets to be revealed, accidents to happen, lives to change.

Fiona wasn't sure what she could do, but that had never stopped her before...

5

FIONA

Fiona preferred to use the word *focused* rather than *obsessed*, which had such negative connotations. Jocelyn would say she was fooling herself. Perhaps she was. There was probably a host of articles written about where the line was between focus and obsession but she wasn't going to give them any coinage by looking them up.

Actually, *determined* was probably the better word to use. She liked to think it defined her completely. When she saw something she wanted, she went for it. Her role as investment consultant with one of the biggest London firms was one she'd fought for, working ridiculously long hours to prove herself, knowing that even now in the twenty-first century, a woman had to be twice, even three times better than a man to have a chance at winning.

Through those years when work was her priority, love was always an afterthought. Lust was easily satisfied. Like everything else, when she saw a man she wanted, she went for it. Satisfying sex, no strings, no distraction.

And then Rich had come along, found a crack in her armour,

and wriggled his way in. She could have pushed him out again, of course. And she might have done, if he hadn't quickly, unexpectedly, become part of her. Now she had a choice: give Rich up, or claim him for herself.

She'd booked a hotel room for that charity function. Rich would be at it, whether or not his wife was at his side. Fiona had six weeks to try to organise it to be *not*.

Booking the room was the easy step. She wasn't entirely sure what the other steps to her goal would be. If she was being completely honest, she wasn't even 100 hundred per cent sure what that goal was. Marriage? Did she really want that? She wasn't sure, but she *was* sure she didn't want Rich married to someone else.

Without a clear idea of what to do, she decided being armed with knowledge would be a good first step. To learn everything she could about this woman she wanted to be rid of.

So much of her work took place out of the office, whether it was visiting clients in their homes or places of business, or occasionally working from home; it left her free to do some investigating. She refused to use the word *stalking*, although it popped into her head. Contrary to what her friend imagined, Fiona did examine her life and her thoughts. Examined, then ignored what she didn't like.

Rich and his wife – Fiona knew her name but refused to use it, as if personalising her made her more real, more human. She recognised it for what it was. Guilt. Because she had never wanted to be the type of woman who'd happily steal another woman's man. How naïve she'd been. It wasn't something she'd actively done; it was something that had crept over her against her will at that first meeting with Rich. It had imprisoned her. Made her behave totally out of character.

That's why she was there, in her car, parked at the kerb opposite the house Rich and his wife shared.

She'd no idea what the wife's routine was, whether she left the house every morning to go to work, a gym, or to meet friends for coffee. It was hardly the kind of thing she could ask Rich. After his initial attempt to tell Fiona about his wife, he'd never referred to her or mentioned her name.

He hadn't said where they lived either but that was easy for Fiona to find out. Like her, he worked in finance, and there was always someone who knew someone who had the answers she needed. She peered through the car window and reluctantly admired the large, detached home. What would be described in estate agent speak as a *fine family residence*. She knew Rich had two children, thankfully grown-up and living elsewhere. If she'd been interested she could have discovered where, but finding out they didn't live at home was sufficient for her needs.

There were no children to keep Rich tied to a wife he didn't love, in a marriage he'd outgrown. Of course, he hadn't admitted to either, but Fiona saw how his eyes lit up when she arrived, the way his shoulders relaxed, the lines of tension on his face ease. He was happy with her; he wanted to *be* with her.

From where she sat, Fiona could see through the wide gateway and up the short drive to the front door. She'd searched for photographs of the wife, but she obviously wasn't keen on the public gaze; of the many events Rich had to attend, and all the photographs of him, there were none of her.

Surprisingly, she had little social media presence either. That or she kept her privacy levels high. Fiona, who posted on social media at least daily, was surprised that anyone could stay under the radar in the twenty-first century.

Her desire to see what the competition looked like was reaching desperation level. It was almost tempting to go across and ring the doorbell with some made-up excuse. She would have done too, except there was always the chance that the wife knew about her husband's affair. Since Fiona had a huge social-media presence, if the wife had any curiosity about her, she'd recognise her immediately. Fiona imagined the scene and shuddered at the image of face-slapping and name-calling that sprung to mind.

Luckily, she could work from the car, so the time wasn't completely wasted. She opened her laptop and answered a few emails. At the end of every sentence, her eyes flicked upward and she stared at the door, then she went back to her emails.

It wasn't until nearly eleven, two hours after she'd arrived, that the front door opened and a woman appeared. The laptop was dropped quickly onto the passenger seat as Fiona scrabbled for her mobile. The gods were looking out for her because instead of jumping into the snazzy BMW parked in the driveway, the wife left the house on foot. She walked past Fiona on the other side of the road, and strolled along without a care in the world.

Fiona caught it all on video.

When the wife was gone from view, she replayed it, slowly, stopping now and then to zoom in for a closer look. She was a dyed blonde – no criticism there, so was Fiona. But unlike Fiona, the wife was showing signs of her age, with sagging jowls and thinning hair. She'd probably chosen the unflattering baggy jacket to hide curves that had become far too curvaceous. A bad choice – all it had done was to emphasise her size. And the colour – Fiona wondered with a snigger if the wife was perhaps colour-blind.

Comparisons were always unfair to someone, and usually, Fiona didn't stoop to making them. There was always going to be someone more successful, more beautiful, slimmer, richer. But she was only human, and in the comparison stakes with Rich's wife, Fiona knew she won hands down.

It should have made her feel better. But it didn't. Because this was the woman Rich was choosing to stay with. The one he went home to after spending hours with Fiona. Hours where they'd had dinner, drinks, walked hand in hand back to her apartment, and had wild and incredibly satisfying sex.

She watched the video again and again. Each time, the viewing irritated her more. This overweight woman, going to seed, was holding on to the man Fiona wanted.

She hadn't become a successful businesswoman by waiting for things to happen. She'd learnt that if you wanted something, if you wanted it bad enough, you went after it and got it.

And nothing, or nobody, got in her way.

6

LYDIA

I wasn't sure when things started to change.

'It's empty-nest syndrome,' my friend Alice said, nodding as if she knew the answers to all the world's problems. Or perhaps she'd found them at the end of what was her third (or was it her fourth?) drink.

She wasn't right. The twins had left home several years before when they'd chosen to go to university in Edinburgh rather than London. They'd come home for holidays and for a couple of months between jobs, but I knew they'd never live at home again. It didn't make me sad. I'd brought both up to have the confidence to cut the family strings and make their own way in the world. Granted, I didn't expect them to go quite so far, but when Missy went to work in Sydney three years earlier, I knew it was only a matter of time before her brother followed her trail.

When he did, Rich and I went to visit, and we fell in love with Sydney as the twins had done. For a short time, we'd considered moving there too, but for one reason or another, nothing had come of that idea. I might envy my children with their supreme self-confidence, their belief that the world was theirs for the taking, I might even miss them at times, but it wasn't their absence that had caused my life to shift ever so slightly off its axis. Not enough to make me completely miserable, but enough to make the weight of every day just that much more difficult to bear.

'Perhaps you're right,' I said to Alice, because I was suddenly sorry I'd brought it up. The couple of drinks had made me unusually unguarded, enough to ask my friend if she ever felt that life had suddenly taken a wrong turn. Perhaps if we'd been closer friends, I might have admitted the truth. That it was my relationship with Rich that seemed to have changed. Back in university, there had been friends I would have opened my heart to, friends to whom I'd have told everything. We'd lost touch over the years and it seemed I'd also lost the ability to make friends like that.

No, that wasn't quite true. I hadn't made new friends because I hadn't needed them. I had Rich, our relationship was so good, so close, that I could tell him everything, anything.

I'm not sure when that stopped. When I noticed his eyes glaze over as I spoke, his noncommittal replies, the lack of genuine – or any kind – of interest in what I was saying.

When had he started to find me pathetic rather than amusing? I'd seen the extra lines that had appeared almost overnight on my face and the slight sagging along my jawline. And the thickening of my waist, no matter what damn diet I tried, no matter how many bloody repetitions of whatever new faddy exercise that shouted itself to be *the* one that would make the difference.

Was that the simple, sad answer? That I was getting old and he no longer found me attractive, entertaining – *fanciable*?

God, had we sunk to that awful cliché? Had he found someone else – someone younger, more vibrant?

Or after forty years, had he finally decided he wanted to see what else was out there? We – or maybe it was just I – had prided myself on the fact I'd only ever slept with one man. Rich used to be able to say he'd only ever slept with me; would he be able to say that now?

Or had he stopped being able to say that a long time ago? Maybe I was fooling myself – seeing life as I wanted it to be, not as it was. Life as it was – when had it become so dull? Was that it? Had Rich gone looking for excitement and found it with another woman? I pictured him in his smart suits, the crisp, white shirts I ironed, the silk ties I chose, the grey at his temples only adding to his good looks. A silver fox: is that what they'd call him? I'd seen women at those ghastly functions we used to attend, giving him the once-over. Glamorous, attractive, charming, *exciting* women.

Exciting women with dynamic lives and high-powered jobs. I had thought about going back to work when the children were old enough, but somehow, there was always some family emergency that stopped me. By the time they went to university, and I'd seriously thought about getting back into the workforce, my basic computer skills excluded me from anything I wanted to do. Instead, I took a volunteer job at a local charity shop for two afternoons a week. I thought it'd give me something to talk about, but I can't remember the last time Rich and I had talked about anything.

If he'd gone looking for excitement, if he was having an affair...

'...so I thought we'd go as Tweedledee and Tweedledum; what d'you think?'

Since I was at that precise moment imagining Rich in a tryst with some slim, gorgeous woman, the arrival of the rotund twins into the conversation came as a surprise and it took a few seconds for my brain to catch up with the conversation. It wasn't difficult. Since we'd decided to go to it the previous month, Alice had brought up the Art United fancy dress charity ball every time we'd met. It was still six weeks away, so I suppose I'd better get used to it being a continuous topic of conversation.

So what did I think? I'd met Alice's husband, Trevor, a number of times over the years. Like her, he was a small man, but unlike her, who had managed to remain somewhat slim, he was almost as round as he was tall. He also had incredibly thin legs. If they were going to go with non-Christmas characters, Humpty Dumpty might have been a better choice but that would have meant being cruel, and I might be sad and pathetic, my husband might have swapped me for a younger model, but I refused to be cruel. I settled for voicing my confusion. 'It's not exactly Christmassy though, is it?' I said, because it wasn't, unless I was missing something. Like a new movie – *Tweedledum and Tweedledee Do Christmas*, perhaps.

Alice laughed as if I'd said something hilariously funny. 'You're so behind the times,' she said with a dismissive shake of her head. 'Angels, fairies and elves are passé. These days, it's fantasy figures. Lewis Carroll's *Alice in Wonderland* is particularly popular.'

I was tempted to launch into a discussion about the importance of tradition, to have sung the praises of Santa Claus and elves in an attempt at misdirection, to force my brain to think of anything apart from the scene that kept forcing itself into my head. Because now that I'd convinced myself Rich must be having an affair, nothing would do for my imagination but to paint full-colour photographs of his mistress on the back of my eyelids. She was tall, tanned, slim – of course – and was stretched out on cream satin sheets. Not naked. That would be tawdry. No, but what she was wearing were wisps of lace-embellished silk that barely covered her nipples and showed that she was an advocate of Brazilian waxes.

She wouldn't be a woman who bought her bras in Sainsbury's for convenience. A three pack usually. Always in beige. And I bet her knickers always matched her bra. I couldn't remember the last time I'd bothered to do that. Had I ever? Or was I always a grab the first bra and knickers that came to hand kind of girl?

My sigh had Alice raise an eyebrow and stop whatever she was saying. I doubt if it was anything interesting because it rarely was. I looked at her and saw a reflection of myself. Two dull, uninteresting women with little to contribute to anything.

Even this Christmas ball. I wasn't exactly sure what the charity did apart from a vague idea that it provided funds for emerging artists. Or something along those lines anyway. I was pretty sure if I asked Alice, she'd give much the same elusive answer. It was our husbands who were involved in it; both Trevor and Rich were patrons of this and other charities.

Alice was still waiting for me to explain that hefty sigh so I came up with the first thing I could think of. 'I'm wondering if I should have made more of an effort with our costumes.'

Her eyebrow stayed raised for a few seconds, as if to emphasise that she didn't believe worrying about what fancy dress to wear could be responsible for such a weighty sigh, but then, unsurprisingly, she shrugged. Alice believed in keeping things light, superficial, unchallenging. God forbid that she'd have to think, make a decision, or give advice. Her eyebrow descended to join its twin as she went with my comment. 'What had you planned to wear?'

I hadn't planned anything – the fifteenth was weeks away – but backed into a corner, I quickly came up with something suitable. 'We're going as Mr and Mrs Claus.'

The response was a blank stare, as if she didn't understand.

'You know, Santa Claus and his wife.'

'Well, it's seasonal,' she finally said, as if in her head, she'd censored the comment, had decided to delete the *if not very imaginative* that had originally been part of it.

'Someone has to do the boring, traditional bit,' I said. She could sit back and accept things the way they were turning out, where being boring and banal was the norm, where the most exciting thing was to go to the ball as bloody Tweedledum and fucking Tweedledee, and where having a fling with some floozy was perfectly acceptable. But someone had to stand up and fight for the status quo. For the way things were supposed to be. For Santa Claus and fidelity.

I clenched my hands into tight fists under the table as I thought of my husband with another woman. If he was having an affair, it would just be a fling, wouldn't it?

It wouldn't be serious.

He wouldn't be planning to leave me.

Because if he thought he could, if he thought that, after forty years, he could swap me for a newer, younger, shinier model, he didn't know me at all.

7

FIONA

Fiona sat in the car, fingers drumming on the steering wheel. If she could have frowned, she would have done, but thanks to regular visits to a very expensive beauty salon, the ability to express emotion by creasing her face was kept at bay. If only she could have eased the irritation so easily. Botox for the spirit. Therapy by any other name.

It was illogical to direct her ire at a woman she didn't know, but then there was no logic in love. *Love.* She rolled the word around her mouth. It was a much sweeter word than lust even if lust was far more honest. If she considered her situation with her practical, pragmatic hat on, she'd have used the word *obsessed* rather than love for what she felt for Rich.

It was the whole rightness of him. Apart from being married, that is. Every attribute, every character trait, every quirk of his personality wrapped up as they were in an attractive package, made him the embodiment of the perfect partner.

He was her last chance.

It was a stupid comment made by a friend at her thirty-eighth birthday bash two months previously that had forced Fiona to reconsider her future. She'd invited a group of friends and acquaintances to celebrate with her at London's latest trendy nightclub, paying the club a ridiculous amount of money to cordon off one section for their sole use and to provide canapés and champagne.

Everyone she'd invited had turned up. A few were genuine friends. Most were acquaintances or work colleagues she was hoping to impress. The canapés were amazing, the champagne flowed fairly freely, the music was loud and energetic and it had been a very successful evening until her friend Debbie had swayed over to her side.

'Great party,' she said. She tipped her almost-empty glass against Fiona's nearly full one, then turned and with slightly slurred words that said she'd had more than one or two glasses of bubbly, added, 'D'you remember when we were that age?'

The section cordoned off for their use was on a dais set above the general dance floor. Fiona turned to look in the direction Debbie was indicating and saw a group of younger women gyrating with more energy than rhythm. The nightclub had a minimum age requirement of twenty-one. Fiona guessed some of these women were using fake IDs. She put them at seventeen, maybe eighteen.

'Yes,' she said, answering the question. 'It doesn't seem that long ago.'

'Until you realise how much extra you have to pay every time you visit the beauty salon to stay looking this good.' Debbie drained her glass and looked around with unfocused eyes for the waiter. 'Until you realise you've missed the boat.' Without elaborating on which *boat* she felt she'd missed, she drifted away, the glass held high like a beacon.

Fiona didn't move. It was irritating, but her friend was correct about visits to the beauty salon. She'd noticed the last couple of times she'd been to hers that the beautician, or *aesthetician* as she liked to refer to herself, was suggesting more and more tweaks and treatments. Thirty-eight. It wasn't old.

She let her gaze drift around the rest of the nightclub. It was, as befitting the latest in-place, packed with beautiful people. *Young*, beautiful people. She suddenly felt old, like a bloody dinosaur. What had possessed her to book a nightclub? A restaurant would have been better. Who was she trying to impress? Worse, what was she trying to prove? That she hadn't, as Debbie had put it, missed the boat?

Her friends – the real ones – would be leaving soon. Returning to their partners, husbands, wives, children. And she – well, unless she made an effort and hooked up with someone – she'd be heading home alone. She glanced over the potential candidates, her attention caught by one attractive man in a well-cut, dark suit. Tall, well-built, he'd be her choice. She could invite him to cross the cordon and join them. Perhaps tell him that she was the birthday girl and give him a hint that he might be her birthday gift.

She smoothed a hand over the silk dress she wore, lifted her chin and assumed her best sultry look – the slightly narrowed eyes and pursed lips she knew worked so well – and prepared to hunt down her prey. A last glance in his direction told her he was on the move. Perhaps he'd noticed her regard and was coming across to speak to her. It suited her; she was quite happy to change roles, to be the prey rather than the hunter.

But it seemed she was destined to be neither. He was on the hunt, but his prey was one of the gyrating women. One of the *younger* women.

Fiona didn't wait to see if he was successful or not. She turned back to her party, wishing it was over. That she could go home, change out of the shoes that were killing her and the dress she thought might have been an expensive mistake, and curl up on the sofa with a good book.

Like the older woman she was.

The irritation had lasted the remainder of the weekend and had carried into the Monday morning, making everything more irksome, delaying decisions, slowing her thoughts. It was the same irritation that had made her late for the meeting and had her rushing down the street with her thoughts in a tangle.

And then, there he was. Rich. A balm for her damaged pride. A sticky plaster for the wound to her ego.

Looking back, she thought it was that very moment, that second of impact, when she'd looked into her future and decided to change its trajectory.

8
FIONA

Of course, a change of trajectory required clearing a path. Fiona stopped tapping her fingers on the steering wheel. She hadn't got to where she was by sitting and waiting for things to happen. Being proactive and dynamic. That was the secret.

That's what made her push open the car door, grab her coat and bag, and speed walk after Rich's wife.

It wasn't difficult. Wherever the wife was heading, she wasn't in a rush to get there and Fiona caught up with her within a couple of minutes. She slowed her stride to remain a safe distance behind, her eyes sliding critically over the wide expanse of rear end that swayed ahead of her.

It was no wonder Rich had run a hand over her backside with such obvious admiration when this was the alternative. She'd wanted to ask him if he still made love with his wife, but she was afraid of the answer he might give. Worse, he might trot out that old chestnut, *my wife doesn't understand me,* leaving Fiona with no choice but to dump someone who'd utter such shite.

But she hadn't asked, and he hadn't volunteered any information, neither good nor bad, about his marriage.

She wondered if he'd be happy to continue as they were. Talking every day, often several times, but only meeting once or twice a week. Usually for dinner, in the same out of the way restaurant where neither was likely to meet anyone they knew. He, because he wouldn't want to meet anyone who was going to run with tales to his wife, and she, because she didn't want to see someone's eyes lighting on the gold band Rich wore, and their eyes widen in surprise before flicking to her face with varying degrees of condemnation. Because when it came to a relationship between a married man and a single woman, the criticism would always be aimed at the woman.

He could have removed the ring, could have slipped it into his pocket on his way to meet her. Did he think wearing it made him more honest? That it was proof he wasn't misleading her in any way? She could see he was a married man, therefore if she was with him, in possession of all the facts, of course the blame was hers.

Or was she being paranoid? The choice of where they ate had always been hers, not his. Had she suggested one of the more popular eateries, would he have agreed or looked at her in horror?

Another of the things she didn't want to find out.

What she had to cling on to, what kept her going in the moments of doubt, wasn't the 'I love you' he whispered in her ears, it wasn't what he said, or didn't say, it was the look in his eyes when they met, and the sadness in them when he was leaving her.

Perhaps he was happy as they were. Why wouldn't he be? He had a wife and a mistress. Wasn't that called having his cake and eating it?

If anything was going to change, it was up to Fiona to change it.

And this was the first step.

She could do it.

If she wanted something, if she'd set her heart on it, she'd make it happen.

She remembered Phillip and smiled. Making things happen was her forte.

9

FIONA

The financial services company where Fiona had worked for the previous five years was one of the most influential and well-regarded in the city. She'd worked long hours, kissed the right feet, slobbered over the more influential of the company's directors while staying just this side of politically correct.

She had a lot in her favour. She was beautiful, slim, sophisticated, charming – and most of all, she was far more intelligent than her peers. It did not, however, prevent less intelligent, and far less deserving men being promoted ahead of her. Anyone who thought things had changed in the twenty-first century didn't work in finance.

Worse was having to accept these promotions with good grace.

She did. For the first four years. Then early this year, when a senior financial advisor role had risen, she was sure it was her time. She'd worked for it, she deserved it, and when it was given to smarmy Phillip Coren, she'd wanted to go to the CEO and poke his eyes out.

It would have been just about acceptable if she'd thought

he'd won the promotion on merit. But what was Phillip's skill? Was he the best negotiator? The canniest financial guru? Of course not. What he was though, was a bloody marvel at golf. Because while Fiona was working all the hours God sent her, evenings and weekends, he was perfecting his shots down on the golf course.

And that's what had swung it for him. Not being the best at what he did, but the best at hitting a little round ball into a little round hole.

Fiona was having lunch with a group of colleagues when she heard the news about his promotion. She'd felt all their eyes on her, waiting for her response, probably hoping she'd explode. Instead, she did what she did best and put on her most charming expression. 'Oh that's good news, isn't it? He's the perfect candidate for the role. It couldn't happen to a nicer guy either.' She saw disappointment in some eyes that they weren't getting the show they'd hoped for, approbation in others for the opposite reason, and she knew she'd pulled it off.

She'd left the office on time for a change that evening and had taken a slight detour to a bar she seldom frequented, drinking double vodkas until the anger had reduced to a simmer. Then she'd drunk a few more bought for her by a guy who'd been eyeing her from the far end of the bar, the gleam in his eye growing as she knocked back drink after drink.

'Has anyone ever told you that you're gorgeous?' he said, running a finger over the hand that was wrapped around the glass.

It was so unbelievably trite that drunk as she was, she couldn't stop the curl of her lips. 'Has anyone ever told you you're an idiot?' She brushed away his hand, lifted the glass and drained it in two quick gulps. 'Thanks for the drinks.'

'Hey!' he said, reaching for her hand again. 'You can't just leave!'

'Why? Because you think buying me two drinks gives you rights? Well, I hate to break it to you so bluntly, but I'm guessing subtlety is wasted on you, so I'll tell you in simple words you can understand: free drinks get you a thank you and nothing else.'

He wasn't taking no for an answer. She knew his type; she'd guessed he wouldn't. When she stood, he did too, moving aggressively close, his breath a waft of booze and nicotine that almost made her gag. The thought of that mouth coming in contact with any part of her body made her reconsider, but she needed this. Needed to get some kind of justice, even if what she was about to mete out was on the wrong man.

'Well, okay,' she said, reaching out to touch his chest with the point of her manicured nail. 'Maybe you're right and you do deserve some payback.' She tipped her head towards the exit. 'Let's go outside, shall we?'

She didn't wait for his reply. It wasn't necessary. She could see it in the quick softening of his mouth, the gleam in his eye. If she looked lower, if she could bring herself to, she knew she'd be able to make out a bulge in his pants. Men were pretty predictable.

Night had fallen in the hours she'd been drinking. There were few pedestrians to be seen, certainly none who were interested in an inebriated woman and the man intent on claiming what he thought was his by right.

'There's a laneway,' Fiona said, walking to the corner of the building before heading that way, her stilettos tapping a quick beat the man followed as if mesmerised. 'Down here.' She didn't wait to see if he'd follow; she knew he would. They always did.

The laneway, used for deliveries to the pub, doubled as a toilet for those caught short, the fetor of urine and faeces clinging to the walls despite regular power-washing by the management. It was also occasionally used by those who wanted to score or to use their drug of choice. And even more rarely, it was used for sexual encounters by those who paid for the privilege. What it was never used for was romantic assignations, even for the fleeting, no-strings-attached kind. But then this wasn't what Fiona had in mind.

If the man was surprised he was being led into such an insalubrious space, he was too much at the mercy of his hormones to put it into words and followed much in the way the children followed the Pied Piper. And by the time the musical tap tapping of her stilettos stopped, it was too late.

'You definitely deserve what you're going to get, Phillip,' she said, turning to him.

His expression, softened by lust, sharpened, just a little, and he opened his mouth, probably to argue that his name wasn't Phillip. But she wasn't interested in what he wanted to say, certainly wasn't interested in his name, or anything about him. In that moment, he was Phillip, or Mr Everyman who kept her from getting what was rightfully hers, and as such, he deserved what she was only too happy to dole out.

The heel of her hand to his nose stopped whatever it was he wanted to say. When his hands flew up to stem the gush of blood, she took advantage of both his shock and the hands that protected her from being doused in blood, to give another blow – a knee driven with force into his groin.

The narrow walls of the laneway contained his scream of pain. Fiona felt them echoing in her ears as she stepped around him and swiftly exited onto the pavement. There was nobody in the vicinity to rush to his aid and with a final glance back to where he lay writhing on the ground, she gave a sigh of satisfaction and walked away.

She'd meted out the same punishment to other men on many occasions over the years. Every time she was passed over for promotion, every time she had to smile at some misogynistic comment, when she'd had to ignore the leering glances, or the accidental touches, she'd find some unsuspecting fool to be held accountable.

In a dog-eat-dog world, she'd learnt it was the bitch who survived.

10

FIONA

Fiona checked her watch. Her next appointment wasn't for a couple of hours. There was work she needed to get done, emails to send, reports to write, but she could shoehorn them into her schedule as necessary. Now that she was following the wife, it seemed essential to keep going, to learn something new about her even if it was only where she got her hair cut.

She knew her name, of course. Lydia. Was she called by a derivative of it – Lyd or Lyddy perhaps – or was she the kind of woman who insisted on the full three syllables every time?

Was that why Fiona had reduced her to that one-syllabled word: wife? Or was it some kind of sado-masochistic tendency she had to keep reminding herself that Rich had a wife, while she, Fiona, was *the other woman.*

Fifteen minutes later, as she was beginning to wonder if the damn woman was going to ramble forever, Lydia stopped and pushed open the door of a café.

A coffee always being welcome, Fiona waited for a minute before following her in. Inside, it was the kind of chichi place popular in that part of London with its clientele of yummy mummies, ladies who lunch, and women of a certain age who were trying hard to be several years younger.

Fiona glanced around. The wife was unlikely to have come to have coffee on her own, so someone was joining her, or she was meeting someone already there. There was one table with a single occupant; it was a reasonable assumption that this was the person the wife was going to join.

There were a number of empty tables. It was tempting to choose the one close by, but it might also give rise to suspicious glances and have the two women huddle together and drop their voices to an unintelligible whisper. Much better to sit a table's distance away and hope the two women would relax enough to speak at normal volume that would travel across to her if she listened intently.

The decision made, she crossed to the chosen table, shed her coat and laid it over one chair, thereby claiming it as hers before turning to join the queue. It was only three people long but despite there being what appeared to be a medley of people behind the counter, it moved slowly. It seemed to be the kind of café where nobody was in a hurry, filled with people with nothing to do and all day to do it. She was more used to places filled with the hurly-burly of a business day, lunch or coffee almost inhaled, that or business lunches where little was eaten or drunk but where deals were made.

The slow pace gave her more opportunity to observe the wife, who was in the queue just ahead of her. Fiona was pleased to see her powers of reasoning hadn't failed her when she saw the wife raise an eyebrow and give a shrug when she caught the lone occupant's eye. Perhaps they weren't as happy with the snail's pace as Fiona had assumed.

'I'll have a chicken salad sandwich with all the trimmings, a cappuccino, and a chocolate chip cookie, please,' the wife said when she finally reached the head of the queue moments later.

Fiona resisted the temptation of raising her eyes to the ceiling and giving a critical sniff. No wonder the woman was edging quickly towards fat if this is what she ate every day for lunch. She hadn't even requested a skinny cappuccino! Didn't she know how many calories a full-fat coffee contained? And did she really need a chocolate chip cookie? Of course she bloody-well didn't – nobody needed one.

There had been nothing to interest Fiona on the menu. 'An Americano, please,' she said when it was her turn to order. A mere ten calories. This was why she was slim and trim and it was why she was going to stay that way, even after she'd managed to hook Rich. There was no point in giving him a reason to look elsewhere.

When she returned to the table, she sat with her back to the women, who were sitting back, relaxed as they ate their calorific meals. Fiona angled her chair and cocked her head all the better to hear their conversation.

Since there was no background music playing, it was easier than she'd expected to eavesdrop. She didn't catch every word. The woman whose name she discovered was Alice had a tendency to mumble, but Fiona heard enough. It was when the charity Art United was mentioned that her ear cocked even higher.

It was the Art United Christmas Charity Ball that the two women were so excitedly discussing, the one Fiona had foolishly agreed to go to only two days before. The one where she'd hoped to appear at Rich's side, with the wife consigned to history. Her obsession with him was making her live in a fantasy world; it was a dangerous place to be.

It was better to face reality. Rich would be at the ball, with his wife, and they'd be dressed as Mr and Mrs Claus. The thought made her smile. She couldn't imagine the rather suave Rich dressed as Mr Claus. She wondered if he'd agreed or if it was the wife's idea. As for her friend! Tweedledum and Tweedle-bloody-dee.

At least she knew she'd win in the costume stakes – whatever she wore. She'd already given it some thought.

But whatever she did wear, she'd still cut a lonely figure.

True, she could easily find someone to drag along to it. There were several respectable-looking guys who'd be only too pleased to have the opportunity. A couple of them handsome enough to perhaps make Rich jealous.

But it wasn't what she wanted.

And as she sat and listened to the wife, Fiona knew the time was coming when she would be forced to give Rich an ultimatum; she wasn't willing to be the other woman forever.

He had to choose: Fiona or his wife.

11

FIONA

Two nights later, Fiona was once again in her favourite wine bar sitting across the table from Jocelyn and swirling ice in her gin and tonic. 'I met her,' she said. The words landed into one of those silences that fall easily between two old friends who don't feel obliged to fill the space with words for the sake of it.

Old friends didn't need everything spelt out for them either. Jocelyn immediately slapped a hand onto her forehead and uttered, 'What! How?'

'You're such a drama queen.'

Jocelyn dropped her hand and sniffed loudly. 'And you're not with that blunt, brief, "I met her"?' She picked up her glass and sat back, all ready to hear the details. 'Go on, spill. What happened?'

Over the years, Fiona had learnt that there were some things worth telling, and others worth keeping to herself. That the latter far outweighed the former was the way it was. Didn't everyone have secrets? She thought back to the man who'd followed her from the pub and into the laneway. She hadn't known his name or the name of many of the men to whom she'd dealt a similar hand. Perhaps, she thought, hiding a smile, she had more secrets than others.

It didn't matter. Truth and honesty were overrated. In the world of finance, it was success that counted. To achieve that, it was necessary to bend or break the rules when required. The important thing was not to be caught.

She could have told Jocelyn the truth, that she'd gone out of her way to see the wife, but two words stopped her from doing so. *Obsessive* and *stalker*. She didn't want to be seen as either.

Anyway, she wasn't precisely lying, just bending the truth to suit her needs. 'I was on my way to a consult and since I was early, I stopped for a coffee in this twee little café that I came across. Imagine my disbelief when a few minutes later, the wife came through the door and sat with another woman at a table nearby. You could have knocked me over with a feather.'

'That's because you don't eat enough.' Jocelyn smirked. 'Well, go on, what's she like in the flesh?'

'She's...' Fiona hesitated, unwilling to use the politically incorrect word *fat*. 'Let's be kind and call her plump. Very plump,' she added, deciding political correctness didn't apply to Rich's wife. 'And badly dressed too.'

'And you wondered what he sees in her?'

It had been exactly what Fiona had thought in the relative quiet of the café; it was still what she thought surrounded by the blended sound of voices and laughter and the tinkle of ice in glasses. Perhaps even more so, because this den of sophistication seemed far more Rich's milieu than the café's suburban dullsville.

'They've been married forty years. I doubt if she looked quite so matronly and drab when he married her. But as some men do, he's matured well and possibly looks better now than he did then.'

'So you think it's time he got rid of the old and welcomed in the new, do you?' Jocelyn shook her head but her expression was congratulatory, not critical. 'You'll persuade him to, if I know you. Honestly, it's amazing how things always work out for you.' She glanced around before leaning slightly closer to add, 'Like Phillip's downfall! Honestly, talk about luck!'

Fiona was pleased to see that the ice in her glass didn't as much as tinkle. Luck, as it happened, had had nothing to do with it. There were major benefits in always being the last one to leave the office, in keeping your eyes open while you waited for the perfect opportunity to arise, then sliding into that space and using it to maximum effect. And if it should be the case that the opportunity doesn't arise, Fiona wasn't going to let that stop her. Not when it was so easy. Not when Phillip was such a fucking idiot that she was able to discover the password to his computer in less than a minute.

It didn't take much to destroy him. With access to his clients' details, it was easy to make a change here, an alteration there, adding a bit, subtracting even more. A few emails sent to the right people, or even the wrong ones. No rhyme nor reason to any of it. There didn't have to be. There never had to be to cause chaos.

Then all it needed was for somebody, AKA Fiona, to drop a few words in the right ears, the ones firmly attached to gossiping mouths who were sure to add their own slant to her words before passing them on. Fiona didn't criticise Phillip, of course; rather, she spoke soft words of concern for a valued colleague who was looking a little strained. Then, in a quieter voice, she'd added that she didn't want to be telling tales out of school, but she'd travelled in the lift with him recently and the smell of alcohol was overwhelming. She *had* been in the lift with him, but it had been his aftershave she'd found overwhelming. Truth and honesty were overrated, and also so easily manipulated. 'Poor Phillip,' she'd said with practised sympathy. 'I do hope he's okay.'

The rumours swelled, clients started to complain loudly and vociferously of errors, and before the company was shaded by Phillip's perceived wrongdoing, he was gone. He was still proclaiming his innocence as he was escorted from the building. Innocent or guilty – at that stage, it didn't really matter. In the world of finance, perception is everything.

'I'm absolutely stunned,' Fiona had said, when the CEO, Matt Donaldson, dropped into her tiny office minutes after Phillip's departure.

'We need to plaster over this mess as quickly as possible,' he'd said. 'You know the way these things go.'

She did only too well. Rumours, in the wrong hands, were dangerous weapons.

'You have my full support, of course.' This was the bastard who'd chosen Phillip over her in the first place. 'If there's anything I can do, you know all you need to do is ask.'

Fiona could arse-lick with the best of them when it counted, and it counted now. She could see the irritation flit across Matt's face as he realised he'd made the wrong choice. That some of the fault lay with him for putting Phillip in a position of authority he didn't deserve.

'We'll need someone to take over his accounts,' Matt said.

Under her desk, Fiona was pinching the soft flesh of her inner thigh. This was where she needed to be silent, to sit there looking as if butter wouldn't melt, and leave it to him to make the correct decision. The one he should have made months before.

Humility wasn't in Fiona's nature and it took every ounce of her strength to sit there while the stupid man cogitated.

'The promotion was a close call, you know,' he said finally. 'Phillip simply had the edge.'

Because he was a man, or because he played a good round of golf? She was suddenly tired of playing the game. It wasn't, after all, as if there was anyone else who could fill the position.

'It looks as if that edge rubbed off pretty quickly, doesn't it?'

She saw his eyes narrow and wondered if she'd blown it.

Then he smiled, but it was the merest tilt to the corners of his lips, his eyes remaining hard and considering. 'Indeed,' he said. 'Well, it looks as if the position is now yours, Fiona. Congratulations.'

She waited until the echo of his leather-soled feet on the tiled corridor faded before allowing her expression to relax into one of sheer satisfaction for a job well done. There was no reason to put it off, so she stood, grabbed her handbag and ambled down the corridor to her new office. It was twice the size of the one she'd had, with floor-to-ceiling windows overlooking the Thames. The office of a winner.

She used the desk phone to ring housekeeping and inform them of the change. 'The office needs to be cleaned before I can move in,' she finished. 'And I require a new chair. There are some rather disreputable stains on the seat of the current one.' There weren't, not that she could see with her naked eye anyway, but the thought of sitting in the chair that Phillip's large backside had sat in held no allure.

That had been six months ago, and for a while, Fiona had thought she'd had it all.

But then she'd met Rich and she'd realised she'd been fooling herself. *All* was what Jocelyn and Kate had – professional and personal success. But *all* was once more nearly in Fiona's grasp.

She sighed and tuned back into whatever Jocelyn was saying. Some rambling tosh about luck and good fortune.

What was that expression? Ah yes, *fortune favours the brave*. She swirled her glass again. She preferred the other one. *Only losers need luck*.

And she most definitely wasn't a loser.

12

LYDIA

I fumbled in my handbag for my house keys but there was so much rubbish inside it, I was forced to hold it closer to my face and peer myopically in hoping the low winter sun shining over my shoulder would light them up. It didn't, of course, and I began to frantically push various stuff from side to side. Had I lost the damn things? Maybe dropped them in the café? But I'd have heard them fall, wouldn't I? It was a big enough bunch.

An edge of panic gripped me, making me scrabble more frenetically – and uselessly.

I tried to remember leaving the house – had I locked the mortice lock, or simply shut the door behind me, leaving security in the hands of the Yale? Maybe that's what I'd done, and the keys were sitting in the drawer of the hall table. I'd have to ring Rich, get him to come home and let me in. Again. The second time in as many months. He hadn't been pleased the first; he'd be bloody annoyed to have to do it again.

No, I wasn't going to call him. It'd be better to go back to the café, have some more coffee, maybe even a cake this time, sit and read a book on my mobile's Kindle app. If I was very clever, if I got the timing just right, I might arrive home at the same time as Rich. He'd unlock the door and be none the wiser. Except he'd know then the door hadn't been locked properly. God, had I even put the damn alarm on?

It seemed that I was damned if I did ring him, damned if I didn't.

Maybe I'd return to the café, have another coffee and one of those chocolate eclairs I'd seen earlier. The one I'd decided not to have because I was trying to lose a bit of weight. I shouldn't have had the chocolate cookie either but I'd needed the sugar rush. I needed it again now. With the handles of my bag hooked over my shoulder, I turned away from the door and shoved my cold hands into the deep pockets of my coat. And that was where I found the damn keys. It should have made me happy, not brought tears rushing to my eyes so that I turned with the bunch in my hand and struggled to get the key into the keyhole. Inside, I had indeed set the alarm. I brushed the tears away and disarmed it.

Usually, coming home brought a feeling of calm. I loved our house: a rambling Victorian one we'd bought the month before we married. It had been in the same family for fifty years prior to that and hardly anything had been changed in those years. Everything needed updating or replacing: the plumbing, electrics, roof and windows. We'd got a good deal because of the condition it was in, but the purchase still took every penny we had, leaving little remaining to do the renovations. So we'd done it bit by bit, the essentials first, then the redecorating, room by room.

We'd extended the kitchen and built another bedroom above it as money allowed, and as the house grew, so did our family. The twins had grown up within its walls; they'd left their own somewhat untidy mark on it, from crayon doodles on the walls when they were younger, to posters in their teens. The home had echoed with the sounds of celebrations, parties and get-togethers.

It was a happy place and I loved it. Every room held memories, every item of furniture had been chosen with care, each ornament with love. If the walls could speak, it'd be words of contented happiness. Until recently. Now, I wasn't so sure. The idea that Rich had met someone had taken up residence in my head so firmly that, despite any real evidence that he was cheating on me, I was convinced I was right.

I stood in the hallway and looked around, my eyes drawn to the curve of the oak staircase, then to the gleaming parquet floor. How many times had I polished it in forty years? Hundreds, maybe even thousands? If my suspicions about another woman were correct, and if it was more than a stupid fling, would Rich leave me? The very thought made me feel bereft.

If he left me, I'd lose him, but wouldn't I also lose my home? Because if he was serious about this other woman, and they wanted a home together, he'd need money. He couldn't afford to buy me out, nor could I. It was worth far more than we'd paid for it forty years before. Two million, perhaps more. It would need to be sold. I'd have to leave all my memories behind to be auctioned off to the highest bidder.

I'd have money to buy somewhere else but where the fuck would I go?

Worse, who would I be? An unemployed ex-wife, ex-mother. Would Rich still support me? I'd no idea how it would work. Too late now to regret being a stay-at-home mum, a full-time wife. I should know where I stood financially – fuck's sake, I wasn't even sure how much, if any, savings we had. But I could change. Maybe reinvent myself. I had honed my computer skills since the last rejection, so perhaps I could look for a job.

The keys, still clutched in my hand, cut into my palm as I envisaged my future. It didn't look rosy. With a sigh, I pulled open the drawer and dropped the bunch inside. My fingers lingered on the table. We'd found it in an antique shop when we'd been on holiday in Devon, ten, perhaps fifteen years before. And the keys had been kept in the drawer of it ever since.

If we divorced, would Rich want it? Would we argue over everything we'd bought together? It was bordering on masochism, but I wandered through the sitting room, my eyes flitting from the sofa – where I was convinced the twins had been conceived – to the painting on the wall that we'd fallen in love with in Italy, and which had cost us more to ship home than to purchase. I crossed to the shelves that lined the alcoves either side of the fireplace and looked at the mementos and photographs they held. How would we divide everything?

Why did we have to?

I sat on the sofa and rested my head back. No, why did *I* have to?

For the first time in what seemed like a long, long time, anger uncurled and made itself known. Was I going to simply sit back and let things just happen to me? A punchbag swaying with every blow?

Or was I going to get off my increasingly fat arse and do something?

13

FIONA

Fiona's apartment on the seventh floor was like her: lean and classy. That's how she described it to anyone who asked. It gave the impression that the space was small and so gave her added pleasure when they arrived and saw the reality. Because for London, it counted as being a very spacious apartment indeed. It should be; it had cost her a ridiculous amount of money. Despite her generous salary, she'd struggled to keep up the payments, but she'd known the promotion was in the offing when she'd bought it. It was only a matter of time before her increased salary would ease the burden. When the promotion had gone to Phillip, she had been initially dismayed, then steaming angry.

She couldn't have continued to live in the apartment, struggling as she had been, and had considered selling until the reality of the market hit her a staggering blow. The apartment should have increased in value in the year she'd owned it, but it hadn't. In fact, the one next door had sold the previous month for fifty thousand less than the original price. So if she'd sold, she'd have been financially worse off.

Really, she told herself, the powers that be in Donaldson and

Partners, and Matt Donaldson in particular, had left her no option. The blame lay with them for what she'd been forced to do. The thought made her smile. It made life far easier to be able to find someone else accountable.

The promotion to the position Phillip had enjoyed so briefly brought her financial situation back into the realm of comfortable, but it could be better.

A change to her lifestyle was occupying her thoughts that morning as she sat at the breakfast bar in the small kitchen. If – no, strike that – *when* she married Rich, things would change. Marriage, she'd decided, was her goal.

It would make sense for Rich to move in with her as soon as he could. He liked the apartment, had said so several times, so she didn't foresee any problem. She sipped her coffee, her thoughts spinning. He'd want to pay the mortgage; it was the kind of man he was. But although Fiona loved him, she wasn't a fool. He'd already proved that he could be swayed by a charming woman. If in ten years' time, he was swayed by a younger, more glamorous model, would he leave Fiona for her? If he'd paid the mortgage for ten years, it would give him rights she didn't want him to have. No, she'd keep paying it. But although love, not money, was her motivating factor in their relationship, she'd no intention of being stupid and would come up with some other way to benefit financially from their union.

She was still mulling over possibilities when her mobile rang. It wasn't necessary to look; she knew it would be Rich. Although they didn't ring or message each other with the same frantic need they'd had in the first weeks, he still messaged her every day, and rang every morning as soon as he'd left home.

'Hi,' she said, lowering her pitch to the sultry level she knew he couldn't resist. Normally, she'd be greeted with effusive complimentary words. A variation on, *Hello, beautiful,* or, *Hi, sexy,* and once, thankfully only once or she'd have had to reconsider their relationship, it was, *Hi, baby.*

'Morning, Fiona,' he said.

As if she was his secretary. It was so unexpected that she was immediately on guard. Was this it? He was tired of her. Were his next words going to be, *Listen, we need to talk*? She hated the rush of disappointment that hit her and batted it away, choosing to be angry instead – at him, at herself for being so fucking stupid. It made her voice tight when she spoke. She chose her words carefully. Perhaps she was jumping to conclusion:, a dangerous exercise at the best of times. 'I'm just finishing my morning coffee before heading to the office. I've a full day there today. No flitting about London to meet clients. It gives me a chance to catch up with things.' She was yammering. A nervous reaction. She held her hand over the speaker, took a deep, shuddering breath and let it out in a long hiss. 'So how's your day looking?' she said, relieved to hear her voice sounding calm, unconcerned. As if silence between them was the norm. As if they were some tired, bored-with-each-other couple who'd run out of things to say.

'Busy,' he said.

One word and nothing else. Was he on his way to work? Usually, she'd be able to hear the sound of traffic as he walked, sometimes voices as he passed other people. She wanted to ask, to keep talking and fill the silence with words but, unusually for her, she was afraid.

The idea that he was her last chance had become embedded in her brain. As if she was some decrepit old hag, not a thirty-eight-year-old glamorous woman in her prime who didn't need a bloody man. *But she wanted one!* And there were so few decent men out there. Plenty for good times, for one-night stands, for earth-shattering sex. But to make a future with? Men like that were harder to find.

And now that she'd found one, now that she'd realised she didn't yet *have it all*, she was damned if she was letting go so easily.

'Sorry,' Rich said, the word coming on the crest of a sigh. 'I've a lot on my mind. I don't mean to take it out on you. I'm looking forward to seeing you tonight. I'll have your favourite wine opened and ready to pour when you arrive, and I promise you'll have my undivided attention, okay?'

A lot on his mind? Had the wife found out about them? Yes, that must be it. She'd found out and was making his life hell. Fiona hoped so. It would work in her favour. She desperately wanted to ask but she'd been careful never to bring his wife up in conversation; she didn't want to start now, especially over the phone. Tonight, at their regular dinner in what had become their favourite, out-of-the-way restaurant, she'd find an opportunity to pry.

'That sounds perfect,' she said, using her sultry voice again. And then, because she couldn't help herself, she added, 'Is everything okay? You sound a bit low, and it's not like you.'

She wanted to add that he'd sounded fine when they'd spoken the night before, that he was chatty, effusively complimentary, the way he usually was. So what had happened in the hours in between? It had to have been the wife. That blasted woman. She needed to go.

Fiona waited for him to explain, hoped he'd finally admit he was having problems with his wife and give Fiona an opening, but to her annoyance, he brushed her words aside.

'Oh it's something and nothing, don't worry. Same time as usual tonight?'

What was it about the words *don't worry* that immediately caused the recipient to do just that? Fiona gripped her mobile so tightly she was surprised it didn't shatter as she asked. 'Yes, and you'll come back with me, won't you?'

'Ah,' and there was a wealth of meaning in that one extended non-word. 'Maybe not tonight, Fi, if you don't mind. I have a lot on at the minute; I need to get a good night's sleep.'

'Actually,' she said with a soft laugh that she hoped sounded unconcerned, 'that suits me perfectly. I have an early-morning consult with a new client tomorrow and need to look my breezy best.'

'Good, good, right, well, I'll see you tonight.'

Fiona, waiting for some form of endearment, was left with her ear pressed to a dead phone. Never, in the multitude of phone calls between them, had he ever left without some form of compliment, or saying, as he had done not more than ten hours before, *I miss you already*.

In the evenings, when he rang her, it was from what he referred to as his office. Like her, he often worked from home and the space allowed him the privacy to make illicit phone calls. Was that where he was phoning from that morning? Not on his way to work as usual? He was, she'd discovered, a creature of habit, so something must have occurred to have jolted his routine out of sync.

The wife had to have found out and he was wracked with guilt. It was the logical explanation.

Fiona slammed her mobile down on the counter and swore. She'd invested time and energy into this relationship. Not so long ago, she'd thought love was for eighteen-year-olds, or for older women with little sense, not for thirty-eight-year-olds who understood that love was ephemeral, that it was the capacity to like someone, to enjoy their company and at the same time find them sexually compatible, that made a relationship last. But now, she understood there was no age limit to falling in love; that age didn't preclude falling ridiculously hard, and there wasn't much difference between an eighteen-year-old in love and a thirty-eight-year-old. Except, at thirty-eight, Fiona recognised the touch of desperation, more than a smidgen of realisation that this could be the last chance saloon, and the newly fledged desire to finally have it all.

She drummed her nails on the counter, the rhythm increasing with her thoughts. For a woman who liked to be in control, for whom sitting around waiting for the world to turn was never a good idea, the situation she found herself in was unbearable. She'd got rid of Phillip; how difficult would it be to get rid of a woman who was desperately clinging on to the shadow of her dying marriage?

All Fiona needed was a plan. It helped that she was a firm believer in the ends justifying the means.

14

LYDIA

I had always avoided confrontation. It was a habit ingrained in me from childhood when running was a more sensible option than standing my ground to get beaten up by Sally Green, the bane of my junior school years. *Fine, whatever,* became my standard reply, reduced to a simple *fine* when I was older. It effectively shut a conversation down before it descended into an argument.

Alice says it's being passive-aggressive.

I say if it works, don't knock it.

But as I walked around the home Rich and I had shared for so many years, seeing the ghostly outline of scenes from our past, hearing the faint echo of laughter from days gone by, I felt an unaccustomed rage build inside me. Everyone, even the mildest, most laid-back of people, has the capacity for violence somewhere inside. Buried deeply perhaps, but it's there, just waiting for something to crack apart the layers that society and conditioning have built around it. I could feel it bubbling inside me, waiting for direction. Oddly, it felt comforting, as if knowing I had some defence made things more bearable.

Defence. As if I was under attack. It was a sensible way to regard it, because if Rich was having an affair, it was bad. If he was going to leave me for this other woman, it was worse. Things were going to get very messy. Being non-confrontational wasn't going to work. Sitting back and ducking the blows wasn't going to work either. I needed to dip into my capacity for violence and fight back. I had to be proactive. I was no longer in junior school, facing Sally Green. I might not technically have any skills, but over the years, I'd coped with family disasters: the time when Missy broke her arm, followed only a day later by her brother doing the same. I'd coped with plumbers who'd left work half-done, electricians who thought they could pull the wool over my eyes, builders who would turn up when they felt like it. Facing this new catastrophe, it was time to get on the offensive and attack first.

But attack needed strategy.

I was still trailing around the house. There was a photograph of us, taken only the year before while we were on holiday in India. We looked happy, relaxed. We looked fucking content. Or was I seeing what I wanted to see? I took the frame closer to the window and peered at it. I was looking adoringly at Rich and laughing, perhaps at something he'd said, I couldn't remember. I was looking at him; he was staring at whoever was taking the photograph.

My fingers tightened on the frame. I remembered. The photographer was one of the other tourists on our organised holiday, a young, pretty, flirty woman who seemed to find everything ridiculously funny, and whom I'd dismissed as being a little dim-witted. She was travelling with her elderly parents, who were finding the heat draining and as a result, they didn't go on all of the trips our guide had organised.

There was a choice of which excursion to go on almost every

day. Some were more interesting for me than others, and it was the same with Rich. So it made sense to split up. The other travellers were a friendly bunch, but I don't remember this woman being on any of the trips I was on. Which meant she must have been on the ones that Rich chose.

'My name is Candice, but everyone calls me Candy,' she'd told us on the first day. She gave a huge, toothy grin before she added, 'Because I'm so sweet.'

She had undeniable sex appeal, but also an excruciatingly annoying habit of hijacking conversations to talk in far more detail than was warranted about herself. Within a day or two, most of the women had learnt to avoid her. I don't think Candy cared. She was far more interested in the men's company.

Had she spent more time with Rich than I'd realised?

I lifted the frame again, examining his face. I'd never noticed before, because I hadn't been looking, but now it was blindingly obvious. That softness in his expression, a certain warmth in his gaze. It was the way he used to look at me. How had I never noticed its absence? Worse, how had I never noticed he looked at other women that way? The way he was looking at Candy.

Had I stopped noticing, or stopped caring?

I wasn't sure.

Had I simply coasted through life, seeing what I wanted to? Believing in the fairy-tale happy ever after that didn't exist? Had I wanted to believe that Rich had stayed faithful to me, because I had to him? I'd never even been tempted. We were cited as the couple who'd made it. Forty years of wedded bliss. The envy of many of our friends.

How many of them, I wondered, knew the truth about his philandering? I'd almost bet that some of his work colleagues knew. Some of his golfing buddies too. Did they laugh at me, those overweight, heavy drinkers who letched after women young enough to be their daughters? I'd seen them at those thankfully increasingly rare work events I'd felt obliged to attend. The ones held in five-star hotels with their epicurean dinners and their endless self-congratulatory after-dinner speeches.

I'd assumed the decrease in these events had come down to cost-cutting, to the tightening of economic belts, but perhaps there too I had been fooling myself. Did the noticeable drop in these jollies coincide with a rise in nights Rich had to spend away at business conferences?

I'd never thought to question him about these nights away. Why would I? I trusted him.

How blind I'd been. How fucking stupid.

I looked at the photograph in my hand, but all I could see was the way he was staring at the photographer. Had he discovered just how sweet Candy had been?

I threw the frame across the room, wanting it to smash to pieces. But it seemed I couldn't even do that properly. It landed on the seat of the opposite sofa, ending upright so it seemed as if Rich was staring at me.

I knew better now. He hadn't looked at me in any way for a long time and definitely not in the way he was staring at the so sweet and biddable Candy.

There was no doubt in my head any longer. He was cheating on me and probably had done before.

The signs had been there; I had simply refused to see or acknowledge them.

15

FIONA

Fiona would never have considered herself to have an obsessive personality. Not until recently. It was definitely obsessive, the day after her last visit, to be sitting outside Rich's house, waiting to see if his wife would appear.

Unlike most of her plans, the one with Phillip for instance, this one was lacking in focus and strategy. Perhaps it was because there was no desired outcome. Although, that wasn't exactly true; the desired outcome was that the wife would fuck the hell off out of Rich's life, but Fiona needed to focus on how to achieve that.

She could wait until the stupid woman was crossing the road and run her down. There was a problem with this plan, though. Although she acknowledged that she was manipulative and cunning and had a sufficient tendency towards violence to be able to pull it off, there was no guarantee that running her down would kill her. And the last thing she needed was a disabled wife that Rich would feel too guilty to leave.

She rang her office and told her secretary she'd be working from home that day. It wasn't unheard of, although was usually planned in advance. The news was taken with little surprise and even a hint of pleasure. Fiona knew why. She was a demanding boss. With her out of the office, Trish would take a long lunch break and several tea breaks. She was a hard worker, reliable too. Fiona didn't begrudge her having an easy day.

There were several emails she needed to send and calls she needed to make, but an hour or two on reconnaissance wouldn't have too much impact. *Reconnaissance.* The word would have made her smile if she could find anything remotely funny about her situation. Here she was, an intelligent, successful woman, resorting to spying on her lover's wife. What did it say about Fiona? That she was becoming obsessive – definitely – but did it also mean she was verging on the desperate, and pathetic?

It was only a blink of an eye, wasn't it, since she'd been twenty and her whole life stretched in front of her, a runway of lights filled with the promise of glorious, endless opportunities. It was true, she thought bitterly: youth *was* wasted on the young. In another blink, she'd be sixty and facing retirement. The thought of retiring didn't faze her; it was the idea of doing it alone that scared her.

Alone and single. The pool of eligible men would shrink until all that was left were the ones as desperate as her. She'd sign up on every dating app, lie about her age and have more and more work done on her face. More fillers, more Botox, more fucking everything until when she looked in the mirror, she'd barely recognise herself. She sometimes got a shock when she looked in the mirror now; she imagined herself being twenty, but her reflection, even with the work she'd had done, was the face of her mother.

She opened her eyes, turned her head towards Rich's house and willed his wife to appear. The sight of her might be enough to break the logjam in Fiona's head. A bright idea would arrive, fully formed and ready to implement. Everything would fall into place. The wife would be history. Fiona and Rich would be the future.

But willing something to happen never did work and the house stayed stubbornly quiet. Perhaps the wife already knew about Rich's infidelity and was even now inside packing a suitcase for him. Did she look like the kind of woman who'd give up easily? They'd been married for forty years. A lifetime. Fiona couldn't imagine being with one man for so long.

For the first time, she wondered about Rich. Forty years with one woman. Had he strayed before? Perhaps he was a serial strayer. She needed to tie him down before he became bored with her. Or had he already? She thought back to their earlier conversation. Was that it? Had she misread it all? It was nothing to do with the wife, and all to do with Fiona.

That night, was he going to tell her that he was sorry, but their relationship had run its course?

If he thought she'd be that easy to dismiss, he didn't know her.

He didn't know her one little bit.

She allowed the anger to simmer as she glared towards his house. If he wanted trouble, she'd be only too happy to give it to him. She could hammer on his front door until the wife appeared and tell her the intimate details of their relationship. The sexual gymnastics they'd indulged in.

Anger dimmed as quickly as it had appeared. Accosting the wife would achieve nothing. All it would do would diminish Fiona more, cement her position as being as disposable and worthless as yesterday's newspaper. She shut her eyes, pushing one hot tear out to slide down her cheek. Just one. What a fucking cliché she'd become.

This was why she'd never wanted to be the mistress. The

other woman. It robbed her of every iota of rationality. Turned her into a monster. Or was she already one? She thought of Phillip. She'd seen him that last day, clearing out his office, a stricken look on his face. Had she felt the merest hint of guilt? She couldn't remember anything apart from an intense feeling of satisfaction. Justification even. The promotion should have been hers, and now it was. The promotion, the bigger office, the recognition, and the increased salary to make her life so much more comfortable.

What she'd done to Phillip had been justified. Colleagues who were competitors were fair game as far as she was concerned. Finance was a tough business. In its world, it was survival of the smartest, the wiliest.

But this, she thought, looking at Rich's house, this was different. She'd never wanted to be the kind of woman who'd destroy a marriage. She wanted to believe Rich's had already reached the end of its life before she'd wandered so accidentally into it. Why else would a man like him, a man who seemed so honourable and honest, have been tempted to stray?

But destroying the marriage when she was going to ride off into the sunset with Rich was one thing – and bad enough for all that – but to destroy it out of malice because she was being dropped, if that was what was happening that evening, was something else. So no, she wouldn't accost the wife on her doorstep.

The unknowing was killing her. Surely, Rich wouldn't be bringing her to a restaurant that had become 'their' place to tell her it was over? Or was it his way of breaking it to her gently?

What would she do? Take it like the lady she wasn't? Carry the pain with her and leave him sitting at the table? That was as far as her thoughts took her, because she opened her eyes, looked across the road, and saw the wife.

Was Rich really choosing her over Fiona?

Anger seared her at the thought. Without a plan, she stepped out of the car and followed.

16

FIONA

Fiona had no idea what she was going to do; all she knew was that the woman who was standing between her and the man she loved, was walking a few feet ahead, her chin in the air, her badly styled hair curling over a hideously unstylish, mud-coloured jacket. It should have made Fiona feel better, but it was having the reverse effect. Because if she was right, if Rich was going to tell her it was over, it meant that he'd chosen this dowdy ageing-badly woman over her. And it questioned everything Fiona thought about herself. That self-belief, hard-won as it was, crumpled and turned to dust, shedding as she walked.

She wasn't surprised when the wife stopped at the same café. Women like her were always going to be creatures of habit.

Fiona passed by, walked to the end of the street, then turned to retrace her steps to her car. But when she reached the café, instead of passing by as she should have done, she pushed open the door and went inside.

It was surprisingly quiet, with only one table occupied by two young mothers, their babies sleeping peacefully beside them in strollers. The wife had already been served a coffee and what looked like an enormous eclair and was crossing to a table in the window.

'Can I help?'

It was said with a level of impatience that told Fiona it wasn't the first time the assistant had asked the question.

'Sorry, daydreaming,' she said with a smile. 'An Americano, please.'

'Anything else?'

'No, thanks.' And then, because she thought, why the hell not? Why should the wife have all the fun? 'Actually, yes, I'll have one of those eclairs, please.'

She took her purchases to a table in the corner where she sat and regarded the eclair with something akin to disbelief before picking it up to take a bite. She couldn't remember the last time she'd indulged in something so fattening and so luscious. It was an oddly satisfying experience. When she'd finished it, she picked up her coffee and sat back. The sugar hit seemed to have calmed her agitation and allowed her to gaze across the café to where the wife was sitting. On her own, not meeting a friend this time.

Was she doing what Fiona had done, and trying to cure heartache with calories? If so, she was making hard work of it. She was eating her eclair with a fork, breaking a piece off, pushing it around the plate before finally, almost reluctantly, spearing it on the tines and lifting it to her mouth. Sometimes, the tines were driven in with such force that they scraped the plate noisily. Was she wishing she could stab a fork into the woman her husband was having an affair with?

Because of course, she'd have known. She and Rich had been married for forty years; she'd probably known from the very beginning. Perhaps Fiona was the last in a long list of women he'd cheated on her with, and Fiona's belief that he was an honourable man and what was between them was something special, was nothing more than wishful thinking.

This was why she'd never wanted to be *that girl*. The constant self-doubt, the stupid second-guessing, the bitter feeling as she watched her self-worth corrode to rust and flake away. It almost wasn't bloody-well worth it. Almost.

She dragged a finger through the remnant of chocolate and cream on her plate and lifted it to her mouth to lick it away. It was tempting to order another. To sit there all day and stuff her face with every cake in the damn café.

Instead, she sat sipping her coffee and staring at the wife. Married for forty years. Forty! Two children, grown-up and gone. As far as Fiona could tell, the wife didn't work. So what did she do with her days? Perhaps she wondered where the years had gone. Maybe she wondered, as Fiona sometimes did, if she'd missed the boat.

Would the wife have been happier as a successful businesswoman? Would Fiona have been happier as a wife and mother? Having children had never appealed to her, but being a wife... it might not have done before, but it appealed to her now. And Rich would be the ideal husband.

The wife was still playing with the fork. She looked sad. Worn. Old. Fiona tried to feel some sympathy but she didn't have any to spare.

Because the truth was, one of them was going to lose.

Maybe the wife was as desperate to hang on to Rich as Fiona was. Perhaps, after all, they had a lot in common.

17

LYDIA

The café was my go-to place to meet with friends, but also a place I'd go to on my own when I needed to be in the company of others. It was a place frequented by young mothers and their children and often echoed to the sounds of cries or laughter. Both were a happy contrast to the silence of my own company. The staff were friendly and never pressurised me to leave even when I lingered an hour or two over a mug of coffee. I'd bought the eclair I'd wanted to have the previous day. It was probably delicious, but after a mouthful or two, I found myself pushing it around the plate. It seemed wrong to be sitting and doing something so normal as eating cake when my heart was breaking.

I was probably being self-indulgent. Sitting there feeling sorry for myself. As if I had the woes of the world leaning heavily on me, instead of merely being the next in a long line of women who'd made the discovery that their husband was a cheating shit.

The previous evening, Rich had come home, eaten the dinner I'd prepared, barely spoken to me and left immediately after with the excuse that he had work to do. That morning, he was equally quiet. If I was right and he was having an affair, either he was taking no pleasure in it, or was feeling so guilty that he couldn't look at me.

I gave up trying to eat the eclair, pushed the plate away, and stared out the window as I drank my coffee. The dull winter's day was perfectly matched to my mood. It was dark enough to turn the window into a mirror that reflected the interior of the café back at me. I frowned at myself and lifted a hand to push my hair back. It needed to be cut and I'd noticed in the mirror earlier that my roots were showing. My daughter, in that half-joking, half-critical way she has, calls it 'the badger look'.

The brown jacket didn't do much for me either. It had been an expensive mistake. When I got home, I'd bundle it up and put it into a bag for the next charity-shop drop.

The young mothers at the table behind, by contrast, were stylishly dressed, their blonde-streaked hair tied up in messy buns that I bet took ages to arrange. Their chatter was a pleasant sound and for a moment, I envied their obvious happiness. Once, I had been just the same.

But although I enjoyed watching them in my private viewing screen, it was the woman behind who kept my attention. Like me, she was on her own. Like me, she'd indulged in an eclair, but whereas I'd struggled to eat mine, she'd slid hers into her mouth and held it there for what seemed a long moment before biting down. There was something sensual and erotic about the way she ate it. Or perhaps it was because, unusually for me, sex was uppermost in my mind as my overactive imagination kept sending me images of Rich *in flagrante delicto* with a variety of females who bore more than a passing similarity to Candy.

The woman behind, finally, thankfully, finished eating and picked up her coffee. She was younger than I. Perhaps thirty-five, maybe a little more. She was the kind of woman I envied.

Elegant, stylish, well-maintained. As I looked at her reflection, I had the oddest sensation that she was staring at me. Her expression was intent. It struck me then that she looked familiar and I rattled my brain to think if I knew her from somewhere.

It took a minute before it came to me. I'd seen her before. Here, just the day before. I'd noticed her staring at me then and thought I'd been imagining it. Now here she was again. And I wasn't imagining it; she was fixated on me. Even as I looked, I saw her expression change. It took on angry lines and suddenly, I knew, without a shadow of a doubt, exactly who she was.

No, not who, but what.

Rich's mistress. His lover. His bit on the side.

I sat watching her reflection until she finally stood. I wondered if she was aware of my regard. Her actions were slow, almost deliberate as she picked up her coat, shook it, then swirled it around her shoulders. Like a witch's cape. Or the Devil's. She flicked her hair from under the collar. I watched it bounce around her shoulders, catching the light from the overhead lights.

A wave of hate swept over me, hot and searing, almost overwhelming. I wanted to rush across the café and grab her, tell her about what she was doing to me, to my life, to my marriage. And as she sauntered away without a care in the world, I wanted to grab a knife from one of the yummy mummies and ram it into her cheating, whoring, black heart.

18

LYDIA

Back at home, years of habit, years of being the loving, dutiful wife, made it easy to slip into automatic pilot. I changed the bedsheets, put on a load of washing, took out the ironing board and tackled the mountain of shirts. There was comfort in mundanity. By mid-afternoon, I was calmer. By late afternoon, as I set about preparing dinner, the burning anger had been reduced to a flicker.

Oddly though, the flame of the earlier anger had burned away the debris that had been clogging my vision. For the first time, in a long time, I could see clearly. The most startling thought that hit me was the truth about my relationship with Rich. I didn't love him. Not any more. I wasn't even sure I liked the workaholic golf fanatic very much. Somewhere in the last few years, he'd changed.

No, that wasn't quite right. He hadn't. I had. I wanted more than evenings and weekends spent alone. I was only sixty; it wasn't too late to find someone who wanted to be with me.

Or perhaps I was wrong and he had changed too – perhaps what *I* wanted was exactly what *he* wanted.

We just wanted it with different people.

* * *

I was still in the kitchen when Rich came through the door that evening.

'You're early,' I said, my tone carefully neutral, the flicker of anger held in check. 'Dinner won't be ready for a bit.'

'I just need something small,' he said. 'I have to go out again.' He turned away, unbuttoning his overcoat, keeping his face averted as he took it off and folded it over an arm. 'One of my clients needs to see me. She sounded a bit stressed so I thought it better not to put it off. She's one of my best. I don't want to lose her.'

It wasn't unheard of for some of his more demanding clients to ask to meet outside normal office hours. It was, Rich maintained, part and parcel of being a successful hedge-fund manager. And like many things, I'd never questioned the necessity of keeping these clients sweet. But in the past, when he'd needed to go, I'm sure he didn't need to so studiously avoid meeting my eyes.

'One of your clients?' I opened the oven door, checked the casserole, poked it unnecessarily with the fork I was holding, then shut the door again with a slam before turning to him with a smile that made my face ache. I must have looked slightly demented because he took a step backwards, shuffling the coat he held from one arm to the other. I had debated how to approach the problem, but suddenly weary, I decided to go for it. 'Would that be the one you're having the affair with?'

He laughed uncertainly, then stared at me with wide eyes. As if he wasn't sure what was going on. As if he was horrified by what I'd said. 'I don't know what you're talking about, Lydia. It's business, I swear.'

'You swear!' I shook my head.

He sounded genuinely affronted by my accusation. But I was right. Wasn't I? I hadn't imagined the woman in the café staring at me.

'You swear on our children's lives that you're not having an affair?'

He tossed his coat onto a nearby chair and took a step towards me. He reached for me, pulled me closer, his arms holding me so tightly, I was sure I could feel his heart beat. His breath was warm on my cheek as he spoke. 'It is a woman I'm meeting, but I swear on our children's life that it's business.' He held me close for a moment before pulling away and looking into my eyes. 'I don't know where you got that idea.' He kissed me lightly. 'I know I've been a bit distracted recently. I promise I'll make it up to you soon. When this current sticky bit of business is done with, okay?' He kissed me again. Harder, with passion I hadn't felt in a while. 'I wish I didn't have to go,' he said, kissing my neck. 'I'll try not to be too late.'

And as his lips trailed along my skin, I wanted to believe him because suddenly, I knew I'd been fooling myself. I loved him as much as I had the day we married. I didn't want to find someone else.

I wanted to believe he was telling me the truth, that he wasn't having an affair. But when he'd gone to his business meeting, when I was sitting on the sofa, the TV screen flickering, the sound on mute, I replayed the conversation in my head again and again. The words he'd used. The ones he hadn't. I'd asked him to swear on our children's lives that he wasn't having an affair, but he hadn't, had he? He never actually said he wasn't having an affair; he'd said it was 'business'. A politician's answer.

Perhaps I should have followed him. Seen the truth for myself. I tried to shift back into the mood I was in earlier. The one where I was tired of him, of our life together. The one where I saw myself sailing into the future with someone else. There was a bit of me that hated him in that moment, hated him for making me want him again, for making him the only man I could ever think of wanting.

Hated him for the passion he'd ignited in me that had me longing for him.

Hate. I stoked it with thoughts of that woman from the café, with her bouncing, shiny hair, her slim, trim figure. The beautiful face that I wanted to pulverise.

Maybe I was wrong and she wasn't the one, but it'd be someone like her. Someone younger, fitter, more beautiful.

I hated her, but suddenly, I hated him more.

19

FIONA

Fiona had stayed in the café for far longer than she'd planned. Not wanting to draw attention to herself, she'd put her phone on silent and had continued to ignore it when it vibrated angrily in her coat pocket. It wasn't until she was back in her car, almost two hours later, that she looked at it to discover several missed calls from her secretary.

'Sorry,' she said when she rang the office. 'I was with a rather difficult client and it took me far longer than I'd allowed for.' It was a plausible lie, her colleagues would have taken it at face value without batting an eyelid, but her secretary was a different matter. She knew all the clients, knew when they were booked in for a visit. But Fiona had learnt the art of lying. State it clearly, don't waver, don't back down. 'Was there something important?'

'Mr Donaldson was looking for you.'

Matt Donaldson, the CEO. *Shit*. 'Oh right, I'll give him a call.' As if Fiona was completely fine with being unavailable for the CEO in the middle of a working day. 'Was there anything else?'

'He's rung five times. I told him you were working from home. Like you told me.'

Fiona grimaced. The message was clear. She and the secretary might have a good relationship, but the woman wasn't intending to go out on a limb for her immediate boss. 'Thank you. Now, if that's it, I'll get on with my day.'

She hung up and stared at her mobile for a moment. What could Matt possibly want from her that required him to ring five times? Whatever it was, she wasn't going to find out by staring at the damn phone.

Sitting up straighter, she rang his number and pasted a smile on her face that he wouldn't see but she hoped would be heard in her voice. 'Matt, good morning. Sorry I wasn't available to take your calls. I was in a meeting with a potential client.' She laughed. 'One of those who wanted everything spelt out for him. You know the type.'

'Your secretary said you were working from home.'

It was a statement, not a question, and it shimmered with suspicion. Fiona could have said the secretary had made a mistake, could have hung her out to dry. She didn't. She refused to be the kind of woman who would sacrifice other women to get to the top. 'That's right, and I was until I had a call from a potential client.' The second lesson in how to lie: do it with aplomb. 'A Japanese IT whiz kid with an unpronounceable name who's looking to invest his somewhat dodgy cash.' The third lesson: spin a tale that was almost believable with vague details that were impossible to check. 'It might be a bit too dodgy for us, though. I'm going to do some research before taking it any further and running the risk of getting Donaldson and Partners into trouble.'

There was silence before he replied. 'Hmmm, right, well keep me posted on that one.'

'Yes, of course. If it sounds too precarious, I'll point him towards one of our competitors.'

This drew a laugh.

Fiona waited till it had faded before jumping in. 'So I apologise for not being available when you rang. Was it something important?'

'No, no, it wasn't anything. I thought you were in the office today so when I noticed you weren't there, I asked your secretary.'

And then he decided to check up on her. Fiona gritted her teeth. He wouldn't have checked up on Phillip, who was renowned for taking a few hours off to play golf.

'I was hoping you weren't sick. When I couldn't get hold of you at home... well, you can understand, I was concerned.'

The lying bastard. The only thing he was concerned about was money. 'You're so good, Matt. I'm sorry I caused you such worry. In future, I'll make sure to keep Trish updated.' Fiona was being nauseatingly obsequious but there were times when it was necessary and this was one of them. She wasn't going to risk her very well-paid job if a bit of arse-licking would do the trick.

'Good, good. Well, I'd better let you get on with it. Keep me in the loop regarding that Chinese guy.'

'Japanese, and of course I will.'

She'd send him an email in a few days to say she'd researched the gentleman thoroughly and felt it was too big a risk for Donaldson and Partners to commit to. And that, hopefully, would be that.

***

Once home, Fiona did a quick catch-up with emails, finished some reports, and made a few phone calls. By five, she was exhausted and would have liked nothing better than to have had a long, hot bath and a few glasses of wine.

She could cancel dinner with Rich. Ring him, get her pennyworth in first and tell him that perhaps it was better if they called it a day. Or perhaps, she wouldn't ring him, just not show up. He'd sit there at *their* table in *their* restaurant, and wait expectantly, his eyes flicking to the door every time it opened. How long would he wait before the truth hit him that she wasn't coming? She could stay home and drown her sorrows in a surfeit of alcohol.

But as she imagined him sitting there, her expression softened. She had to be wrong. He couldn't be ending it. Not after all the words of love, that almost tangible chemistry between them. She hadn't bloody-well imagined it.

And in that spirit, she had a long shower, smothered herself in her favourite moisturiser and sprayed herself with matching scent. Barely-there underwear, her favourite little black dress and, with a glance in the mirror, she knew she was looking better than ever.

A taxi dropped her outside the restaurant a respectable ten minutes after the appointed hour. And there he was, waiting at their table in the window. She stood on the pavement and watched him for a moment, unable to prevent a smile curving her lips or that stupid warm glow where her cold heart should be. Perhaps she was desperate, maybe even a little obsessed, but she faced the truth there on the pavement as the chilly winter air seeped through her thin coat: she loved him. Absolutely, completely, ridiculously.

Perhaps it came harder when you got older. There had been so many men; she didn't remember feeling this way about any of them.

If, as she feared, he was going to tell her it was over between them, what would she do?

She'd like to think she could take it like the tough, successful woman she was, but as she stood there looking at him, she knew it would break her as nothing before had ever done. The chilly evening helped; it cut her to the bone, strengthened her resolve so that she pushed through the door with her head held high, and a swing in her step.

'Fiona,' he said, getting to his feet and holding out a hand to her. 'You look stunning.' He kissed her cheek. 'And you smell amazing.'

She put her hand against his cheek and held it there for a moment as she looked into his eyes. They were soft with admiration and desire. And then he kissed her, and she knew she'd been mistaken. He wasn't about to tell her they'd reached the end. Perhaps she'd got the wrong end of the stick altogether – perhaps he was about to tell her that he was leaving his wife.

'I've had one of those days,' she said, sitting in the chair he pulled out for her. 'I've been looking forward to this.'

'A glass or two of your favourite wine and you'll feel more the thing.' He lifted the bottle and poured wine into her glass before topping up his own. 'And I bet you've not eaten all day, have you?'

She thought of the eclair she'd had earlier, sitting across the café from his wife. 'No, I've been manically busy, so I've just been inhaling coffee.'

He handed her one of the menus. 'Probably better if we order before we drink too much in that case, eh?'

'Sounds like a plan.' She barely glanced at the words, knowing she'd order what she had done on every visit. It seemed to fit. Same restaurant, table, wine, meal. It was becoming a little obsessive, as if to alter any one of those items would jinx things. And she especially wasn't going to change now that her fears seemed unfounded. So it would be the same *pasta al forno* that she'd had on each visit. It had been tempting to wear the same dress each time too but that was one step too far. She was wearing the same set of underwear, though, and she was damned if it was going to go to waste.

'I was thinking,' she said, holding her wine glass towards him, waiting as he did the same before touching it gently, hearing the satisfying clink as glass met glass. She hoped he'd get the message.

'That glass shouldn't be having all the fun?'

She laughed. He never disappointed. 'Exactly! So how about we eat, then go back to my place to prove it doesn't? I promise you'll still be home in time to get a good rest for whatever excitement you have planned for tomorrow.'

They ate slowly, savouring the food, enjoying the wine, both of them anticipating what was to come.

And for the moment, she was able to put her doubts behind her. They hadn't been completely dismissed, though, lingering there like a bad, unidentifiable odour that caused her now and then to sniff the air and wonder if she was imagining it.

* * *

Three hours later, Fiona slipped from Rich's arms. Sexual gymnastics had left her physically satisfied but strangely confused. It was as if she didn't really recognise this woman she'd become. She reached for the pillow that had fallen to the floor and dragged it under her head. The sound of Rich snoring softly beside her made her smile and turn to look at him. She should wake him. He'd told her he couldn't stay long. An early meeting, he'd said. She didn't believe him, guessing it was something to do with his wife. Perhaps Fiona should have asked him gently if everything was okay at home. It would give him an opening to tell her exactly how the land lay.

It was a conversation that would have to happen eventually.

She was damned if she was going to stay a mistress forever. Rich would have to be brought around to the facts of life: he couldn't have his cake and eat it. At least not this cake.

With a sigh, she turned to look at him. She'd read somewhere once that you could influence someone's decision by whispering in their ears while they slept. She'd thought it was a crock of shit, but desperate times called for desperate measures.

'Rich,' she said softly. When there was no change in the volume of his snores, she moved a little closer. 'It's time I left my wife. I love Fiona. She's my future. I love Fiona. I really love Fiona.' She repeated the words, wondering if they were worming their way into a part of his brain, if they'd sit there like seeds, waiting for the right moment to burst into life. Would he be at work tomorrow, and the thought suddenly hit him that he needed to be with her? That she was his future and he needed to tell his wife their marriage was over?

Fiona knew she should wake him, but she had the irrational notion that she needed to let those whispered words settle into his brain before she did. She sank back onto her pillow. She'd done what she could, hadn't she? Short of killing the wife, she wasn't going to be able to get rid of her. Short of killing her... and on that thought, she fell asleep.

20

RICH

Rich couldn't complain. He shouldn't have fallen asleep. He checked his watch for the tenth time since climbing into the Uber – but compulsive checking wasn't going to make the time go backward. It was almost one. How was he going to explain being this late? Hopefully, Lydia would be asleep and he wouldn't need to. She'd floored him earlier when she'd asked if he was having an affair. He thought he'd carefully covered his tracks, but obviously, he hadn't been careful enough. How had he thought he could hide anything from a woman he'd known for so long?

He thought he'd allayed her suspicions. It was easy to be credible when telling the truth or even half the truth. It was business. Or at least it had been. Now he wasn't sure what it was. That final kiss with Lydia – the passion had been genuine. He loved her. It was just... He shut his eyes, thinking about Fiona and what she did to him.

He checked his watch again. He needed to shower. Usually, he'd have one before he left Fiona's but waking as late as he had, he'd pulled on his clothes and fled with a brief kiss to her sleeping cheek. He opened his jacket, bent his head and sniffed, relieved to smell nothing out of the ordinary. The electric shower at home was noisy. If Lydia was asleep, it was sure to wake her and lead to more explanations as to why he was having a shower. He missed the days of smoky pubs which would have given a perfect excuse to need a shower.

He rested his head back and shut his eyes. How the hell had he got himself into this situation and what, apart from his sanity, was he going to lose before it was over?

Guilt. That had been the driving force. It still was, but now it had multiplied exponentially until he seemed to be bathing in the sticky, consuming mess of it. Worse, he couldn't see a way out.

How could he have said no? How could he say it now?

He'd lied to Lydia. That had been the start. 'Keep telling yourself that,' he muttered, staring through the taxi window at the rain-washed city street. He saw his reflection in the glass, the rain and the darkness taking years off his age. And for a moment, until street lights washed the image away, he saw the boy he had been when the whole sorry mess had begun.

If he could turn the clock back years, he'd have changed the whole course of his life. If he could turn it back even a few weeks, he'd have made a different decision. He'd have told Lydia everything. Thrown himself on her mercy. She loved him and he knew she'd have forgiven him. Instead, he'd kept his secret and done what was asked of him. And one lie had led to another and another. Lies to Lydia, to Fiona, to himself.

And behind it all, the guilt and regret for something he'd done so many years before.

Like the boy he was then, the man didn't know what to do to make things right.

21

LYDIA

I headed to bed early. It was a cutting off my nose to spite myself move, because the more I tried to convince myself that I hated Rich, the more the longing for him seemed to overwhelm me, like an addiction to something I knew was bad for me. Too agitated to be remotely sleepy, I switched out the light and lay in the darkness to await his return. I'd wait until I heard the clunk of the front door shutting, the proof he was home, then I'd shut my eyes, curl over on my side, and he'd get the hint that he'd had all the passion he was going to get from me that day. But with the heat of longing still warming my blood, I wondered if I'd be able to resist reaching for him when he slipped in beside me and I felt the familiar warmth of his body.

After a while, I did turn on my side, but only to watch the luminous hands of the old-style clock move slowly, slowly around the dial. It was hypnotic and I felt my eyelids growing heavy and the agitation easing. Sleep was a good idea. It would end a day of confusion, of disbelief and self-doubt. But when my eyes shut completely, I saw Candy's sugary face appear on the back of my eyelids.

Maybe she and Rich had stayed in touch. I tried to think back. When had I noticed him being a bit more distracted? There were always periods when he was busier at work and he'd be tired and withdrawn some evenings, but it was only recently, perhaps in the last couple of months, that his mind and thoughts continuously appeared to be elsewhere.

I frowned as I tried to remember where Candy lived. Not London – that I'd have remembered. But maybe she'd moved to the city recently.

It was the problem with lying in the dark. Things that might seem preposterous in the cold, bright light of day seemed eminently possible in the shadow world. So yes, of course that saccharine woman might have drifted back into Rich's orbit. It was possible, but was it likely?

Four hours of staring at the dial didn't give me any answers. Nor did the passage of time bring Rich home. It wasn't until the small hand on the clock pointed firmly to one that I heard the sounds I'd been waiting for: a car pulling up outside, the soft clunk as its door was shut, the dull thud of our front door closing.

It had been a very long *business* meeting.

I curled up on my side, shut my eyes, and waited. Would he have a shower? The giveaway of every cheating husband the world over.

He didn't, but he should have done. A shower might have made me suspicious, but the scent of the woman he'd been with still clinging to his skin when he slipped in beside me went a step further. It confirmed what I'd known, and that he'd lied to me.

There was no satisfaction in being right, when it was as wrong as this. My faithful husband proving himself to be a faithless cheat. Any longing I'd felt for him was swept away on a tide of hatred so intense, I had to bite my lips to stop a scream of sheer rage escaping. I curled up more tightly, a foetal protective position that was no defence against the scent that seemed to intensify as Rich's body warmed under the winter duvet. It caught in my throat, tickled my nose and made me want to vomit. Had this strange woman rubbed up against my husband to mark him as hers? Like the she-cat she was?

After a while, I couldn't stand it any longer. I slid from the bed, grabbed a robe, and went downstairs. The old house didn't keep the heat and the chill of a November night made me shiver. I could have switched on the heating, but it was an old system and it rattled, burped, and gurgled as it started up, the noises loud enough to wake the heaviest of sleepers. Not that I cared about disturbing Rich, but it would have brought him down to investigate and I didn't want to speak to him. Not then when I felt so raw. So betrayed.

I needed time to consider my situation.

I had already, but that was with some airy-fairy notion that he *might* be cheating on me. The fact of it was a painfully different story.

Was I willing to stay with him, now that I knew he was being unfaithful? What should I do? Tell him to pack his bags and leave, or keep my mouth shut and hope it was a passing phase? A mid-life crisis.

Was I willing to fight for him?

I looked around the chilly room with its clutter of memories. If I fought for him and lost, I'd also lose my home.

And that wasn't at all acceptable.

I'd always avoided confrontation.

But that didn't mean I couldn't face it when I needed to.

That didn't mean I was just going to sit back and take whatever shit life was going to throw at me.

22

'Are you any closer to finding anything?'

'It isn't that easy! It's going to take time.'

'Time! My life is on hold until this is sorted.'

'I'm doing my—'

'Spare me the fucking clichés. If you were doing your best, I'd have what I need by now!'

'I'm close to getting it. You just need to be patient. If I rush now, I could lose everything.'

A sigh hissed down the line. 'Okay, okay, I just hope you're not lying to me. Because if you are, I have nothing else to lose, do I?'

'Threatening me isn't going to get you what you want any faster.'

The voice when it came again had a vicious edge to it. 'That wasn't a threat; that was a promise. Get me what I want or I can make your life very unpleasant indeed.'

23

LYDIA

I stayed in bed the following morning. I'd barely slept and was feeling physically and mentally exhausted as I listened to Rich getting ready for his day as if everything was hunky-dory. I suppose in his world, everything was.

When he walked into the bedroom in his dark suit, wearing the shirt I'd ironed so carefully for him, and his tie with its usual neat Windsor knot – as if everything was as it always was – I wanted to jump from the bed and tear the tie from his neck. Or maybe to tighten it instead, until his tongue protruded and turned black, until he gurgled and took his last breath.

'You not feeling well?' he said, standing in the doorway, his face creased in concern.

I blinked away the image of him dying at my hand and managed a shaky smile. 'A bit of a headache,' I said, resting a hand on my forehead. 'I'll be fine in a bit.'

He came over and sat on the edge of the bed. 'Would you like me to bring you up a cup of tea or something?'

I'd already asked him for the truth, and he hadn't given me that. There wasn't anything else I wanted, except for him to leave.

Only then could I hope to get my thoughts untangled enough to see where I wanted to go. 'No, thanks, I'll head down for some breakfast in a bit.'

He reached for my hand, holding it tightly, his thumb sweeping to and fro. Perhaps it was supposed to be soothing, maybe in another time it would have been, but in that moment, with my senses on high alert, it was intensely irritating. It took all my self-control not to pull my hand away. Until I knew what I was going to do – until I knew what I wanted – it was better to leave him thinking that I believed the tall tale he'd told me. I hoped he'd go and leave me in peace, but typically, he wanted to set his own mind at rest. Wanted to be certain his lie had been accepted.

'I'm sorry I was a little later than planned last night. I hope you didn't wait too long for me.' He pulled my hand to his mouth and planted a kiss on the back of it. 'You were certainly out for the count when I got in. Sleeping the sleep of the happily contented.'

I smiled, genuinely amused. He'd taken my fake deep sleep as a sign that I believed him. I kept the smile in place as anger shot through me that he was taking me for a fool. In that second, I hated him as much as I loved him. Or maybe more.

When he left, after kissing me with far more passion than was the norm before leaving for the day, I flopped back on my pillow with a heavy sigh. Until I knew which way I was going to go, I needed to play it carefully. Hard as it might be to do, it would be easier to allow Rich to believe my suspicions had been put to bed.

If I decided separating was the way I was going to go, he wouldn't know what hit him. If I decided to fight for our marriage, his bit on the side wouldn't.

I'd no clear idea which way I was going to go since I was still struggling with the *I hate him, I love him* conundrum.

Whatever my feelings were for him, I knew exactly how I felt about that woman: I despised her, hated her ability to attract Rich, and at the same time, envied it. What had she got that I hadn't?

Perhaps it was time to find out.

I was almost certain it was the woman from the café. I'd seen her twice in the same place and each time, she'd arrived after me. As if she'd followed me there. And I'd swear she'd been staring at me. Or was it that I was staring at her? She was beautiful, glamorous, the kind of woman I assumed would be attractive to men. Was that it? Was I blaming her because she was everything I wasn't?

No, no, that wasn't it! I wasn't that stupidly pathetic that I was seeing every attractive woman as a threat. There was something about her. It wasn't simply that she'd been staring at me; it had been the *way* she'd been doing it. As if she hated me, as if she wanted me dead. I hadn't imagined it. I was sure I hadn't. *Almost sure.*

If I went back to the café, would she be there again? If she was, this time, I'd face her, and I'd know for certain. I'd challenge her. I could see myself in the role, like an avenging angel, calm and controlled as I confronted her and she cowered before me. The fantasy felt good, as they often did, but I guessed the reality would be different. Anger would come out in every word I uttered, and I knew I'd end up screaming my pain at her. Did I really want to make such a scene in a café I enjoyed visiting? Anyway, did I really expect her to promise to stay away from my husband simply because I asked her to? A woman like her was hardly going to be persuaded so easily to give up what she wanted. After all, if she'd followed me there, as I believed she had, didn't that show some determination on her side?

No, I wouldn't challenge her outright; I needed to be cleverer than that. But how was I going to find out who the bitch was?

I wasn't going to get far lying in bed. Nor would I succeed without an injection of caffeine to get my sleep-deprived brain cells working.

It was the need for coffee rather than any desire to start searching for information on a woman who might have displaced me in Rich's heart, that finally made me throw back the duvet. There didn't seem to be any reason to get dressed. I used to go to the gym for a few hours every morning. I used to volunteer in a charity shop two afternoons a week. I *used* to do a lot of things. I wasn't sure when that had changed.

I looked at the robe hanging on the back of my bedroom door – a cerise velour one that Rich had bought me for Christmas the previous year. It was soft, cosy and practical. On that Christmas night, when I'd pulled it on, I'd noticed the label stating it was a size sixteen. Sixteen! I'd laughed, tightened the belt around my waist, and never mentioned what I had assumed to have been his mistake. Now I wondered if it had been, or had he noticed my shirts pulling a little tighter around my sadly expanding midriff and decided to go up a size?

Although comparisons were always going to be a bad idea, I couldn't help but wonder what kind of robe *she* wore. A slinky, silk one that left nothing to the imagination. Or maybe she wasn't a robe person at all. I imagined her bouncing around a stylish, minimalist apartment in a camisole and lace-trimmed French knickers.

I left my robe where it was and pulled on a high-waisted pair of baggy jeans and a crew-necked sweater. Fuck sexy glamour. I needed comfort. I ignored the little voice shouting in my head that comfort didn't need to look quite so... I shut the voice up before it finished the sentence. It could only have been a mean, cruel word, and I was feeling demoralised enough without it.

Downstairs, I made a pot of coffee and sat with it to mull over things. Whether I decided to separate or fight, it seemed essential to find out as much as I could about Rich's bit on the side. But how? I didn't know who she was, or where she lived. The only thing I knew about her was that she was fucking my husband.

The caffeine finally gave me a nudge. Rich was a consultant for the company he worked for and, as such, was classified as self-employed. He was religious about keeping receipts to give to his accountant at the end of the tax year. He kept them all in a box in the small back bedroom he used as an office.

He'd started to keep the door locked after the twins had got in one day when they were seven or eight and crayoned over some papers he'd left on his desk. When they were older, he kept locking it to stop them from 'borrowing' stuff. These days, he kept it locked from habit.

But I knew where he hid the key.

He'd no reason to hide things from me. No reason to believe I'd go poking about in his things. So the key was where he'd aways left it.

Was I really going to do this? Of course I bloody-well was. He'd left me no choice, had he? I'd given him the opportunity to tell me the truth and he hadn't. By lying to me, he'd pushed me into this. Into being the kind of woman I never thought I'd be. One who was twisted with suspicion, mired in anger, struggling with envy for a woman I didn't know. And there was guilt there too – whether it was deserved or not – for not being woman enough for Rich, for pushing him away, for making him stray. Stupid thoughts, but I couldn't shake them off.

Before the thoughts rendered me incapable of action, I took

the key to Rich's office, unlocked the door, pushed it open and stared inside. What had I expected? Glaring evidence of his infidelity? A cardboard cut-out of his new love? But there was nothing out of the ordinary in the neat, tidy room. A place for everything, and everything in its place.

It would have been perfect to find a diary filled with notations for the days he was meeting the bitch. But technology had scuppered the easy ways to do things. Rich kept his diary on his mobile. His laptop was sitting open. I knew the password, but I was afraid I'd leave some kind of trace if I used it. Anyway, he was hardly going to have details of his affair on it.

No, what I wanted was the box of receipts. If there was anything to be found, it would be there.

It was in the bottom drawer of his desk. A box that had at one time held expensive toiletries, a gift from Jocelyn for my birthday one year. I'd loved the toiletries; Rich had loved the box with its dramatic black and gold pattern. 'It'd be perfect for keeping my receipts in,' he'd said, not even trying to be subtle. I'd laughed and handed it to him.

I took it out, put it on the desk, and ran my hand over its surface before lifting the lid and putting it aside.

It was a relief to see that the receipts were simply tossed in, in no particular order. It meant he'd be unlikely to notice them being disturbed.

This late in the year, there were hundreds. It was going to take time. I might as well make myself comfortable. I sat in the leather chair we'd bought at the same time as the desk, in a shop that had closed down many years before. In all the intervening years, I'd never sat in it. Even in those days when I looked to escape from the twins' chatter, I'd never thought to come in here, even when it was empty all day while Rich was at work. How strange that was. How stupid I'd been.

I was still shaking my head as I picked up the first receipt. It was for last night. Despite his late return, my dear husband had been efficient. It wasn't unusual for him to bring clients out for dinner and he always took them to the same French restaurant close to the office. But not last night. This receipt was for dinner in an Italian restaurant. One Rich had never brought me to, although Italian was my favourite. They'd had wine, of course. A bloody pricey bottle too. The scarlet whore had expensive taste.

They'd had dinner, wine, and then what – had they gone to a hotel, or to her apartment? Had they got naked together, had sex? Had she deliberately rubbed her damn scent all over him to lay claim to a man who wasn't hers?

I laid the receipt face down on the desk and reached for the next. It wasn't till several more had joined the pile on the table that I came to another for the same restaurant. It was for a night the previous week when Rich had said he'd needed to work late. The same wine, and one of them had ordered the same dish: a *pasta al forno*. Her, I guessed; Rich liked to vary what he ate and would usually work his way through a menu.

There were three more receipts for the same restaurant. A couple for the French one which I guessed were real business dinners. And that was it. No other restaurants. I examined all five receipts for the Italian restaurant carefully. Each time, they'd ordered the same wine, and she – because I knew it had to be her – ordered the same dish. I knew it was more than a coincidence and fear shot through me.

I'd been dismissing the woman as a man-stealing bitch, and Rich's involvement as middle-aged desire for excitement, as a last-ditch attempt to get a new model when the old one was getting worn and tired. What I hadn't really anticipated was this – this *romance*. Because looking at the receipts, that was the story they told. They went to the same restaurant – their special place.

The same wine and food – because the first time had been so good. I could almost see them sitting across from each other, could almost hear the tinkle of glass as they toasted each other, could almost feel the lust coming off them in waves.

This was more than a passing fling. This man-stealing woman seemed to be besotted with my husband. Maybe even obsessed with him. That made her more dangerous and would make her harder to get rid of.

And if he was besotted with her too – if it wasn't simply excitement, lust, and the lure of the new – that would make it almost impossible to fight against. Because if I pushed him to choose, wouldn't he prefer the new over the old?

Perhaps the better option was to wait till the flame of their passion burnt out. To allow it to cool, maybe to die, leaving nothing but ashes of regret in its wake. It would be a risky move because there was always the danger that the hot heat of infatuation might turn into love.

There was nothing else to be learnt from the receipts. Especially since it was hard to see through the tears that I couldn't seem to stop.

Tempting as it was to leave the proof of his adultery on the desk for him to find, I returned the receipts in the same order and put the box back in the drawer. I needed to play the game until I decided what to do.

I rocked to and fro in the chair and drummed my fingers on the desk. I was no closer to knowing who the woman was, but at least now I had a lead. The restaurant. If they always went to the same place, all I needed to do was to wait for the next day Rich said he needed to work late and do a stake-out of the restaurant. I wouldn't have long to wait; it seemed to have become a weekly meeting. On the same day, of course.

I'd watch, wait, and follow them when they left. Perhaps they checked into a nearby hotel for a few hours of passion. Of course, she might live nearby. That would be my preference. I could follow and find her lair. Unless of course, she too was married. If so, I'd wait till they left whatever hotel they frequented for their coupling, then I'd follow her home.

I drummed my fingers faster, harder. It wasn't going to be easy, but it should work. I'd find out everything I could about the bitch.

Then I'd decide what to do. Whatever happened between me and Rich, it wasn't going to end well for her.

24

'You promised you'd help me!'

'I know, and I will. I just need more time—'

'That's what you say every damn phone call. Are you even trying to help?'

'I am, I promise, it's just—'

'Don't say it's difficult! My life is being flushed down the damn toilet! That's fucking difficult in a fucking nutshell!'

'I'll get it for you.'

'It's only two weeks to the fifteenth. I want to have it then, to make a big to-do out of revealing the truth.'

'I'll get it by then. I promise.'

'You better, because if you don't, I'll be revealing a different truth, one that'd shake up your fucking cosy life.'

'Don't threaten me!'

But the line had already gone dead.

25

FIONA

Fiona had no idea if it had been the words she'd whispered into Rich's ears that were responsible in the following days for an increase in the romantic, sexy messages from him, the even more frequent calls.

'You'll get me into trouble,' she said, answering the fifth from him in so many hours. She'd forgotten to put the mobile to silent after the third, and the fourth call had interrupted a meeting with a new client. 'My apologies,' she'd said, glancing briefly at the screen before switching it off. 'My sister had surgery this morning. Her husband said he'd ring once to tell me that she was through safely.' The client didn't need to know there wasn't a sister, just that it was an important family matter that had momentarily distracted her, and not another client claiming her attention.

Fiona thought she'd pulled it off, but she'd had to make more promises than normal to swing the client her way, and she cursed her stupidity in leaving her phone switched on.

'I'm sorry,' Rich said. 'Messages aren't good enough; I needed to hear your voice.'

The weekend was looming. It was rare they got to meet over those two increasingly long days. Perhaps a subtle hint was in order.

'I don't suppose there's any chance of meeting over the next couple of days... No, forget I said that, I'm being silly; I know how you're fixed.' That he was a married man with obligations. 'Next Wednesday can't come fast enough.' She had baited the hook; now she needed to stay silent.

'Well...'

Fiona held her breath.

'I might be able to free up some time tomorrow. I was supposed to be playing golf with some old buddies, but—'

'But you can play golf anytime.'

'Exactly. I'd much prefer to spend the time with you. And often, after golf, we end up drinking too much, and occasionally, I've had to stay over at a friend's house.'

This was better than she'd expected. *I'm* a friend.'

'I'll play a round of golf, make my excuses, and get away early. We could go somewhere else for dinner if you'd like?'

It was tempting to push him further, to mention one of the more popular restaurants where they might bump into someone they knew. It'd force his hand, wouldn't it? Make him bring their relationship out of the shadows. But meeting on a Saturday, and having him stay over for the first time, it was progress. *Baby steps*, she thought. 'No, I love our place,' she said, 'let's not change.'

'Okay, I'll book it. Seven?'

It was early for a Saturday-night dinner, but it had been the time they'd always met up, so once again, she decided not to tempt fate by changing the time. 'Sounds perfect.'

They chatted for a few minutes more, tying up the logistics of where he'd park, and how long it would take him to change from his golf gear and shower.

'Five minutes if I'm showering alone,' he said, 'but if I can persuade you to join me, it'd take a lot longer.'

Fiona, who had made appointments for a haircut and facial on Saturday morning, had no intention of spoiling either by spending too long under hot water for a messy quickie. But there was no harm in giving him a little hope. 'I can be quite persuadable when I want to be,' she said, giving a throaty laugh. 'Let's see what the night brings.'

* * *

She should have relaxed, safe in the knowledge that their relationship was going forward – slowly perhaps but moving in the right direction. She *should* have relaxed. She certainly shouldn't have continued with her obsessional need to find out more about the wife. It would be called stalking, she supposed, as she sat once more in her car outside Rich's home on the Friday afternoon. She'd been distracted since his earlier call and was forced to make apologetic excuses when she'd lost concentration during a meeting with a client who'd been less than impressed.

Even her normally laid-back secretary looked at her askance when, shortly after lunch, Fiona said she had a headache and was heading home. She'd have looked at her even more strangely if she'd seen her peering through her car window at Rich's house less than an hour later.

Fiona had no idea what she was doing there. The wife might be out. She could even be meeting Rich. Perhaps they had a regular Friday-night dinner arrangement. Maybe – the thought made her mouth go dry – maybe he took her to the same Italian restaurant. She shook her head. No, he wouldn't have done something so crass. They'd have their own special place. That thought didn't cheer her in any way.

It was a grey day; the light was already fading by the time she arrived, the day continuing to darken as clouds gathered overhead. As she stared at the house, one of the upstairs windows glowed briefly, as if someone had switched a lamp on and off. A minute later, a downstairs light came on, and stayed lit. It seemed the wife was at home. Waiting for Rich to return. Fiona checked her watch. Almost three. He wouldn't be home for a good while yet. His last message had said he was crazy busy and might have to genuinely work late. It had made her smile.

So there they were: the wife waiting inside, Fiona waiting outside. It was a crazy situation. Things were moving slowly, but perhaps it was time to give them a nudge to get them moving a little more quickly. She was convinced the wife had to be suspicious. She had to be. Fiona had only known Rich a couple of months, but she could already almost tell what he was thinking. After forty years, the wife would know his every expression, every twitch. He'd never be able to hide an affair as exhilarating as theirs was from her. Or was Fiona fooling herself again?

The thought angered her. Of course the wife must know, but on the off chance her head was firmly buried in the sand, perhaps it would be a good idea to give her a hint.

Fiona pulled a notebook from her briefcase and tore a page from it. What to write? She'd have liked to come up with something poetic but pointed. Unfortunately, her brain was mathematical, not literary. She dismissed *who's being a naughty boy, eh?* as being too pantomime-villain sounding. Since she couldn't come up with anything clever, she decided to be clear and blunt: *did you know your husband was seeing another woman?*

She used a black felt-tipped pen she found in the bottom of her briefcase and wrote the words in large, jagged block capitals. She hesitated before writing *seeing*; she'd have liked to have written *was in love with*. Instead, she decided to substitute a cruder, in-your-face word.

DID YOU KNOW YOUR HUSBAND WAS FUCKING ANOTHER WOMAN?

The resulting message looked quite dramatic. A little threatening, and just a tad creepy.

If the wife didn't know by now, if she was deliberately being blind to what was going on in the hope it was simply a fling and Rich would come back to her, if she was pretending that all was well in her small little world, this would shake her up. Perhaps it would be enough to force her to confront Rich and his relationship with Fiona could be dragged kicking and screaming out into the open. If the wife presented him with an ultimatum now, while Fiona and he were still in the red-hot throes of love, she was sure he'd choose her. Absolutely positive. Almost 100 hundred per cent sure – or maybe 99 per cent anyway.

It was a risky strategy. But Fiona was a good strategist. All she needed to do was to play the game and she'd get the outcome she desired.

This note was just a first step.

She almost changed her mind at the last minute. She stood on the doorstep of Rich's house and wondered if the wife was in there getting ready for a relaxing evening with her husband. Perhaps she was busy in the kitchen, cooking him his favourite meal, an apron tied around her waist. Fiona had always sneered at such domesticity. She still did. It didn't mean she didn't want Rich. But they'd be a dynamic duo. A social pair. If they had to eat at home – and it would be a rare occurrence – there was the wonder of the takeaway.

So it wasn't envy of the domestic scene she imagined inside

that made her push open the letter box to post the note; it was the fact that Rich was coming home to his wife and not spending Friday night with Fiona. She'd pictured the pristine, white sheet with its dramatic message sailing through to land inside, but it wasn't working out that way. She struggled to get the single sheet through the letter box's ridiculously thick draught excluder. Instead of sailing through, it was going to land in a crumpled heap. The bloody wife would probably think it was trash and throw it into the bin without reading it.

Back in her car, Fiona sighed. It was possibly one of the stupidest things she'd ever done, and she wasn't really sure what she hoped to achieve by it. She sighed again. That wasn't true; she knew exactly what she wanted to achieve: to move things along faster. To get a proper commitment from Rich before things began to cool between them. Tension eased at the thought and she smiled; that wasn't going to happen anytime soon. There was something special between them. She was a pragmatic woman, and wasn't normally given to flights of fancy, but from the beginning, from the moment they'd literally bumped into each other, hadn't it been a little bit magical?

She was sure Rich felt the same way – almost sure. He just had to take that final step. If the wife did read the note, perhaps she'd give him the push he needed.

Fiona put her head back, shut her eyes, and spent a few minutes fantasising about the future when Rich and she would be together.

It was the rumble of a van passing that made her open her eyes again and frown. When had she become so dependent on a man for her happiness? She was a successful professional. She needed to get a grip. Her obsession with Rich was beginning to interfere with her work. If she wasn't careful, she'd end up the same way as Phillip.

It was time to put both Rich and his wife from her head and get back to work. She checked her mobile, answered a couple of emails, and returned a call from her secretary. 'Everything okay there?'

'More or less. Mr Donaldson was looking for you. I explained you weren't feeling well so you went home.'

Fuck! 'Right,' she said, far more calmly than she was feeling. What the hell did he want this time? Or was he simply checking up on her again? She needed to step carefully. She hadn't gone to all that trouble to get rid of Phillip to end up being thrown on the trash heap herself. 'I'll give him a buzz.'

'He's not in his office,' the secretary said. 'He mentioned going to play golf.'

'Right.' Fiona knew better than to contact him if he was out on the golf course with some of his buddies – or as he'd refer to them, 'business contacts'. Phillip used to do the same thing. Tell everyone he was speaking to a business contact – on the golf course. It was probably true too. The number of deals that were done over nine or eighteen holes was ridiculous. It was, Fiona, had decided, why Phillip had got the promotion over her in the first place. She supposed she should be grateful there was no other golfer in the company biting at her heels. 'Okay, I'll no doubt find out what he wanted on Monday. Have a good weekend.'

When she hung up, she realised the secretary hadn't asked her how she was feeling. Fiona frowned. Her fake illness obviously hadn't been believed. But had the secretary shown that doubt to Matt? Fiona slammed her hands on the steering wheel. She'd have to have a word with the stupid woman on Monday to see if she could get some inkling before she met with the CEO. Forewarned being forearmed and all that.

In the Friday-afternoon traffic, it took longer to get home.

That evening, as on every Friday, there was a standing arrangement to meet friends, acquaintances and business colleagues for drinks, dinner, and usually a late-night bar or club. Fiona was part of the core group of five who'd been meeting for years. They were all of an age, and were either married, divorced, or on their second or third marriage, apart from Fiona. The rest who turned up were usually younger, single, out for a good time. The one thing that united them: they were all successful, glamorous, and with money to splurge.

There was a time when it was her idea of the perfect evening. Now, the thought of the night ahead with its superficial chat, the desperation to be seen to be having fun, and the artificiality of it all, made her weary.

More wearying though would be to stay at home and wonder what Rich and his wife were doing. And worse, to wish he was doing it with her.

So she had a shower, changed into her finery, put on her make-up, and went out to party. None of her friends and acquaintances would have guessed that her thoughts were firmly elsewhere as she laughed, chatted and danced into the wee hours of Saturday morning.

26

LYDIA

Friday night used to be family night. The twins would come home from school, then college, and even after they'd moved out, they'd return for a few hours and we'd eat a meal together. There'd be arguments, discussions, laughter. I remember those evenings with fondness, even with a little longing. When first one, and then the other moved to Australia, I'd suggested we continued the Friday evening get-togethers by Facetime, but they'd laughed.

'You usually eat dinner at seven thirty; that'd be four thirty on a Saturday morning here in Sydney, and much as we love you, Ma, that's a bit early!'

So Rich and I ate on our own and it wasn't long before the importance of Friday family nights became less so. I was never sure if it was a coincidence or not, whether it had been the draw of the children that had brought Rich home, but since they'd left, he frequently needed to work late, and often I'd eat my dinner on a tray in front of the TV with a good movie for company.

He'd usually ring if he was going to be delayed, or sometimes, if he was particularly busy, I'd get a brief message. So when my mobile pipped, I wasn't too surprised to read:

> Crazy busy. Be home nineish.

One of the worst aspects of suspicion was the way it made you doubt everything and look for hidden meanings behind every word. I read the message again. Read it aloud, trying desperately, pathetically, to find some kind of underlying message. But after reading, rereading, and rereading again, there was nothing suspicious between the lines. The *crazy busy* didn't appear to be a euphemism for spending the evening with his trollop. Not if he was planning to be home by nine. The nights he'd gone to the Italian restaurant with the floosy, he hadn't been home till far later than that.

Self-pity was exhausting. I tried to jolly myself into a better mood. Rich would be home at nine. He wasn't spending Friday night with her. That was a good thing. A reason to be positive. There was an open bottle of white wine in the fridge. If I had a glass, it would help relax me more. I decided to take it through to the sitting room to watch TV while I waited for him to come home. I was sipping the wine as I moved, already beginning to feel a little more chilled. *The power of positive thinking,* I told myself just as I reached the kitchen doorway, my eye immediately drawn to the crumpled, white paper that lay on the polished floor by the front door.

Premonitions are strange. I didn't know what was written on it, but I knew absolutely that it was going to be something nasty.

I brought the glass I was holding into the sitting room and put it down on the coffee table, the glass rattling on the wooden surface as my hand shook. Then, because I knew I'd need Dutch courage, I picked it up again and drained it.

With a childish hope that perhaps I'd imagined what I'd seen, I peered around the edge of the doorway. But no, it hadn't been my imagination. As I approached, I could see that this side of the page was blank. I stood over it for several minutes before bending to pick it up. Carefully, by one corner. Using the tips of two fingers. I was careful because I didn't want to be contaminated by whatever it was that was written on it.

Whoever had pushed it through had been in a hurry. Probably afraid to be caught. Because they'd shoved it through with little care, the paper becoming crushed and torn on the thick draft excluder that edged the letter box.

I smoothed the page out, my hands trembling. They hadn't bothered sugar-coating the message, nor had they bothered with euphemisms. They were determined to make the message clear. No ambiguity here.

DID YOU KNOW YOUR HUSBAND WAS FUCKING ANOTHER WOMAN?

I didn't need to be a rocket scientist to know who'd sent this. Did she really think I didn't know about her? That I didn't smell her stink clinging to his skin when he came from her bed to mine? It was almost a relief to have my suspicions confirmed.

I guessed she knew I was aware my husband was fornicating with some skanky mare. This note, this overly dramatic missive, had been sent to force my hand. It looked as if she was bored waiting for Rich to leave me. Did she hope to push me into making him decide between his wife and his mistress? Did she really think I was that stupid?

I took the note through to the kitchen and pulled open a drawer to find the box of matches I kept there. Then I took great pleasure in setting the note on fire, holding it by a corner till the very last second before dropping it into the sink where the last of the flame fizzled out. A spray of water from the tap rinsed it away.

But not the words, nor the intention behind them.

If that hussy thought I was going to make it easy for her, she'd have to think again. She'd shown her true colours with this move. Showed just what kind of woman she was. One who was willing to go as low as she could to get what she wanted.

I saw it clearly now. My mission was clear. If I couldn't persuade Rich to stay with me, I needed to rescue him from the clutches of this bitch.

27

LYDIA

I considered myself to be one of those what you see is what you get type of people. Friends said I was refreshingly honest and blunt, those who didn't particularly care for me called me rude. Rich said I was simply too lazy to make the effort to dissemble or to be polite to people I didn't like.

Of course, because he knew me best, Rich's assessment of my character was closest to the truth. I couldn't see the point of pretending, of showing one face to some people, a different one to others. But perhaps it was simply because I'd never had the need.

With that horrible note reduced to ashes and rinsed away and the words that had been written on it imprinted on my brain, I knew I'd need to give an Oscar-winning performance that evening if I was going to succeed in rescuing Rich from the harlot's clutches. She'd expect me to show him the letter, rail at him, perhaps throw him out. That would work in her favour, because he'd go straight to her. She'd offer him a shoulder to cry on, a fuckable body to hold on to, and she'd drip poison in his ear about me.

But then she didn't know me at all, did she?

It'd been a long time since I'd made any effort on a Friday night.

I saw Rich's eyes widen in surprise when he opened the kitchen door just after nine o'clock to find I'd set the table with the best glasses and had soft music playing in the background.

'This looks nice,' he said, coming over to plant the usual dry kiss on my cheek. 'I haven't missed an anniversary or something, have I?'

I laughed. It was a forced, brittle sound that made him step away and look at me so suspiciously that I laughed again in genuine amusement. I patted his cheek gently. 'No, silly, you haven't. I just thought we'd have a nice romantic dinner together.'

'Right.' He sounded puzzled, which wasn't surprising as we ate together most nights of the week.

'It's your favourite,' I said, nodding towards the oven. 'Beef bourguignon. And I bought a nice bottle of Rioja to go with it.' I smiled as I watched his face for the slightest hint of guilt. I'd searched Waitrose's wine shelves for the exact bottle of wine he and his floozie had had in the restaurant. Of course, they didn't have it, but it had been a Rioja so it was as close as I could get. 'Go and get out of your suit. It's almost ready.'

It was a good meal. I'd given him most of the beef but I still struggled with the little I had. Since that note, everything tasted like ash. I kept the conversation flowing, talking about the twins, what they'd said when I'd Facetimed them last, how they seemed to be so happy. 'I was thinking maybe we could visit next year. Maybe stay for a few weeks. There's a train journey I'd quite fancy doing from Sydney to Perth. The Indian Pacific. It's three nights. We could do that, then spend a few days in Perth and fly home from there. What d'you think?'

'Three nights on a train?'

His tone of voice said he wasn't enamoured with the idea. Or maybe it was spending three nights in such close proximity with me that he wasn't keen on. Or maybe, it was that I was talking about next year at all.

I struggled to keep enthusiasm in my voice as I went on about the trip. 'We get a cabin. It's en suite. And all the meals are served in a restaurant carriage. It looks really good; will you think about it?' *About the future we could still have. The past we've shared. The children we'd raised.* 'We'd need to book soon. It's very popular.'

He wasn't saying no, or yes. It didn't matter; I'd put the idea into his head. Hopefully, it would linger there even when he was with her.

'Have you room for dessert? I bought tiramisu. That Lidl one that you raved about the last time we had it.' I got up to clear the plates away as I waited for his answer. He'd say yes, of course; he could never resist dessert.

He still hadn't answered by the time I'd loaded the dishwasher and I turned to him, surprised. 'Don't tell me you're turning down tiramisu?'

He was staring into his wine as if the answer lay within. He wasn't listening to me at all. I opened the container and spooned a generous helping of the luscious dessert onto a plate for him. Normally, I'd have a portion too, but my appetite appeared to have been rinsed away with that note.

'Here you go,' I said, putting the plate on the table before him, but it was another few seconds before he dragged himself back from wherever he'd gone to pick up the spoon and begin to eat.

'There's a good movie on tonight I thought we might watch. *Conclave*. It's had great reviews.'

'Sure, sounds good.'

I sat and sipped my wine. If he'd noticed I wasn't having dessert, he didn't say anything. He seemed to be enjoying it, taking a long time to eat each mouthful. It was a sweet, luscious dessert. Perhaps he was wishing he could be with his sweet trollop instead of having to endure the presence of his wife and sit with her watching some stupid movie about cardinals. I should have chosen something romantic. Perhaps something family centred. Or maybe I should have searched for a movie where the whore got her comeuppance. *Fatal Attraction* sprang to mind. From what I could remember, she got shot in the end of that movie. Not that I was wishing death on the slut. Well, not at our hands anyway.

'I've bought a second bottle of this,' I said, emptying the last of the wine into his glass. 'We could open it, have a glass while we're watching the movie if you like.'

It mightn't have been my best idea. In my mind, I'd seen us sitting close together on the sofa, sipping wine and enjoying the movie. I saw us holding hands, maybe leaning gently against each other. The way we used to. Instead, I sat on one end, and when Rich came through a few minutes later, he sat on the other. I did sip my wine, but I noticed he emptied his first glass in a few mouthfuls, refilling it and drinking that almost as quickly. Before the movie was over, I had finished my one drink and Rich had finished the bottle.

'That's me done for the night,' he said, draining the last drop. 'I think I'll go up. It's been a tiring week.'

I reached for the remote. 'We can finish watching it tomorrow.' The evening was supposed to end with us going up together, perhaps kissing along the way, both of us sure how the night was going to end. It was to be a contrast to the sordid little quickies he was having with the slapper. It was going to be a reminder of how good we were together.

'No.'

In the face of that harsh, blunt word, with an almost audible pop, the fantasy and cosy little image I'd created was gone. I looked at him, unable to speak as disappointment and heartbreaking sadness swept through me and robbed me of words.

He got to his feet, staggering slightly. 'You stay and finish it. It's not really my kind of movie, to be honest.' He leant down and planted a clumsy kiss on my cheek. 'I'll probably be asleep by the time you come up. I'll see you in the morning.'

I still couldn't speak. But what was there to say anyway?

28

LYDIA

I sat watching the movie until it was over but if anyone had asked me what happened in the end, I'd be unable to tell them. I was lost in my thoughts. An uncomfortable place to be.

It was two hours after Rich had gone up before I followed. He had always been a heavy sleeper. I could switch on the light and do my usual nightly preparations without any fear of disturbing him. There were nights, still fresh in my memory, when I'd wake him to make love. I stood in the doorway, in the dark, and wondered if I should try.

But when I slipped into bed beside him, when I reached a tentative hand towards him, I pulled back. If I woke him, and he rejected me, it would be more than I could bear. Or if he responded and called me by the wrong name – by *her* name – I'm not sure what I'd do.

So I did nothing. Not even sleep. I lay there, stared at the ceiling and made plans.

* * *

I was sitting in the kitchen with a pot of tea and a slice of toast when Rich appeared the following morning.

'The tea's fresh if you want a cup,' I said, tapping the pot. 'And you can have that slice of toast if you like; I've had enough.' I'd forced myself to eat one slice; the second would stick in my gullet now that he was down, looking ridiculously handsome and stupidly cheerful. He was dressed in his golfing kit, so I guessed that was going ahead as usual.

'Thanks,' he said, taking the slice and slathering it with butter.

I poured tea into a mug, added milk and pushed it towards him. 'What time d'you think you'll be home?'

He'd taken a bite of the toast. He chewed, swallowed, and took a mouthful of tea, all the time avoiding looking at me.

I was almost amused to watch him desperately searching for the appropriate words and tone. I could have spared him, told him I knew what he was going to say. That he'd be late, maybe even later than normal, and not to keep dinner for him. It wasn't unusual when he was with his golfing buddies. He would meet them, of course, he wouldn't forfeit a day's golf, but I guessed he'd skip the post-game drinks in order to spend the evening with the harlot.

'It's going to be a late one.' He reached for the pot and topped up his mug. 'Den is celebrating a promotion and you know what he's like. He won't want the evening to end.'

My expression was carefully fixed in neutral but I was screaming inside. I knew what he was going to say and it was too much to bear. I wanted to beg him not to speak. Not to tell me his plans. I wanted to tell him that I knew. But fear was a contrary friend: sometimes, it made you brave; sometimes, it made you freeze. So with ice in my veins, I waited for him to spill his lie.

'So I thought I might stay over at his place tonight. I should be home in time for lunch tomorrow.' He laughed, the sound forced and unreal. 'Unless we all have massive hangovers and are unable to move!' He crossed to the dishwasher, opened the door and put his mug inside. 'You don't mind, do you?' he said, turning back to me and looking at me for the first time.

'Of course not,' I said, the lie almost choking me. 'Maybe we could go somewhere nice for lunch tomorrow when you get back; what d'you think? I could book a table for one, maybe.'

He had the grace to look embarrassed when he answered. 'Might be a bad idea. It could be very late before we get to bed, and if we've drunk a lot, I won't be fit to drive until early afternoon.'

Dinner, followed by a night of passion. Maybe in the morning, they'd shower together and have sex under the spray. We used to indulge, but that was before the twins. They were fractious babies and in the first year, I rarely managed to eat a proper meal. I took to grazing on chunks of cheese, packets of crisps, sausage rolls. Anything I could grab and eat as I nursed one or other of the babies. Once they were walking, and into absolutely everything, I managed to lose some weight but I never managed to get rid of the belly fat.

I'm not sure if it was the continuous exhaustion, or my newfound self-consciousness about being seen naked, that had reduced our sex life to a missionary-position quick fumble every few months. We never regained that pre-baby sexual freedom. I'd thought it was simply that we'd grown up, had responsibilities and commitments, but perhaps we'd just stopped trying.

I told myself that our sex life was pleasurable and comfortable, insisting to my questioning inner voice that months without making love didn't mean anything. I assumed Rich was happy with the situation – assumed because we never spoke about it. Now I wondered why we hadn't. Why I hadn't said something years before? Why I hadn't made an effort to get some of that early magic back into our marriage? Perhaps if I had, Rich wouldn't have had to go looking elsewhere. I could almost feel the pain of the lash as I whipped myself because, of course, it was all my fault that he was a lying, cheating bastard.

'Maybe we could go out to dinner tomorrow night? Somewhere special, eh? To make up for it.' Totally oblivious to the thoughts scrambling my brain, he smiled at me, as if it was all a done deal.

And it was, of course. I could start screaming at him, but I'd only lose more. 'That's a great idea,' I said, accepting the consolation prize with as much enthusiasm as I could manage to squeeze out. 'I'll book somewhere nice.'

'Good, good.' He checked his watch. 'Right, I'd better get ready and go, or I'll miss the T-off.'

I stayed where I was, my hands curled around the empty mug. It was a heavy pottery one I'd bought at a market somewhere. Rich had left the kitchen door open. From where I sat, I could see the bottom of the stairway. I felt the weight of the mug in my hands. I could wait until he was on the bottom step, then throw it. Aim for his head. It'd knock him unconscious. Then he'd have to stay. I'd look after him and he'd forget all about that other woman.

The blow might kill him.

But he'd die as mine.

The thought startled me. I hadn't realised it was in my nature to be so vindictive. It seems I wasn't too old to learn new tricks.

When he came down the stairs a few minutes later, he was holding the leather holdall I'd bought him for Christmas the previous year. He used it when we went for weekends away. It wasn't meant to be used for overnight stays with the tart. My hands, still wrapped around that damn mug, tightened further. Would he be startled if it was crushed to dust? Or would he simply laugh, turn around and go anyway?

His expression was easy to read. Relief that he was getting away with it blended seamlessly with excitement for what lay ahead. Shattering a mug that I liked between my hands to make a point seemed silly. Anyway, who was I kidding; I wasn't the Incredible Hulk with superhuman strength. Nor was I going to throw the damn thing at Rich. I wasn't a monster.

What I was, was a betrayed woman with a mission. That thought put some steel in my spine. I released my grip on the mug and stood to walk with Rich to the door. His golf clubs were already in the boot of the car. He put the holdall in beside them and turned to kiss me goodbye.

'I'll ring you later,' he said. 'Before we've drunk too much and I find it hard to string words together.'

In other words, I wouldn't hear from him late in the evening. And I wouldn't be able to complain because he'd warned me, hadn't he? Such a kind, considerate husband as he was.

'I'll message you tomorrow to let you know what time I'll be home, okay?'

There was nothing *okay* about any of this. Rage surged through me again. Suddenly, I wanted to dash to the car, jump in, start the engine and run him over. I wanted to hear his bones crunch under the tyres. To know he'd never cheat on me again. Once more, the thought sizzled in my brain: *he might be dead, but he'd die mine.*

I didn't run him over, of course; I swallowed my ire, forced the corners of my mouth up in what I hoped was an approximation of a smile, and nodded like an idiot. 'Enjoy the golf.' But not the evening, or the night, or the morning with *her*.

I watched his car as he pulled out onto the road, then stood staring into space for a long time before turning to go back into my big, beautiful, empty home.

29

FIONA

Fiona's first thought when she woke on Saturday morning was *never again*. But that was a frequent wish after a late night of heavy drinking. She reached out a hand, hoping she hadn't been wasted enough to have done something stupid, relieved to find the other side of the bed empty. There had been some mornings when she'd eyed the man beside her with something akin to horror as she'd realised she'd no idea who he was. Or what they'd done.

She'd been a changed woman since Rich. A born-again one-man woman. It was a dramatic change for someone who'd always maintained that variety was better, that unlike swans, humans were not designed to mate for life.

It took a gallon of water and a couple of paracetamol before she was feeling well enough to join some girlfriends for their regular session in the beauty salon. By the end of the morning, there wasn't a part of her that hadn't been clipped, buffed and polished. She'd even had time to pop into one of her favourite boutiques and buy a new dress that she knew would make Rich's jaw drop.

The slick hairdo and dress would make it very clear that a quickie in the shower was not on the cards.

It didn't matter. They were going to have all night together. And he'd be there in the morning when she woke. It was his first time to stay overnight. A first step towards their future together.

Only now and then did she allow a niggle of worry to bother her. Would the wife show him the note? It was what Fiona had wanted, after all – to get the truth out there – but perhaps it hadn't been one of her cleverest ideas. If the wife did show him the note, a number of things could happen: he'd deny it, then feel obliged to stay home with her that day to prove it was nonsense, or admit it was true, then spend the day arguing with her about it. Or she'd throw him out, and he'd arrive at Fiona's feeling guilty. Each outcome would ruin a night Fiona had been looking forward to, and she kicked herself for having posted the note – or at least for having sent it when she had. She could have waited until Monday.

If the wife showed it to him – *if* she'd even read the damn thing.

Fiona was used to feeling in control, to being in charge of what happened. She hated this new and constant, unsettling doubt that seemed to have taken over her life. In the past, she'd always been so sure she was on the right path, but now it seemed to have been absorbed by a surrounding wilderness and she couldn't see where she was going.

Deciding it was important to think positive, she put a bottle of their favourite white wine into the fridge to chill. She fussed around, plumped cushions, rearranged the couple of ornaments, and stared out at the view. Then she checked her mobile, in case he might have sent her a message, and the time that was passing slowly, tick by tick.

When the doorbell sounded, she gave a yelp of relief that

half-amused, half-appalled her. What kind of a woman was she turning into? She was still wondering as she pressed the buzzer to let him in. She was beautiful, sexy, successful and she deserved this chance at happiness. Rich would choose her eventually; she hadn't needed to try to force it with that stupid note. It had been a mistake she wouldn't make again.

By the time he'd taken the lift to the seventh floor and knocked gently on her apartment door, she had beaten some sense into the wimp who seemed to have taken up residence in her head, and was able to greet him with a smile and a glass of the wine she'd hurriedly opened.

'Here you go,' she said, putting it into his hand and leaning closer to kiss him on the cheek. 'I've been looking forward to this night for days.'

Rich kissed her on the lips, then stood back, his eyes sweeping over her in obvious admiration. 'You look amazing.'

Fiona reached for her glass and touched it gently against his. 'You make me feel amazing.' She took a sip of her wine and smiled. 'But I'm starving, so why don't you get ready and we'll go and have that dinner.' She lifted her glass to him in a toast. 'You need to eat to keep up your energy. You'll need a lot of it later.'

* * *

Later, in the Italian restaurant, they ordered the wine they always ordered, she looked at the menu but chose the same meal. They ate, drank, and talked about everything and nothing. There was no shade in his conversation; he chatted freely, shared some amusing anecdotes about people he'd worked with over the years. Fiona in turn told him an edited version of how a colleague had been promoted over her.

'Honestly, it was simply because Phillip played golf. His

financial skills were debatable, he made several questionable decisions, and it wasn't long before they regretted choosing him over me.' She didn't mention her part in his downfall. Some things were best left unsaid.

'You really disliked the guy, didn't you?' Rich shrugged. 'You've mentioned him a few times and you get angry when you do.'

'Do I?' Of course she bloody-well got angry. Someone incompetent had been promoted over her after she'd worked her arse off to prove herself. She relaxed her shoulders and gave a quick laugh. 'I suppose I do a bit, but I didn't dislike Phillip, just the old-boys-together attitude that got him promoted to a position I deserved.'

'So what happened to him?'

She got rid of him. 'He made too many errors. Clients complained and he was finally let go.'

Rich smiled. 'So they saw sense and gave the position to you, did they?'

'They did. I was probably lucky there were no other golfers on the way up.'

That made Rich laugh. 'Maybe you should take it up. It's a very social game and I have to admit, I've done a bit of business on the green myself.'

Fiona's smile was forced. 'Even if I did play, I couldn't join the club that Phillip and my boss play in. It still has a men-only policy. Every year, they take a vote on whether to allow women, but it's for form's sake; it never passes.'

Rich's shrug, as if to say it was the way things were, made her grit her teeth, and the evening might have been spoilt if she hadn't suddenly seen the funny side of it. She was going to get into an argument about golf of all things!

Luckily, Rich mentioned a book he'd read and the conversation turned to books and from there to plays they'd both enjoyed. Fiona relaxed, finished her meal, sipped her wine. This was what she'd wanted. There was no rush to get home. No barely satisfying quickie to fit in before Rich needed to leave to return to his wife. He was Fiona's for the whole night.

Rich, as usual, was having dessert and was poring over the menu as Fiona sat back, relaxed, letting her eyes drift around the restaurant. With nothing interesting inside, she turned to look out the window. It was a cold but dry night. Street lights and neon signs made the outside almost daytime bright. The road, busy by day, was quieter at this time and she could see across to the far side.

Because they'd recently been talking about Phillip, when she saw a figure standing there, looking their way, at first, she thought it was him. But as she stared, the figure was lit by the full beam of a passing car. It wasn't Phillip's craggy face under the beanie hat, but it was one she knew well. The wife.

How on earth did she know they were going to be in that restaurant?

It seems like her note had had an effect on the wife all right, just not the one Fiona had wanted or expected. She'd wanted the stupid woman to tell Rich, to back him up against a wall and force him into making a choice. She'd expected the wife to be devastated, not to come out fighting.

Fiona stared at the unmoving figure. Although she was well wrapped up and wearing a hat, it looked to be an effort to stave off the cold rather than any attempt at disguise. She didn't seem to care that Fiona could see her or that Rich would if he looked that direction.

The wife was standing just that bit too far away to be able to judge her expression. What was she thinking as she stood out there in the frigidly cold night, watching her husband of forty years dining with his lover?

Fiona smiled. She'd bet a year's salary that the wife never referred to her that way. The smile faded as a litany of names dropped one after the other into her head. They seemed to be written in the same black, jagged writing that she'd used in the note. *Whore... slut... tramp... hussy... slag.* It didn't matter that Fiona had never wanted to be *that girl*. In falling in love with a married man, she'd become one.

It was galling that there were no equivalent words for a man. After all, although she might be breaking some unwritten female code by falling for another woman's man, she wasn't the one who was married. The worst he'd be called was an adulterer. She'd be the one blamed for breaking up the marriage.

Rich was still obsessed with the dessert menu. 'I can't decide between an affogato or a tiramisu,' he said, almost to himself.

It seemed appropriate that he was trying to decide between a sweet, soft, almost sickly dessert, and one where the sweetness was drowned by a shot of very strong, bitter coffee.

She took a final glance at the wife before smiling at Rich. 'Go for the affogato. It's the winner. Every time.'

Because it didn't matter what name the wife called her; that night, Fiona *was* the winner. It was she who was sitting over a romantic dinner with Rich, the wife who was the *other woman*.

If the note had forced the wife to see the truth, it hadn't been such a mistake after all.

Maybe things were going to go just as Fiona had wanted.

30

LYDIA

It was a bitterly cold day and I'd heard on the weather report that they were expecting the temperature to dip to minus two that night. Not the best time to be mounting a stake-out. But I needed to. I wanted to see the woman for myself to know exactly what I was up against. And to end that lingering doubt that I was imagining it all just to add some excitement to my life. Because I had to admit, it had done. I felt more alive than I had in a long time. How crazy was that? That it took the possibility that Rich was cheating on me to wake me up.

I'd had the clues – the stink of a woman's perfume on his body, the restaurant receipts, his distracted behaviour – but I needed more tangible proof. I wanted to see them together.

From the receipts, I knew they normally ate at seven. But that was during the week. They'd possibly eat later on a Saturday.

Especially when he wasn't rushing home to his wife.

I was more alive, but also more emotional. Bitterness swept over me in a wave that left me weak and tearful. *Pathetic.* That was the word. This is what they'd done to me, he with his cheating, her with her thieving. They'd made me a snivelling, pathetic mess. Anger swept the bitterness away and energised me. I was going to do this.

A lack of certainty as to when they might eat meant I needed to be outside the restaurant early if I wanted to see them arrive. I'd had a look at the restaurant's website. It had some artfully lit interior photographs which showed me all I needed to know. It wasn't very spacious and thankfully, lacked those nooks and crannies that would have made spying on them more difficult. I could arrive early – six thirty, perhaps – and go inside, pretend to be interested in booking a table for some date in the future, have a look around to be certain of the layout, then make my getaway.

Then it would be a case of waiting across the street until they arrived. I was almost positive they'd turn up. They seemed to treat this restaurant as their special place and since this was the first night Rich had spent away from home since he'd met the trollop, it made sense that they'd begin their night there.

It was what I'd have done. Perhaps, after all, the tramp and I had something in common apart from Rich. We were both hopelessly romantic fools.

* * *

The afternoon passed slowly. I tried to fill it with things I used to consider important – housework, laundry, supermarket shopping – but everything seemed such a waste of time and effort.

When Rich rang at five, I stared at my mobile but couldn't bring myself to answer it, relieved when, a minute later, he sent a message.

> The golf went well. We're in the bar already – it's going to be a long night! Hope you have a nice evening. xx

In the bar already! It was such a blatant lie that it might as well have had neon, flashing lights encircling it. I didn't bother to answer. I wondered if he'd notice, or worry, or if he had already put his mobile away and forgotten my existence.

At five thirty, I dressed for my stake-out. I donned several layers in the hope they'd prevent me dying from exposure in what might be a long wait. They might turn up at seven, they might turn up at eight, or nine, or not at all. I wasn't sure how long I was going to wait.

The restaurant was exactly the kind of place I'd have enjoyed. Flattering lighting, nice décor, elegant without being over the top. The waiter who approached when I opened the door kept a pleasant smile on his mouth but his eyes were telling me a different story. They were telling me that it wasn't the place for frumpily dressed women.

'I'd like to make a reservation for next week,' I said, following him to the desk. While he checked the computer, I had a chance to look around. Rich and his floozie weren't there yet, but that was what I'd expected. In fact, this early, there were only a few tables occupied.

'What day were you hoping for?'

Hoping? As if he was already planning on my rejection.

'Saturday.'

He turned down the corners of his mouth. 'I'm so sorry, we're fully booked on Saturday. Weekends tend to book up very quickly, you understand.'

'Of course, not to worry. Thank you.'

He had turned away before I'd finished speaking. Perhaps, after all, it wasn't my kind of place.

Outside, I waited until the traffic slowed before dashing across to the other side of the street. Shops on this side had shut at six. It left convenient doorways for me to stand in, offering shelter from the biting wind that swept along the street. Sneakily, it managed to slide between my layers so that before long, I was stamping from foot to foot, trying to stop myself freezing to death.

My breath was puffing out in white clouds. Like smoke signals. I wondered if they'd make me stand out. If Rich would look across and read, *I'll save you, Rich*. Or if the whore would look over and see a different message: *bitch, I hate you*.

I was being ridiculous but it passed the time to imagine what signals I could send.

With no idea if they'd arrive by taxi, or if she lived near enough to allow them to walk, I continuously scanned the pavement in each direction and peered into every taxi that passed. As the time ticked closer to seven, I stopped pacing and upped my surveillance, straining my eyes to see as far as I could, almost afraid to blink in case I missed them.

And then, just as I was beginning to think they weren't going to come, or they were coming later, by which time, I'd have died of hypothermia, I saw them. In the distance. A blurry twosome. I knew it was him, even before the shapes took form. I'd have recognised Rich's rather bouncy walk anywhere, and the woman by his side, almost as tall as his six-foot-two, was exactly what I'd feared. Even from afar, when I couldn't make out her features, I knew she was beautiful. It was the way she walked. As if she was certain of her place in the world. And although she was wrapped up against the cold night, I could tell by the way she moved that she was slim under the layers.

There was no fear that they'd see me. They were totally absorbed in one another. Anyway, in my unflattering layers, I'd rendered myself invisible. Glamorous women like her didn't see women like me, and men, even husbands, weren't immune to being dazzled by the sparkle of women like her.

Unlike Rich, the bitch didn't bounce as she walked; she glided. As they spoke, their breaths, puffing white in front, blended into one and danced before them as they walked. I still couldn't see her face; it was turned to look at him. Pretending she was enthralled by him. The bitch was good.

Hate, envy, dismay, heartbreak – every negative emotion that existed oozed through me as I watched them approach the restaurant. Then they were inside, and I was left outside with my thoughts. My mission might be to save Rich from the slut's talons, but it didn't stop me, right in that minute, from hating him for falling for her in the first place.

They sat at a table in the window, the frosted lower half doing little to hide them from my gaze. But it was still hard to see her face, and I wanted to; I desperately needed to see my nemesis.

They were so engrossed in each other that I guessed even if I stood with my nose pressed to the window, they might not notice. But I didn't want to risk it and give the game away. Not yet when I was still uncertain how I was going to proceed.

It seemed safer to cross over and walk casually past. I waited for a break in the traffic then raced across at an angle that brought me slightly further along the street. Walking past the restaurant, I'd be able to see her face, and Rich, who might possibly recognise me, would be unlikely to identify me from my receding rear.

My plan worked – almost too well. Because I saw her face

and immediately recognised her. I wanted to stop, to bang on the window and shout, *I know you!*

The woman from the café.

I'd been right; she'd followed me to the café on both occasions. It seemed the woman was as curious about me as I was about her.

And perhaps she was looking for ways to get rid of me, as I was searching for a way to get rid of her.

31

LYDIA

With my curiosity satisfied, I crossed back to the far side of the street. I could have gone home at that stage. After all, I'd seen what I'd come to see. But now I needed more. I wanted to know where she lived.

I'd become oblivious to the cold. It's amazing how anger heats every part of you.

The window of the restaurant became my own private movie. I watched the waiter come to the table with their meals, take plates away, stand to refill their glasses. I watched as he held the bottle and looked at Rich. I couldn't see the waiter's lips move but I knew he was asking if they wanted another. I hoped they would. More alcohol would make it less likely that they'd spot me as I followed them to whatever lair she'd lead him to.

Moments later, I saw another bottle being opened and poured and I smiled. Things were working in my favour.

It was almost ten by the time they finally left the restaurant. They'd made it easy for me to follow them, the alcohol making them both careless and slow. And amorous. Four times on the ten-minute walk between the restaurant and the apartment block where they finally stopped, they swung into doorways for what could only be described as a snog. *Sucking face* as we used to say in school. I wanted to be disgusted, to sneer at their lack of control, but instead, I quivered with both anger and desire. I wanted to be her, to have my husband so intoxicated with me that he'd throw constraint out the window. Had he ever? In the beginning, there were coy glances, gentle kisses, holding hands, the odd, almost embarrassed fumble. Our first night together was less than earth-shattering and I distinctly remember thinking, *is that it?* even as I was telling him how amazing it had been. The pleasure had come with practice, but passion?

It angered me that I couldn't ever remember feeling the kind of emotion that seemed to spark between my husband and the woman he was fucking. It made me want to scream out my frustration.

I was relieved when their journey finally ended at a multi-storey apartment block. Once they were inside, I was out of the loop. It didn't matter. I knew exactly how their journey would end.

I waited a few minutes after they'd gone inside before I approached the building. Unsurprisingly, there were numbers beside the doorbells, but no names. I pressed my nose to the glass door and peered into the foyer. There were rows of postboxes. Her name would be there but there were two problems. I was on the wrong side of the door, and I had no idea what her name was.

In TV shows I'd watched, the baddie would wait until someone was going inside, then run in after them before the door clicked shut. I'd have thought Londoners were too safety-conscious to be that stupid, but with no other plan and nothing to rush home for, I stepped away from the door into the shadow of a tree and waited.

The first person tapped in the code on the keypad and slipped in when the door was barely open. Annoyingly, it shut behind him before I could get to it. I was luckier with the second, who'd obviously had a very enjoyable night. He swayed alarmingly as he tapped in the code for the outside door. It blinked red and he swore. I took the chance that he was too drunk to notice and moved closer as he swore again, loudly, and slowly jabbed each number with unnecessary force. It allowed me plenty of time to memorise the numbers: 5612.

I didn't need to use them this time. He pushed the door open so hard, it bounced against the wall behind, and before it shut, I was inside. I'd already noticed the CCTV camera, so knew to keep my face averted. Once the drunk had disappeared into the lift, I moved to the bank of postboxes. Some only had numbers, others surnames, and a couple had both first and surnames.

I was no wiser. But she struck me as a woman who'd be on Instagram. If she was, I might be able to find her. I took out my phone and snapped a photo of each group of boxes. Then I scarpered.

By the time I pushed open my front door, I was exhausted. Not merely a physical tiredness but a mental one. It was my imagination's fault, because although I couldn't know what was going on in the apartment, I pictured it. Every thrust and grunt, every cry of satisfaction, every orgasmic moan.

Exhausted, but I couldn't think of going to bed until I found out who the bitch was. I opened my laptop and went into Instagram, then one after the other, I searched for the names I'd photographed on the postboxes. I imagined her to be the kind of woman who wouldn't be happy to hide behind a number. I hoped I was right. The first couple of names I checked, irritatingly, had used avatars, the next was of a much older woman, the following one a man, but the next... I tapped in Carlton and there she was. I thumped the table in my excitement. *Fiona Carlton*. To make it easy for me, she'd posted several photographs of herself in various poses, most of which left little to the imagination. She was definitely a woman who liked to show off her body. Looking through the photos, I grudgingly admitted that if I had a body as good as hers, I'd show it off too. She wasn't as young as I'd thought, though. Maybe closer to forty than thirty. But still a good twenty years younger than me.

Now that I had the information, I was no clearer in knowing what I was going to do with it.

But I knew one thing.

Fiona Carlton might be beautiful, she might have a stunning body, but she was a whore and I was going to make her pay.

32

FIONA

Fiona smiled as Rich tucked into the affogato with obvious enjoyment.

'You sure you don't want a taste?' he asked, holding a spoonful of coffee-laced ice cream towards her. It immediately dripped onto the white tablecloth, leaving a round, brown stain that reminded Fiona of dried blood. It made her shiver.

Noticing, Rich laughed. 'Goose walk over your grave?' He took the spoon back and put it in his mouth.

'Something like that,' she said. She could feel the wife's eyes boring into her from across the street, surprised that Rich was totally oblivious to them. Perhaps Fiona was wasting the opportunity. Maybe she should point the wife out, bring the elephant in from the cold. The thought made her smile. Dressed as she was, that was exactly what the wife looked like. A baby elephant.

'What's so funny?'

No, it was the first night they were spending together; she wasn't going to ruin it by bringing his wife in to spoil it. 'Just watching you enjoying that dessert. You're like a child.'

'Like a child?' He looked slightly taken aback but then laughed. 'Wait till we get home; I'll show you otherwise!' He dropped the spoon on the plate and reached for her hand. 'Let's give coffee a miss.'

As they exited the restaurant minutes later, Fiona glanced across the street. The wife, that shuffling mound, wasn't making much of an attempt to be inconspicuous. She must know that she'd been spotted. By Fiona anyway. As far as she could tell, Rich had remained totally ignorant of her presence. Or was it a case of none so blind as those who don't want to see? Perhaps, he, like Fiona, didn't want the wife to intrude on their night together.

After all, what could he do? Go over and tell her to piss off?

'It's a chilly one,' he said, draping an arm over Fiona's shoulder and pulling her close. 'We could get a taxi; what d'you think?'

She shook her head. 'It's only five minutes; walking will warm us up.'

'I know something else that'd warm me up.' He pulled her into a doorway and kissed her. She could taste the coffee as his tongue dipped into her mouth, feel the warmth of his hand as it crept inside her coat and under the edge of her blouse. But even as she felt herself melt under his onslaught, she was aware that somewhere not far away, eyes were watching.

Minutes later, when they moved on, she stopped to straighten her coat, using the pretext to search behind them, but there was no sign of the wife. Perhaps worse than seeing her husband having dinner with another woman was the sight of him canoodling in a doorway with her.

Feeling an unwanted ache of pity for the wife, and stinging regret for sending that note, Fiona reached for Rich's hand and held it tightly. How long would he and his wife have stayed together if Fiona hadn't come on the scene? Not long, she guessed, as Rich pulled her into his arms again.

It was simply bad timing that she and Rich had met before he'd realised his marriage was over. It would have made it neater, and kinder to both women, if he'd ended one relationship before starting another.

It was why Fiona had sent that note, wasn't it? To force the wife into challenging him about his affair. Once she had, he'd be pushed into cutting that final string that held him to a woman he no longer loved. The note hadn't been sent simply to be cruel. Or mean. Fiona wasn't that kind of woman.

She tried to put the wife from her head. It helped that the thought of spending the whole night together had made Rich more than usually amorous. Their five-minute journey took far longer, as time after time they stopped to kiss like teenagers. But despite her best efforts, she couldn't get that bloody woman out of her head.

For the first time in a long time, and the first time ever with Rich, Fiona faked her orgasms that night. Too well, obviously, her response egging him on to a repeat performance she wasn't in the mood for. Nor was she in the mood for more amorous advances early the following morning. She resisted the temptation to snap at him to leave her alone when she felt his hand sneak over her belly at – she opened a weary eye to see the time – fucking four o'clock! 'You're insatiable,' she said, hoping he'd at least be quick so she could get back to sleep.

When she woke again, she was surprised to see the other side of the bed empty. Checking the clock, she groaned. Five. Too early to be awake on a Sunday morning. She shut her eyes, hoping to get back to sleep, and she probably would have done if the silence hadn't disturbed her.

Rich wasn't using the en suite. Perhaps he was being considerate and had gone to the main bathroom for whatever he needed to do. She waited, expecting to hear the flush of the toilet. When the silence continued, she threw the duvet back and slipped from the bed.

He'd hardly gone, had he? They were going to spend the morning together. The plan was to go to her local pub for breakfast. Perhaps he'd sensed her lack of interest in their earlier lovemaking. She thought she'd pulled it off but maybe she wasn't as good an actress as she'd believed.

She stood in the doorway, head cocked. The door to the main bathroom was open, so if Rich was still in the apartment, he wasn't there. She crossed to the door of the open-plan living room that extended the width of the apartment. Normally, the door stood wide open, so to find it shut puzzled her. Then she smiled. Of course, he was being considerate, afraid the sound of the boiling kettle might wake her. She opened the door quietly. If he was sitting looking out the window, lost in his thoughts, she didn't want to startle him and risk him dropping a mug of coffee on her off-white carpet.

She was smiling as she opened the door, the smile fading to puzzlement when she saw Rich, not as she expected, sipping a coffee and admiring the view, but on the sofa, his face creased in concentration as he stared at the computer screen of her laptop.

Her laptop!

'Rich?' The *what the fuck are you doing* was left unsaid but it hung in the air between them. She waited for an explanation, feeling stupidly foolish in her nakedness. He, she noticed, had pulled on the golfing clothes he'd worn on arrival the previous day. She also noted the glimmer of guilt that had crossed his face. 'Is that my computer?'

It was a superfluous question. They both knew it was.

'Yeah,' he said with a smile. 'And thanks again for letting me use it. I still can't believe I forgot to send that email before I left the office. It's your fault, of course; you have me bewitched!' He tapped a key, then shut the laptop.

She felt as if she was missing part of the story. 'How did you know my password?'

He jerked his chin back. 'Don't you remember? Last night, when we got back, I remembered I'd forgotten to reply to an email and you told me I could use your computer.' He looked at her, his expression perplexed. 'Of course, we'd had a bit to drink, but you don't remember?'

She didn't. Not his story about needing to send an email, nor her offer to use her computer, and certainly not giving him her password. But she had drunk a lot of wine. A bottle at least. Perhaps more now that she thought back. The waiter had been very attentive, and she'd a vague recollection that Rich's glass was emptying far slower than her own.

Maybe she had been drunk. She must have been to have forgotten about the email. Very drunk indeed to have handed over her password. Must have been, because if she hadn't, then Rich was lying to her, and that wasn't possible, was it?

'No,' she said. 'I don't remember.'

'Gosh, I'm sorry. I wouldn't have bothered, only it was rather important the email was sent this morning.'

He looked suitably dismayed. Because she couldn't remember, or because he was caught and had needed to lie? But why would he want to access her computer? They both worked in finance; had he been hoping for some inside information? Maybe details of her clients? If so, he'd have been disappointed.

'That's okay,' she said, although she wasn't sure it was. It was no big deal, really. There was nothing important on her computer. *But he wouldn't have known that.* No sensitive information. *But he wouldn't have known that either.* Nothing too dodgy in her search history either. Not unless he looked very deep. It was no big deal, except it was if he'd lied to her. Because if he had, everything she thought she knew about him was suddenly uncertain. 'If you're finished with it, I'll put it away.'

And later, when he'd gone, she'd change her password.

33

Voicemail:

'Are you avoiding me? This is my third time to ring without getting an answer. I'm getting very impatient. Remember you have to find out what I need before the fifteenth. Let me know how close you are to getting it, okay? Don't make me have to call you again.

'And just in case you think you can back out of our arrangement, remember you're in even more deeply now. I don't like to threaten, but I will make your life a misery. I'll destroy you if you fail me.'

34

FIONA

Fiona was relieved when Rich showed no interest in returning to bed with her. She left him watching a news programme on his phone and tried to get back to sleep. But when she shut her eyes, the previous night's conversations buzzed around in her head. Alcohol may have made the edges a little blurry, but the gist of each was clear, and nowhere could she remember any conversation which finished with her giving Rich the password to her laptop.

Yet, she had to have done. Unless he was some kind of tech wizard, or... She might not remember the details of the conversations they'd had the previous night, but she did recall one they'd had weeks before, both of them laughing at the number of passwords they were forced to remember. She'd boasted that she could remember every one of them, but laughingly admitted when pressed that she kept them written down in a notebook just in case.

Her notebook. She kept it in the drawer of the coffee table. It wouldn't be hard to find if you were looking for it. Her style was minimalist. There was one bookshelf in the living room that held only a few books, old favourites she occasionally reread, a couple of ornaments she'd purchased on her travels, and that was it. If someone wanted to search for something, they wouldn't have had too difficult a job.

If Rich had needed to send an email, of course she'd have allowed him to use her laptop. But she'd have unlocked it for him, wouldn't she? Not given him her password. She loved him, but she wasn't sure she completely trusted him. How could she when he was lying to his wife? That the lies benefitted Fiona was beside the point. He lied to his wife; didn't it follow therefore that he could lie to her?

Why had he wanted her laptop? She didn't believe his story about needing to use it to send an email. He could have used his phone.

It was her personal laptop. There were no details about any of her clients. No financial information. She didn't like where her thoughts were going. Was she seriously considering that Rich, the man she loved, was using her? That he was involved in some kind of dodgy industrial espionage?

Wasn't that all a bit B-movie?

As B-movie as sending that stupid note, and the wife stalking them.

Perhaps that's all this was. Her stupid overactive imagination. Seeing the wife outside the restaurant had really thrown Fiona. Perhaps the guilt of being the other woman was making her a little paranoid. She had been very drunk the previous night. Drunk and determined to make Rich's first full night with her a success. Determined, desperate, and so obsessed with making sure it would be a night to remember, a taste of the future they could have together, that she'd have done anything he'd asked.

So she probably *had* given him the password to her laptop. It would have been easier for him than using his phone. She'd seen the way he peered at the restaurant menu, obviously too vain to wear glasses. She could understand. In the last year, she'd noticed she was having a similar problem. Growing old was inevitable; looking old was a different matter altogether.

She curled onto her side and pulled the duvet up around her shoulders. A little more sleep and she'd feel much better, and less likely to jump to ridiculously suspicious assumptions. But as soon as she shut her eyes, she wondered what Rich was doing alone out in the living room.

She immediately thought back to the moment she'd gone in and caught him using her laptop. He'd looked guilty. Why would he, if she had in fact given him her password and permission to use her computer?

Or maybe she was overthinking it. Maybe he'd looked guilty because he was up and dressed instead of lying beside her on their first morning together. Yes, that was more likely. And she *had* given him her password. But even as she tried to convince herself that everything was perfect, the worry that something didn't add up niggled. Too much to allow her to fall asleep. She flung the duvet back, got up and grabbed a robe from the en suite door.

Rich was sitting in a chair by the window when she went back to the living room. 'Hey,' she said, crossing to him and resting a hand on his shoulder. 'Would you like me to make you some decent coffee?'

He reached up, took her hand and kissed it. 'That'd be good. A strong one, please.'

She nodded and went to the kitchen where the Nespresso machine was the only piece of equipment that she allowed herself to keep on the countertop. 'You didn't sleep well?' she asked as she took pods from the cupboard.

'I've had a lot on my mind recently.'

'Well this will help you keep your eyes open,' she said, putting a black coffee in front of him, then returning to make one for herself. 'We can go to breakfast at ten when the pub opens, if you'd like.'

'Sure, that'd be good.'

Was she imagining the lack of enthusiasm in his voice? Perhaps she'd made her feelings clear when she'd seen him using her laptop and he'd been annoyed at her change of mind. After all, she'd told him he could use it, and she'd given him her password. Hadn't she? That doubt uncurled again. As she sipped her coffee, her eyes slid to the expensive, white, beech coffee table in front of the sofa. It had been one of her most expensive purchases after she'd bought the apartment. The design was perfectly simple, with one single drawer set underneath the tabletop. When shut, as it was now, it was almost imperceptible. It had seemed a safe place to keep her notebook.

Had she opened the drawer while Rich was nearby? Or had he found it while searching for the TV remote?

'You should have turned on the TV,' she said. 'It wouldn't have disturbed me.'

He shook his head. 'I saw all I wanted to see of the news on my phone.' He indicated the window with a jerk of his thumb. 'It's nice to sit and look out the window.'

They chatted about nothing much until they'd both finished their coffee. 'I'll go and get dressed,' Fiona said, taking the mugs and putting them into the dishwasher. 'I won't be long.' She wondered if he'd suggest going with her and having the shower sex he'd mentioned the previous evening. She was relieved when he simply smiled and let her go.

Back in her bedroom, relief changed to disappointment. Okay, she wasn't interested in sex, but she'd have preferred if he had been. Maybe she was simply tired and contrary but something felt just a bit off.

After a shower, she felt a little better and was even able to laugh at herself. Seriously, had she really wanted him to follow her into the shower? She remembered when she was younger, and the men were too – in those days, nothing seemed impossible, but fit as Rich was, she wasn't sure he'd be able for the gymnastics required, despite his best intentions and desire. She frowned; he hadn't shown any desire though, had he? Then she remembered that 4 a.m. wake-up and smiled again. She was just being silly. He was dressed, probably thinking of his breakfast.

But no matter how much she reassured herself that everything was fine, she continued to feel a little on edge and found herself over-compensating as a result. Being that little bit over-the-top cheerful as they did the short walk to the pub, a tad too enthusiastic about a breakfast that was barely above average, and perhaps way too rapturous about what a wonderful night it had been.

They had bought the newspapers on the way to the pub. After they'd finished eating, conversation dribbled to a halt and they buried their heads in the pages, occasionally raising their eyes to comment on an article they were reading.

From the beginning, there'd been an easy rapport between them and even the silences, when they occurred, were comfortable. But that morning, the gaps between the words seemed filled with expectation. As if they were both waiting for something to happen, something to explode.

Fiona found herself constantly glancing towards the entrance. Was the wife going to burst through at any moment to cause a scene? Stand there in all her virtuous wifely indignation and point a finger at her husband and his whore? Because, Fiona guessed, that was the word the wife would use to describe her.

That blasted wife. The image of her standing out on the street, staring in at them, was bothering Fiona. And making her mentally kick herself once more for sending that note. It had been an unnecessarily stupid thing to have done. She'd poked the bear and now it was coming for Fiona with her dream of happy ever after.

It was the thought of the wife that was unsettling her. Nothing to do with the image of Rich's face when she'd found him with her laptop. Nothing to do with the doubt that had raised its ugly head – that maybe she was wrong about him.

Their relationship had been impossibly romantic from the very beginning. She'd fallen for his charm, for this perfect man who'd wandered into her life. Was it really all an illusion?

35

LYDIA

I sat in the living room as the house cooled around me and I was shivering before I finally stood and headed upstairs. I hadn't switched any lights on. It didn't matter; I knew my way. One step in front of the other, slow and sure, and I'd get where I wanted to be.

The whore didn't know that about me. That I wouldn't rush into doing something stupid. I'm guessing it was what she'd hoped for with that pathetic note. That I'd challenge him, make a fool of myself by playing the poor, abandoned, rejected wife, force poor Rich into making a choice.

Now that I'd seen her, I was no longer sure what that choice would be.

I needed her to make the decision to fuck off and leave my husband alone.

A few minutes under the duvet and I was warm. But still wide awake. My thoughts were fixated on what my husband and his tart were doing. She'd be adventurous in bed, of course. I bet she'd read the *Kama Sutra*, bet she'd tried every one of the positions in it. I imagined her long limbs entwined with Rich's.

They'd probably not sleep at all. He'd come home, looking all heavy-eyed and weary and blame it on late-night drinks with the lads. If he did, I wasn't sure I'd be able to keep from scratching his eyes out.

Unable to sleep, I kept thoughts of their sexual gymnastics from my head by coming up with various scenarios for getting rid of her. Murder was out – not because I didn't want to see the bitch dead, not even because I wasn't sure I had that capacity for violence, but because I didn't think I'd be able to kill her without being caught, and spending the next several years in prison seemed to be self-defeating.

But there were other ways to destroy someone.

By the time I'd come up with what I was considering to be a first step, it was after 7 a.m. and starting to show traces of the day to come. He'd be home in a few hours. I needed to get some sleep or I'd look like an ancient, worn-out hag.

The thought of the comparison with that image and the woman I'd seen the previous night was enough to keep me awake a little while longer, but somewhere before the day arrived, I fell asleep.

* * *

When I woke, I was surprised to see I'd slept for three hours. I didn't feel completely rested but not exhausted either. I took extra care with my ablutions and applied the kind of make-up I normally reserved for special nights out.

The restaurant we were going to later was smart. I searched through my wardrobe for something suitable and pulled out a dress I hadn't worn for a while. When I tried it on, I remembered why. I'd put on a few pounds since I'd bought it. Who was I kidding? I'd probably put on a stone.

Dragging it off, I shoved it to the back of a shelf. It was going to have to be trousers and a floaty top to cover the curves. Being winter made it easier. Black trousers, and a black, long-sleeved top that skimmed over my excess bulges.

When I looked in the mirror, I wanted to cry. The lack of sleep had made me more than usually pale and in my effort to compensate, I'd been far too heavy-handed with the make-up. I looked like a bloody clown. The black trousers and top were also a disaster. I was a clown-faced bat who'd obviously eaten far more than her fair share of bugs.

Twenty minutes later, having tried and discarded several combinations, I settled for the black trousers, a black, scoop-necked sleeveless top, and a black blouse with a fine grey pattern that was at least one size too small but looked fine left open.

I stood in front of the full-length mirror and smiled in satisfaction. With my make-up toned down, I looked good. Okay, being realistic, I couldn't compare with the other woman but I didn't need to. Rich and I, we had history. Over dinner, I was going to talk about the twins and what they were doing. When that conversation ran dry, I was going to reminisce about the months we'd spent renovating our home and whether we should get it repainted. And when I'd mined that for every atom of shared experience, I'd fall back on gossip Alice had shared with me about a mutual friend.

Forty plus years of intimate knowledge: our children, our home, our friends. It had to count for something. Had to count for more than he had with *her*.

After a final glance in the mirror and resisting the temptation to add a brighter lipstick, I headed downstairs, surprised to see it was already three. Rich hadn't said what time he'd be home, but I'd assumed early afternoon. I checked my phone. There were no messages from him.

Too busy.

Bitterness shot through me. Was the sex so magical, he couldn't tear himself away? Had she totally bewitched him?

My finger hovered over the key to ring him. But if he answered, if he lied about where he was and what he was doing, I wouldn't be able to stop myself from lashing out. And if he didn't answer, my imagination would switch into overdrive as I considered what was keeping him so busy. So instead, I sent a message, keeping it light, friendly, carefully neutral.

> Hi, I hope the hangover isn't too bad. I've booked the restaurant for 6pm. Love you xx

I read it over, deleted the *love you* and added an extra x instead before sending it.

Then I sat and stared unblinking at the screen until my eyes grew gritty, and anger, which never seemed to be far below the surface these days, bubbled up. If Rich had come through the door at that moment, I think I'd have had to reconsider my capacity for violence, because I was sure I'd have killed him.

36

FIONA

In the previous few days, when Fiona had thought about the weekend, she'd expected she and Rich would have one final session between the sheets before he left her to return to the drudgery of his marriage. But by the time they'd returned to her apartment after their pub lunch, she knew that wasn't going to happen. He was in an unusually sombre mood, a little distant, and more than a little cool.

It was almost as if he'd thought their night together had been a mistake. Maybe he'd found her lacking somehow. She wasn't usually so concerned about what other people thought, but this was different. This was Rich, and she minded, probably way too much. She could feel desperation slink around her ankles. It would creep upward on poisonous fingers until it leeched into her voice.

'Would you like some coffee?' she asked, resisting the temptation to add *since you're obviously not in the mood for anything else.*

'We could have had some in the pub,' he replied with obvious lack of enthusiasm.

'Yes, but we didn't, did we?' Her voice was sharp. She added a laugh to soften it. 'Anyway, I make far better coffee.' She nodded towards the dining table. It sat in front of sliding doors that opened onto the tiny balcony. 'Sit, admire the view; it won't take a minute. We can chat until it's time for you to leave.'

'There you go,' she said a few minutes later, putting a mug on the table in front of him and taking the seat opposite with her own. 'Have you a busy week ahead?'

'Coming towards the end of the year is always busy, you know how it goes.'

Being a financial advisor, it was the end of the tax year that caused her more grief. He'd know that, but it seemed pedantic to contradict him so she merely smiled and nodded. It immediately irritated her that she was slipping into the subservient role. As if his every proclamation was right. Did she want to keep him that desperately? Both the *yes* and the *no* were screamed inside her head with equal fervour. Yes, because she loved him, and considered him her last chance at marriage to a decent guy, and no, because she was no longer sure he *was*. She picked up her coffee and held the mug in front of her mouth as she pressed her lips painfully together.

Rich was talking about some meeting he had the following morning, recounting some rather salacious gossip about one of the clients, a tale that Fiona might at one stage have found amusing. It seemed a bit much, she thought, for Rich to be commenting on the client's predilection for prostitutes. She wanted to ask him if his criticism was for the use of prostitutes or was he sneering at the client paying for something that Rich was getting for free.

She put the mug down and sighed. It was loud enough to bring whatever Rich was saying to an abrupt halt.

'Are you okay?'

Was she? Hadn't she'd just compared herself to a prostitute? 'Just a bit tired, perhaps; I might have a nap when you're gone.'

As hints went, it wasn't subtle, but he didn't take it, didn't finish his coffee and leave. Instead, he took up the conversation exactly where he'd left off. At least she guessed it was, she wasn't sure; she hadn't been listening before, and she wasn't now.

What she was, was weary. Many years before, when she'd been younger, and her future had stretched out before her full of promise, she'd sworn no man was going to be in charge of her happiness. And they hadn't. For years, she'd taken what she needed and moved on. Then she'd bumped into Rich and had fallen so ridiculously in love that she'd allowed him to paint her future in bright, cheerful colours. Until that morning... Now, the colours seem faded, greying at the edges.

She tuned back into what he was saying: something about the fundraising charity ball he was attending the following week.

'It's fancy dress, would you believe,' he said with a shake of his head. 'Goodness knows what stupid costume I'll end up wearing.'

Fiona knew exactly which it was going to be, could almost hear the wife's voice as she told her friend they were going as Mr and Mrs Claus. Fiona remembered that she'd sneered. She also remembered thinking that maybe the wife would be history by the time the ball came around. How naïve she'd been.

She opened her mouth to tell Rich she was also going to the ball, then shut it without a word when she realised he was talking about the following Saturday, without any mention of meeting her before as he'd normally have done.

'I have a busy week myself,' she said with a smile. 'Jocelyn has roped me in to go to a few gallery exhibitions.' She chatted on, dropping less than subtle hints about her nights filling up quickly. When he remained quiet, when he didn't come back with an anxious hope that there was room in her busy calendar for him, she swallowed the lump in her throat. She wasn't going to beg.

A horrifying thought came to her. Had he met someone else? Was that it? Perhaps the instantaneous attraction between them had been a spark that had flickered briefly, then died.

Or was it that old story: men wanted you till they had you, then it was easy to let you go.

Despite the doubts that were building up, brick by brick, she was still in love with him. But those doubts would give her strength. They'd help to rebuild the armour that Rich had so easily pierced. It was time to take back control. To be the woman she was before love had rendered her stupid.

She pushed back her chair and stood. 'Right, well, if you don't mind I'm going to throw you out now. I'll need that nap before I head out to meet some friends later. We're going to some new club so no doubt it'll be a late night.'

He stood and looked at her in surprise. 'A club?'

'Yes.' She stretched, pressing her breasts against the silk shirt she was wearing, pleased to see his eyes flick downward. Gilding the lily, she lifted her hair with her two hands, held it on the top of her head for a moment before dropping it to fall around her shoulders. 'So, off you go. Thanks for a nice night.' Nice! Could she have used a more dismissive adjective?

'I'll be in touch,' Rich said, kissing her cheek.

He'll be in touch! It was tempting to tell him not to bother, that the night had been their swan song.

What kind of a woman had she become? Had she really turned into one who would put up with this kind of treatment all in the name of love?

She hated him for making her this way.

Worse, she hated part of herself. The feckless, desperate

woman she didn't want to be. The sad, needy woman who checked her phone again and again over the following hours. The lovelorn fool who hoped there'd be a message from him to say he couldn't wait to see her again.

'Take back control!' She snorted a laugh and tossed the mobile onto the seat beside her.

A minute later, she wiped away tears, and checked it again.

37

RICH

Rich was on his third whisky. It was burning a hole in his belly but wasn't helping him to decide what to do.

All he'd wanted, after all these years, was to do the right thing.

Instead, he'd made a great big fucking mess of everything. And now, he couldn't see a way out. Which was why he was sitting in a pub, a mile from his home, wondering what to do. He hoped he'd find courage in the whisky. Enough to enable him to walk into his house, face his wife, and lie to her yet again.

A bigger lie this time.

One that would destroy her.

If he'd told her the truth from the beginning... but it was forty years too late for that.

If he'd told her the truth recently, instead of trying to make things better, she'd have been angry, but she'd have stopped his life spiralling out of control. A sensible woman, she would never have allowed him to do what he'd been asked to do. A wise woman, she'd have come up with an alternative plan. One that would have worked.

And Rich's life would have continued on its uneventful way.

He'd been happy, hadn't he? Before this. Before he'd made stupid promises he was no longer sure he could keep.

Before he'd fallen madly, crazily, so bloody stupidly in love.

38

LYDIA

It was almost 5.30 before I heard the rattle of Rich's keys in the front door. I was sitting in the living room, pretending I was watching a movie, waiting for him to put his head around the door with an apology tripping off his tongue.

When he didn't appear after a couple of minutes, I frowned, got to my feet and went to see where he was. Still outside, the keys rattling against the door.

Puzzled, I opened it just as Rich lunged forward with a key. My reflexes were slow in disbelief and the key caught me painfully hard on my shoulder.

'Fuck,' he said, rearing back. 'I'm sorry.' He waved the bunch of keys. 'Couldn't get it in the lock.' His titter and the waft of alcohol that drifted to me with every word told me he was very drunk.

I looked behind for the car, relieved he'd had the sense not to drive. 'Where's the car?'

He looked behind, as if expecting to see it, then shook his head. 'Dunno, but it'll come to me.' He lurched past and stumbled towards the kitchen.

I stood at the open doorway for a moment, the cold air cooling my anger. It seemed that all my effort to look nice was going to be a great big waste of time.

'You've been drinking,' I said, stating the blindingly bloody obvious when I rejoined him.

He was downing a pint glass of water, gulping frantically as if the water was going to sober him up. 'They insisted we go to the pub for breakfast. Then someone suggested the hair of the dog. And one thing led to another.'

This was crazy! Did he really expect me to believe him? Maybe it was time to bite that damn bullet after all. 'Rich—'

'No!' He held a hand up to stop me. 'Sorry, but I think I'm going to be sick.'

He dashed away, taking the stairs in twos. A minute later, I heard him retching into the toilet. I should have gone after him and demanded to know the truth. I didn't, for two reasons. Asking someone to explain themselves when they had their face shoved into a toilet bowl struck me as cruel, if not pointless, and secondly, I was puzzled.

He didn't strike me as someone who'd had the night of his life. On the contrary, he seemed more like a man who'd been drowning his sorrows. Maybe the slag had dumped him.

I rang the restaurant and cancelled our reservation, then I sat in my glad rags and waited for Rich to return. Maybe he had come to his senses and ended the affair. If he apologised for being a bit distant in the last few weeks, I'd know we were okay. I'd forgive him for straying. Forgetting was a different matter. If the image of him naked with another woman ever began to fade, I had the words she'd written on that note embedded in my brain to remind me.

Perhaps instead of burning the note, I should have had it framed. I could have hung it on the wall to stop me from ever becoming complacent. Recent experiences had taught me a valuable lesson: that it was impossible to know what the future held. Rich might never be tempted to stray again – but he might. And if he did, that would be it. To forgive might very well be 'divine', as Pope wrote, but I'm not sure he was referring to habitual adultery.

I couldn't pin one thought down. One moment, convinced that Rich's unusual drunken state meant he'd been dumped by the slut; the next, that he'd called a halt to their relationship because he realised how much he loved me. The next, and most worrying, was that he'd decided she was the one he wanted. He was going to tell me the truth: that he was leaving me, and had needed to visit a pub to acquire some Dutch courage in order to break the news.

Worrying, as the minutes passed, it was this last thought that shouted loudest, becoming a shriek that deafened me and scattered the other thoughts.

Was that it? He needed Dutch courage in order to face me and tell me the truth, hoping that another and another shot of alcohol would make it easier. Was that why he was upstairs puking his guts up, still afraid to come down to confront me?

Twilight turned to darkness. I hadn't switched the lights on. The movie I hadn't been watching was on mute, the images on the screen sending a kaleidoscope of lights bouncing off the walls and ceiling. And still he didn't come down.

A vague and irritatingly mundane idea that I should take something from the freezer for dinner came and went without making me move. I wasn't hungry, and I doubted if food was going to be on Rich's agenda for a while.

I reached for the remote and switched the TV off. Then, in the solid silence of darkness, I heard something. The living-room door was ajar. Crossing to it, I slipped through and stood at the bottom of the stairway. With my head cocked, I heard the sound again – it was the soft murmur of Rich's voice.

I crept up, step by step, until I was outside the door of the spare bedroom.

The fancy earrings I'd put on earlier pressed painfully into my neck as I held my ear to the door, tighter and tighter, desperately trying to hear what Rich was saying. It didn't matter; I heard the tone. Loving, conciliatory, gentle. Then, as I pressed even tighter still, I heard the words.

'You know I'd do anything for you, don't you?'

He'd said the words loudly, emphatically, as if he was trying to reassure her. And the voice in my head shrieked the truth again. I stepped back and held my hands to my ears, trying to shut it out, shaking my head as the shriek dissolved into high-pitched, cruel laughter. When it stopped, and the voice spoke again, it told me the hard facts of life. He was going to leave me for her. He'd made his choice.

He just hadn't found the courage to tell me yet.

But it wasn't over until the fat lady sang, and this fat lady wasn't planning to sing anytime soon.

39

LYDIA

I stayed by the spare bedroom door for several minutes. After Rich's declaration, his voice dropped to a low mumble that was impossible to decipher. Words of undying love, perhaps. When even the murmuring stopped, I backed away and returned to the living room.

I sat, and almost immediately stood again to go back upstairs, noisily this time, announcing my arrival almost with a fanfare as I knocked a rat-a-tat-tat on the door.

'Hey, you okay? Can I get you anything?'

It was a few seconds before I heard the faint, but blunt, 'No.'

'Okay. In case you have a bug, perhaps you'd better sleep in there tonight. I don't want to catch it.'

There was no reply.

'I'm heading to bed now. Shout if you need me, okay?'

'Yes, fine. See you in the morning.'

No, he wouldn't. I planned to be fast asleep if he looked in on me in the morning. My plan was simple. If I could stop him telling me that he was leaving me, I might be able to prevent it. I still had a chance to get the whore to back off.

The night passed in restless moments of sleep, waking moments of anger, dreams of violence. I heard Rich moving about – the flush of the toilet, the gurgle of running water from the taps, his attempt to be quiet as he went downstairs, and sometime later, his ascent when he stumbled on the top step and swore softly. I wondered if he'd look in on me. Hoping he would, because wouldn't that show he cared about me? Hoping he wouldn't, because I wasn't sure I'd be able to prevent myself from sitting up and screaming at him that I knew about her.

It was the click of the spare-bedroom door as it shut behind him that released me from my painful wait. And then I was left with thoughts that spun from violent to ludicrous. I pictured killing her in several painfully twisted ways: running her over in my car, reversing over her crushed body – just to be sure. Lying there in the darkness, stretching a hand out and feeling the chill where Rich should have been, right then, if she'd been standing in front of me, right in that moment, I thought perhaps I might have been able to kill.

But daylight brought reality along with it. I wasn't capable of that level of violence. I had to do something, though; after all, I had everything to lose, and everything to gain.

I listened as the house woke with a rattle of pipes as the heating kicked on at 5 a.m. An hour later, I heard Rich stir. He may have stopped and listened at the door but he didn't open it to peer in. I wondered if he'd be relieved or worried when I didn't appear for breakfast. It was becoming a habit. A new norm for us after so many years starting the day together.

He did open the door, very quietly, before he left. I'd liked to have turned to see him, to reach out for him, to get the kiss goodbye that had been mine for so many years. But it was better to keep silent for fear he would, in an early-morning moment of weakness, confess it all. Once that genie was released from the bottle, I'd never get it back inside.

I waited until he'd left the house before sliding from the bed and hurrying to the window to catch a glimpse of him. Usually, he'd stride out, head held high, briefcase swinging from his hand in an in-control, king-of-the-castle, man-of-the-world manner to tell anyone who cared that he was someone who knew what he was doing and where he was going.

That morning, he trudged along, one hand shoved into his coat pocket, the other holding the briefcase still by his side. His shoulders were bowed under the weight of what he might do.

She did this to him, the bitch.

I strained to watch him for as long as I could, until he became a blur in the distance. He wasn't blameless. I wasn't that naïve. But I knew he wouldn't have gone looking for her. The tramp with her long legs and glossy hair had inveigled him. And it was time to teach her a lesson that hopefully, would give her cause to change her mind.

* * *

Two hours later, breakfasted, dressed for what I had planned and armed with the tools I required, I was standing outside her apartment block.

It was a little after nine, and quiet, as if everyone had left for the day. I tapped in the access code for the door, hearing the click with a grin of satisfaction. Thanks to the icy-cold weather, the woollen scarf wound around my neck and head hadn't drawn any strange glances on the journey. I pulled it up to cover my mouth as I pushed through the door. If the CCTV was monitored, which I doubted, they would never be able to identify me.

I took the lift to the seventh floor. There were only four apartments and all were clearly numbered, so it was easy to locate the correct one. I stood by it, wondering if she was inside. I supposed I could knock, have it out with her, tell her to fuck off away from my husband. I'd have done so if I'd thought a direct approach would work, but she'd already proved herself to be a woman of low morals so I doubted that a plea to leave us alone would suffice.

There was no time for second thoughts. I took the can of red spray paint I'd brought from home out of the capacious pocket of my coat. There was no debate about what to write.

<u>A Whore Lives Here</u>

I thought the underline was a neat touch.
On the wall opposite the lift, I added some directions.

Looking for the whore? She's in apartment 40

It would be the first thing people would see when they exited the lift. Then as an extra touch, I added an arrow pointing towards the apartment.

I had the lift to myself. It seemed a shame not to make the most of it. It might be monitored, I didn't care; in a few minutes, I'd be outside and they'd have no idea who I was.

The whore is on the 7th floor, apartment 40

I was on a high when I reached the ground floor and unstoppable. When the lift shut behind me, I took advantage of being alone once more and hastily scribbled on the door.

Whore ↑

And then I hurried away, keeping my scarf pulled up until I was in the tube station. In the toilets, I removed the scarf, left it in the cubicle behind me and mingled with a crowd of women as they exited. If the police were searching for me, which I doubted, they were unlikely to find me.

Nervous energy had me grinning like a fool. I stopped in a pub and ordered a whisky. It wasn't something I ever drank, but I needed to cool the energy down and strong alcohol seemed a good idea. The first didn't do anything, the second helped, and the third did what I needed. I was mellow when I left the pub. Chilled. Game for anything. I even thought about going back to her apartment to paint a big, red arrow on the path outside. That made me laugh so uproariously that people started to give me a wide berth. Perhaps I looked as crazy as I felt.

I had no clear idea how she would respond to my assault. Would she have second thoughts and decide Rich wasn't worth the grief? She'd been to my home, she saw how we lived, how much I had invested in our marriage. Did she really think I was going to give it up that easily?

Did she really think I wouldn't respond to her pathetic note with something bigger and better?

If she was as smart as she was glamorous, perhaps she'd know that I'd only begun and there was much more to come unless she backed off.

40

FIONA

Fiona kept telling herself she hated Rich. That she was stupid to put up with him. 'He'll be in touch,' she muttered again and again, stoking the flames of anger against him, and against herself for being so damn needy. But all it took was one message from him to douse the flames as quickly. One simple message.

> I'm sorry I was a bit distant earlier. It's complicated, apart from one thing… I love you.

It was all she needed to turn her into a grinning fool, to take a couple of dance steps across the floor, spin around, hum a few bars of a soppy love song. It *was* complicated but it was meant to be. They both knew that. They were old enough, wise enough, to grab the chance of happiness, despite the difficulties.

She sat to compose a reply. It was tempting to write, *Love means never having to say you're sorry,* but she wasn't sure even Ali MacGraw could get away with that cliché any more. Several increasingly silly messages later, all thankfully deleted before being sent and immediately regretted, she settled for keeping her reply as simple as his.

> I know it's hard, but remember I love you too.

She waited for his response, the happy glow dimming a little when her phone stayed resolutely quiet. It was late. Perhaps the wife had dragged him off to bed and they were, in that very moment, wrapped around one another. She'd never asked, because she didn't want to know the answer, if he and the wife still slept in the same bed, and if they did, whether or not they still made love. If she was being realistic, she had to admit they probably did. She tried to believe it didn't matter. That she didn't care. But her jaw was tight, her teeth grinding, her fingers curled into fists at the thought of them together.

When love came late, it came hard. She'd read that somewhere and had scoffed. Now, it felt tattooed onto her flesh.

She quickly discovered that imagining the man she loved in bed with someone else – even if that someone else was his wife – was not conducive to a good night's sleep. It was tempting to stay where she was. To ring the office at nine and tell her secretary that she was, after all, working from home that day.

But she'd already been letting things slide recently, and she didn't need Matt checking up on her until she caught up with things. He'd given Phillip far more chances than the idiot had deserved, but Fiona knew she wouldn't be afforded the same leeway. With her, it'd be one strike and she'd be out. Unfair, but then life frequently was.

She'd never let her love life affect her work before, but then she'd never felt this way about any of the men she'd been with. Rich was becoming an obsession that was destroying not only her, but everything she'd worked so hard for. She should end it, get out while she still could. While she still could... She sighed at the thought. It was already too late. Love wasn't only an obsession; it was an addiction.

Before she could weaken, she threw back the duvet and swung her feet to the floor. The combination of an almost-cold shower followed by an extra-strong coffee barely dented the weariness that seemed to envelop her like a cloud. Rereading Rich's message brought a brief smile and a little lightness to her steps as she left her apartment, but by the time she reached her office, the weariness had forced her brain to dwell on the complications of their relationship. How long would it be before they were resolved?

It was hard to keep her mind focused on the day's work. The gallon of coffee she drank didn't help much either. All it did was to send her to the bathroom far more frequently than usual so that she wasn't at her desk when Matt called in to speak to her.

When she returned following her third visit of the morning, Trish looked up from her desk and raised an eyebrow. 'Mr Donaldson was looking for you.'

'Did you tell him I'd just popped to the ladies?'

The eyebrow rose a little more. 'I did. He said he'd be back.'

Just what Fiona needed. More stress to add to her morning. She poured another coffee, then was afraid to drink it. She had to be in her office when Matt returned, at her desk, busy working, which didn't mean staring at her computer with her fingers frozen in place on the keyboard. There were clients waiting for information before they'd make decisions about their investments. Usually, she'd have the figures ready to go, but she was behind with everything. Worse, things she used to take such pleasure in now seemed so dreary.

She was turning into one of those irritating women who let their life slide when a man came into it. The idea was enough to shake some of the apathy away and over the next few hours, she managed to get on top of her outstanding work. Even better, her fingers were flying over the keyboard when Matt returned. He stood in the doorway looking at her with something like approval before she finished and waved him to a seat.

'Sorry, you were looking for me?'

He rested his elbows on the arms of the chair, hands dangling, legs man-spread. It was a pose so desperately casual that Fiona was instantly on alert. Had she made a mistake? Worse, had one of her clients made a complaint? She wondered, with a gut-churning squeeze of guilt, if this was how Phillip had felt at the end. Had that bitch, karma, come to mete out revenge? She tried to stay calm. It wasn't a fair comparison. He'd been generally and consistently incompetent; she'd just allowed her personal life to get in the way for a couple of weeks. *A couple of months?* Bloody Rich. Easier to blame him than to castigate herself yet again for being such an idiot that she'd allowed emotion to eat into all she'd fought so hard for.

She sat back in her chair, trying to look calm, in control, relaxed.

'What's the state of play with that Japanese customer?'

She was startled into blurting out, 'Who?' It was the expression on his face, the one that was saying clearly that he was disappointed in her, that had her mind racing to recover. Even tired, she was good at thinking on her feet. She laughed. 'Sorry, that was my fault for misleading you. He's Chinese, not Japanese. I'd say they all sound the same to me but that's not acceptable these days, is it?' Since she knew the CEO constantly railed against what he referred to as *this modern, PC, woke world*, this comment was sure to make him smile. It did, allowing her to relax. 'I've given him all the information he asked for and more. He wants to discuss it with his partners before making a decision.' She shrugged. 'He sounds serious, but you know the way these things go. If I were asked to bet...' She shrugged again, more dramatically this time. 'I'd say it's going to be a non-starter.

He struck me as being a cautious type and I'd say he'll put his money in bricks and mortar rather than stocks and shares.'

She thought she'd pulled it off but with Matt, you never knew.

'Right,' he said, getting to his feet. 'No harm in giving him a nudge, though, when you have a minute.'

When she had a minute? Was he being sarcastic?

She kept her expression neutral until he'd left, then sighed in annoyed frustration. Did he think they'd made yet another mistake in giving the promotion to her? If she wasn't careful, she'd follow in Phillip's footsteps.

The worry was enough to reignite a spark of enthusiasm and she spent the next hour contacting potential new clients. As a reward, she had another coffee and took out her mobile to ring Rich. There was no answer, which wasn't unusual. She left a message and dropped the phone on the desk.

On the dot of five, Trish popped her head around the door. 'I'm off. See you tomorrow?'

The implied question irritated Fiona. 'As usual. Don't be late.'

This barb hit the mark, Trish being a bad timekeeper. Then she was gone and Fiona sat back with a sigh. She'd leave it a few minutes before her own departure.

Thinking when tired was a bad idea. Immediately, her thoughts went, not to work, but to the note she'd sent the wife. Poking the bear had been a silly idea. Fiona would be lucky if following her was the worst the wife did in return.

She imagined her appearing in the office. Creating the kind of scene that would amuse some and horrify others. Especially Matt. He was the strait-laced type. 'This doesn't reflect well on Donaldson and Partners, Fiona,' she said, imitating Matt's rather reedy voice. 'Fuck him,' she muttered. She pushed away from her desk and got to her feet. She was tired, imagining nonsense. Rich loved her; that was all that counted. Eventually, the wife would realise that fighting the inevitable was a waste of time and give up.

All Fiona needed to do was to hang on. Be patient. Wait.

Keep her temper.

Not do anything else fucking stupid.

41

FIONA

Travelling through London at any time of the day had its problems, but rush hour was in a league of its own for a hellish experience. The Tube was packed. It had been raining heavily and the usual assortment of smells was overlaid with the stink of damp clothes drying in the heat of bodies pressed too closely together for anyone's comfort.

Out on the street, the battle was with other pedestrians wielding carelessly held umbrellas. Fiona's was packed away in her briefcase. Heading home, unless she had further engagements that night, she didn't mind getting wet. Once inside, she'd throw off her clothes, have a shower and relax for the remainder of the evening.

The thought made her speed up, desperate to get home.

In the lobby of the apartment block, she grabbed her post and exchanged greetings with a resident who lived on the floor below her. 'Wet day, isn't it, Mike?' she said, shuffling through the letters, mentally discounting most as rubbish.

He shoved his post into a pocket with little care before nodding in agreement. 'Supposed to be like this for a few days.'

'I don't mind it myself,' she said with a smile as they both headed towards the lift. She guessed they'd have continued the conversation about the weather if they hadn't both been silenced by the word written on the lift door in red paint.

He wiped a finger across the word. 'It's paint. That's a bit weird, isn't it? Who'd do such a thing?'

She'd no idea. 'Maybe it's advertising something.' The lift door opened before she could elaborate. And once the door shut, there was no need. The silence was loud as both occupants stared at the words scrawled across the lift wall.

'Seventh floor, apartment forty.' Mike said the words slowly, as if unable to believe what he was reading. Then, he turned to look at her, his mouth slightly open, eyes wide. 'Isn't that…?' He seemed suddenly to realise it was inappropriate to finish the sentence and his mouth shut with an audible snap. 'Yes, well…' Colour flooded his face as he searched for something to say.

Fiona would have felt sorry for his embarrassment if she hadn't been trying to deal with the shock of her reputation being shredded before her eyes. The bitch! Because she knew who had done it. It could only have been one person. The wife. It seemed stalking Fiona hadn't been sufficient revenge for the note. Or perhaps the note had more than poked a bear; perhaps it had woken a monster determined on revenge.

Mike got out at the sixth floor without saying his customary cheery goodbye, leaving Fiona alone. It seemed to take an eternity for the door to shut, for the lift to travel upward and the door to open again to allow her to escape. She'd find something in her apartment to cover the words, or at least to hide her apartment number. There wasn't paint, but correction fluid might work and she was sure she had an old bottle of that somewhere.

When the lift door opened on the seventh floor, she stepped out and was brought to a halt by the writing on the wall opposite.

She didn't need the arrow to point her in the direction of her apartment. It was possible to become numb to shock, but she hadn't reached that point as yet because the scrawled words painted on her door both shocked and stunned.

Fiona wiped a hand over them. The bitch had taken more time with this one. The words, *A whore lives here,* were neatly written. She'd even underlined it.

Inside her apartment, it took several minutes before Fiona located the bottle of correctional fluid. If she could cover the apartment number, she'd be happy. But when she opened the bottle, she discovered it had dried out. 'Fuck it,' she said, firing the bottle across the room.

Tired, stressed, and now numb, it was another few minutes before she thought of using a permanent marker pen. She found one and hurried out to cover the apartment number on the wall. When the lift appeared, she stepped inside and used a foot to keep the door open while she scribbled over both the apartment number and the floor.

She felt like she'd taken back some control, cheated the wife out of a complete success, but she knew she was fooling herself. There was no knowing when the wife had done the work, or how many of her fellow residents had seen it. Even those who hadn't, they'd soon be informed by those who had. Those who wondered what she did for a living would now be convinced they knew. Not only was she *that* girl having an affair with a married man, but now she'd be seen as someone who did it for a living.

Useless though it might be, she persevered with the marker until the numbers at least were gone. Tomorrow, she'd contact the management company and ask them to get someone to remove it all.

They'd want to know who did it, of course, but she'd play it cool, say she was an innocent victim and had been horrified and shocked by the words.

She was. Not by the words, but by the totally unexpected vindictiveness of the action.

It seemed the wife was willing to play dirty.

She was persistent, and clever too. She had, after all, managed to gain access to an apartment block whose management company were always touting how safe it was. Despite Fiona's annoyance at being labelled a whore, she had to confess to a sneaking admiration for the action. As revenge for the note she'd sent, it was pretty damn genius.

Back in her apartment, she paced the floor, wondering what her next step should be. The wife was proving to be a more difficult opponent than she'd expected. The smidgeon of admiration was replaced by a growing anger that the damn woman wouldn't simply give up. That she didn't have enough self-esteem to tell her cheating husband to sling his hook.

Fiona could tell Rich, but then she'd have to confess to sending that note and she didn't want to let him know that she'd stooped that low. Didn't want him to think that perhaps the devil he knew was better than the one he didn't.

She was used to being in charge, to being the one who called the shots, and she hated this uncertainty, this lack of control. Hated needing Rich so much. Hated even more that she was pushed into playing crazy games with his wife. As if he was the winning prize in some stupid reality TV show.

Trying to salvage some of the evening she'd planned, she had a long shower and slathered herself in her favourite scented moisturiser. Wearing the silk robe she'd bought herself as a reward for managing to get rid of Phillip, she fixed herself a prawn salad and sat at the table with it and a glass of wine. The food was good, but after a couple of mouthfuls, and more time spent moving leaves around the plate, she pushed it to one side and picked up her wine.

When her mobile chirped, she knew it would be Rich. For the first time since meeting him, she was reluctant to answer. It rang out as she waited and then, almost immediately, it beeped to tell her she had a message.

> Ring me back if you can.

She could ignore it. Or perhaps it would be better to send a message to say she was out with friends. Enjoying herself. Partying. Not waiting around for him to decide their future. She could ghost him. End this farcical situation for good. She could... but with a sigh, she picked up her phone and rang him.

'Sorry, I was in the shower,' she said when he answered.

'I wish I'd been in there with you.'

Okay, his fixation with shower sex was slightly cringe-worthy, but the truth was, she'd have been happy to have him there with her even if it did mean getting wet and messy.

'I wish you were here with me now. I'm sitting on the sofa with a glass of wine. We could snuggle together and watch a movie.' Like an old married couple. She shook her head. 'Or we could have gone to a wine bar, had a few glasses, gone to a club, painted the town red and then come back here.' She laughed. 'We'd probably have had to cancel tomorrow, but it'd be worth it, wouldn't it?'

'It definitely would.'

She caught the sound of traffic and guessed he was on his way home. Later than usual – perhaps there were problems in work too that were adding to his lot. She'd liked to have asked, to have discussed their work day over a glass of wine or two. She sighed and waited for him to speak. She wanted him to say they'd be together soon. That he'd told his wife about her and things were moving on. Perhaps that was the reason for the dramatic messages she'd painted on the walls. With a sudden dart of hope, Fiona pressed the phone to her ear so tightly, it hurt. She waited, wanting to hear the words, but they didn't come. Not about leaving his wife, nor about meeting her for their usual Wednesday dinner.

When the silence became painful, she laughed quietly. 'Maybe another night?' And then, because she really wanted to see him, unable to help herself, and hoping she didn't sound too clingy, too damn obsessive, she asked, 'Are we going to meet up on Wednesday?'

'Yes.' He sounded as distant and unenthusiastic as he had the previous day.

'Is everything okay, Rich?'

She waited for him to reassure her, to say he loved her, that he couldn't wait to be with her. How pathetically needy she'd become.

'Yeah, fine. I just have a lot on my plate at the moment.'

And she didn't? Irritation shot through her, and for one delicious moment, she was the woman she'd been before she met him. A strong, successful, nobody-take-her-for-a-fool kind of woman. She harnessed the thought, channelled it into the words that were ready on the tip of her tongue: *it's been fun; perhaps we should leave it at that.*

She was ready to say them when he beat her to it and broke the silence with, 'Just remember that I love you, will you?'

And just like that, she was gone again down that rabbit hole of mixed-up, crazy emotions. 'I love you too.'

'I'll talk to you tomorrow. Have a good night.'

She supposed her reply should have been *you too*, but she didn't want him to have a good night with the wife. Fiona wanted him to be miserable without her. So miserable, he'd face that bitch of a wife and tell her it was over. She'd had her moment with the red painted words of condemnation. Fiona would let her get away with that, because with that *just remember that I love you,* she knew she'd won.

'Talk tomorrow,' she said and hung up.

She picked up her wine glass and sat back. The shadow of her old self lingered. She had won, hadn't she? If he loved her, as he said he did, then it was time to tell his wife. On Wednesday, Fiona would broach the subject. Gently but firmly tell him that he couldn't go on having his cake and eating it. She wouldn't use that worn-out cliché but she'd get her point across. She'd always found subtlety to be wasted on men, so she'd make her point, clear, precise, and very sharp.

As for the wife, she'd done her worst, hadn't she?

42

LYDIA

The whisky had made me brave but not stupid so I resisted the very strong temptation to return to the apartment to do more damage. Instead, with the alcohol making me unusually mellow, I started for home. Unfortunately, it also seemed to have interfered with my capacity to choose the right Tube and I ended up heading in the wrong direction. A journey that should have taken me thirty minutes took me an hour and as I climbed the steps from the tube station near our home, my head was pounding.

I blamed *that* woman for it, of course, not the whisky. Blamed her for making me act so totally out of character. The initial euphoria had worn off to be replaced by a shaky disbelief that I'd done such a shocking thing. The previous few hours had taken on the hazy mistiness of a dream with only the traces of red paint on my fingers to prove what I'd done. I no longer had the can of spray paint; somewhere, and I really couldn't remember where, I'd dumped it.

She'd know I was responsible for it, of course; she was a whore, but I doubt that she was stupid.

Would she see it as just retaliation for the letter, and let it go, or would she strike again? Had we started a tit-for-tat war with the prize for the winner being Rich?

My head was buzzing and it seemed to make sense to stop in a pub near our home to try to get that mellow feeling back.

It took five whiskies and for the bartender to suggest that I'd had enough – a suggestion I took with exaggerated umbrage – before I felt ready to finish the five-minute walk home. I'd been hoping to feel mellow, to be able to put what I'd done down to temporary insanity, but all I could do was worry about what that woman was going to do to me in return.

It was a ludicrous situation and the alcohol wasn't making it any less so, but strangely, it did give me some clarity. There was only one person who could offer a solution, one person who could call a halt to this madness, and I was married to him.

It was time to face the truth. If Rich wanted to be with her, did I really want him to stay with me? To see resentment build, and any feeling he still had for me slide inexorably into bitter dislike?

Wasn't it better to face up to it now?

But as I opened the front door and walked into the home I loved, my determination wavered. Perhaps I couldn't have it all, but I wanted this. If Rich wanted out of our marriage, he could leave, but he wasn't taking my home.

There was an open fireplace in the living room. It wasn't normally lit during the week, but I decided the day needed the extra comfort.

Ten minutes later, having used almost the whole packet of firelighters to speed up the process, I was hunkered in front of a blazing fire. It was another few minutes before I felt warm enough to clamber onto the sofa and unbutton my coat. It seemed sensible to rest my spinning head on a cushion and necessary to shut my eyes.

There was no rest in the alcohol-induced sleep that followed. Either I was chasing after distant, blurry figures, or wide-mouthed, hideously fanged mouths were snapping at my heels, forcing me to run panting into the darkness. Giant paintbrushes with legs instead of handles slapped streaks of red paint that dripped like blood over me and my life. I ran from it all, my mouth open in a continuous scream. At some point, I roused myself long enough to pull off my coat and toss it to the floor.

When I opened my eyes again, daylight had dimmed and the fire was reduced to glowing embers. I stayed alert only for long enough to throw some coal on top, then sank back on the sofa and once more fell asleep.

* * *

It was the front door opening that woke me next. I lay unmoving for a moment, surprised to find that my head wasn't thumping any more, and even more surprised to find my thoughts were clear. It seemed my head and my heart were in agreement. It was time.

I'd left the living-room door open and watched as Rich unbuttoned his coat, took it off and hung it on the bannisters as he always did. The living-room light was out, but the flicker of the fire caught his eye. Only then did he notice me stretched out on the sofa.

'Hi,' he said, coming into the room. He stopped just inside the door and stayed there, staring at me. 'You feeling okay?'

It was time, but I wasn't going to broach the subject of his infidelity lying flat out as I was. I shuffled upright and swung my feet to the floor. 'Am I feeling okay?' I laughed, the sound floating in the air before shattering into sharp, bitter notes. I indicated the sofa opposite with a jerk of my chin. 'Sit. We need to talk.'

He wasn't a fool and must have known what it was that I wanted to talk about but to give him credit, he didn't turn around and leave the room. Instead, with a weary sigh, he crossed to the sofa and sat.

Now that it came to it, I wasn't sure what I was going to say. Come straight out and accuse him of having an affair? Or come at it more obliquely? I decided on the second, aiming for a softly-softly approach. If it didn't work, I had the claws and fangs as a stand-by.

I pitched my voice low and non-confrontational. 'Do you remember the first time we made love?'

He sighed but nodded. 'Of course I do.'

'D'you remember how we thought it was so great that it was the first time for both of us? How we boasted about that for years?'

He'd been sitting with his forearms resting on his thighs, hands dangling between his knees, his eyes down, but at this, he looked up and met my eyes. '*You* thought it was so great, *you* boasted. I never said a word.'

I blinked, taken aback. The memory was crystal clear in my head. We'd been sixteen. Young and in love. We'd fumbled through our first time together; it hadn't been the most exciting of experiences, but I remember... I remember clearly... talking about how amazing it was that we'd shared such an experience, how wonderful that it had been a first for both of us. It was as if we'd been waiting for one another. I'd cherished the memory through the years and it stunned and saddened me that he was dismissing it so lightly. I glared at him, but his expression was giving nothing away. 'I've never been with anyone else. Can you honestly say the same thing?'

Suddenly, his expression changed. He'd always been an even-tempered man and although we'd had our disagreements over the years, I could count on the fingers of one hand the times I remember him losing his temper. It made it all the more shocking that my question made anger furrow his brow, his eyes turn hard, and his lips flatten together as if he was trying to prevent something from exploding.

Then, so abruptly that it startled me, he got to his feet and crossed to the fireplace. The poker was resting against it. With a jerky movement, he reached for it and picked it up.

Fear suddenly swept through me. Rich wasn't a violent man, but then I wasn't the kind of woman who'd paint obscene messages in a stranger's apartment block either, was I? What was that old saying... *desperate times called for desperate measures*.

Maybe I was about to learn just how desperate Rich was.

43

LYDIA

Perhaps I should have picked up my phone and rung the police, or got up and run from the room, screaming for help. Instead, what I did was to sit and wait for the inevitable, which sadly seemed to have become my fallback position. I'm sure I never used to be such a victim. Or was I looking back through those infamous rose-coloured glasses?

I could see his fingers white-knuckling on the handle of the poker. Was this going to be the end of it? Of me? Death by poker?

Maybe the remnants of alcohol in my system were to blame, because suddenly, it all seemed so ridiculously funny that I had to laugh. Aloud. Uproariously. Almost manically as Rich turned to face me, the poker still clasped in his hand. It mightn't have been the best time to sneer or be sarcastic but suddenly, I'd had enough. 'Oh for goodness' sake, put the fucking poker down, Rich; you haven't the balls to kill me.'

He looked at the instrument in his hand as if wondering how it got there, then he shook his head and looked at me in disbelief. 'Kill you? I wasn't going to bloody-well kill you! I was going to poke the damn fire!' He turned back to the fireplace and stirred the coals with far more vigour than the remaining embers required. Then, as if to make a point, he lifted the coal skuttle and hefted a load into the fire before poking it again.

Only then did he put it down, resting it gently against the side. He remained facing away from me as he said, 'I lied to you back then. If I hadn't...' His sigh was long and weary. 'If I hadn't, things might have turned out differently.'

Back then? Suddenly, things didn't seem quite so funny. 'What are you talking about?'

'You assumed you were my first. We were only sixteen, so I suppose it was understandable. Especially since I'd kept to myself since I joined the school almost two years before.' He turned to face me then and I could see both sorrow and regret chasing across his face.

I wasn't his first? He'd led me to believe I had been. Maybe not in words, but by implication. And he'd let me go on believing it, all these years. I'd told the story many times, holding it up as the foundation to our love story. A we-were-meant-to-be tale.

One lie, all those years before. A silly, probably unnecessary lie, surely it wasn't capable of cracking the foundation of our relationship. Was he trying to deliberately confuse me by throwing it into the mix now? A lie told more than forty years before could be discounted. Couldn't it?

'I'm not sure why you're bringing this up now, but I think we have more important things to talk about. Like your more recent lie.' I stood to look him in the eye when I challenged him. 'You said that the woman you were meeting was purely business. That was a lie; I know you're having an affair.'

Rich brushed past me and sat. 'I told you the truth. *Then*, it was business.' He shrugged. 'I suppose you could say it still is.'

I stayed standing. It seemed the better position to be in. It also brought me nearer to the poker. He wouldn't have had the balls to use it; I was fairly sure I wouldn't have the same problem. If he kept lying to me, I might have to teach him that it was a very bad idea. I dragged my eyes from it and looked back to Rich. 'You're not making any sense.'

He looked up at me with puppy-dog eyes. 'Sit, and I'll tell you what I should have told you forty years ago, along with things that have happened more recently.'

It was tempting to take the poker with me but I left it where it was and perched on the edge of the sofa within grabbing distance of it. Just in case. My back was rigid, my jaw clenched so tightly it hurt as I waited for whatever he was going to say.

Rich folded his hands together before speaking in the slow, sombre tone of a funeral dirge. It would have made me laugh had I not been trying so desperately to hold myself together. 'I should have explained back then,' he said. 'Should have told you the truth, but my parents insisted it was to be kept a secret. It was, after all, why we'd moved the length of the country. To escape what had happened.'

I could feel my heart rate increase, the loud thumpty-thumpty-thump of it as I listened to every word he said.

By the end of his tale, I wondered if I'd ever known this man I'd loved for so long.

44

RICH

Rich curled his fingers around the handle of the poker. It was the perfect weapon. If he turned with it in his hand, if he lifted it to waist height and swung it like a golf club, the blow would kill her and that'd be the end to his problems. Or the start of another. He wasn't sure how good he'd be at concealing a crime. True, he'd watched his fair share of crime programmes so he knew some of what the investigating officers would be looking for. The murder weapon to start with. He could take it up to Hampstead Heath, hide it in one of those overgrown patches. It would stay hidden forever, or at least long enough to destroy any DNA that might linger after he'd bleached it. Was there bleach in the house? He wasn't sure.

When Lydia's laughter broke the silence, he sighed. She'd always had the ability to see humour in the most ridiculous places. It was one of the things he'd loved about her. Loved... past tense. It was the first time he'd thought of her that way.

'Oh for goodness' sake, put the fucking poker down, Rich; you haven't the balls to kill me.'

He shilly-shallied for a few minutes, added more coal, poked again, then put the damn thing down before he could change his mind. He wasn't going to kill her; he was going to tell her the truth. 'When I was fourteen, a very young, immature boy, I loved music, especially the violin. My parents encouraged me and paid for extra lessons after school. The music teacher, Ellie, was a young woman who wore long, flowy dresses, and lots of bangles on each arm – a bohemian, arty vibe, I suppose you'd say. I was the only pupil learning the violin and I'd go to the music room every Wednesday after school for an hour.' Even now, the memories could send him back there and he'd swear he could smell the sweet, floral scent she used to wear.

'She was a tiny, slight woman, and I'd just had a growth spurt so I was probably as tall as she was. Sometimes, she'd stand behind me and reach forward to improve the position of my fingers. So close, I could smell her, not only her scent but a...' He shrugged. 'The only way I can explain it is to call it a *woman smell*, which sounds offensive but isn't meant to be.' He remembered breathing it in so deeply that it rippled her long, curly hair. It made her laugh and toss it back. 'By the end of the second month, I had a crush on her that was so strong, it made me weak.'

He looked at Lydia. She was transfixed by his tale and he could see by the pity in her eyes that she guessed where it was going. 'It wasn't until the start of the second school term that her fingers started to linger on my arm. And when she stood behind me to adjust the position of mine on the violin, she'd press against me so tightly, I could feel her breasts through the thin, cotton dresses she wore.'

'And you were how old?'

'I'd just turned fourteen.'

'Shit!'

Rich smiled. 'It didn't seem like that at the time. I was a shy kid, so suddenly having this amazing woman showing an interest in me was like all my Christmases and birthdays rolled into one.' His smile faded slowly. 'She seduced me not long after, and then every Wednesday, instead of playing with my violin, I was playing with her.' He shook his head. 'No, that isn't true. She was playing with me. Or maybe she wasn't.' He heaved a sigh as he remembered. 'She talked about getting a job in a different school so there'd be no scandal, and when I was old enough, when I was of legal age, we could marry.'

Lydia's eyes widened. 'She wanted to marry you? Fuck!'

It was so unusual for Lydia to swear that he couldn't help but laugh. 'Yes, it was pretty crazy. At fourteen, a year seemed a lifetime away, and here she was making plans for three or four years ahead.' He remembered that as being the catalyst for change. Suddenly, the wonder of it all had become a burden no child should have to bear.

'I told my parents I wanted to give up the violin. They argued about it. I think they saw me as some kind of musical prodigy, whereas I was never more than adequate. I stood my ground and eventually, they caved in. But with the cruelty of a child, I never went back to Ellie to say goodbye or to explain.' Looking back, he wondered if he had, if things would have turned out differently. If he'd told her that he didn't love her – because of course, he hadn't – if he'd explained that he was too young, or she too old, it would have been cruel but she might have understood. That he'd been a child didn't seem to be enough of an excuse for simply walking away and hoping it would all be forgotten. And even if it had been enough to have excused him then, he wasn't a child now, so what was his excuse this time for behaving so badly?

'What happened?'

He was startled out of his memories by her voice. 'Sorry, it's hard to go back into the past. It's not something I've ever spoken about.' He ran a hand over his face. 'Ellie took what she saw as my abandonment very hard. She rang my mother to try to get her to persuade me to continue my studies. Her insistence alarmed my mother so much that she rang the school to complain about being pressurised.'

'How old was Ellie?' Lydia asked. 'She sounds completely unhinged.'

He hadn't known at the time but it had come out later. 'Twenty-eight. She looked younger though, and I suppose I assumed she was.'

'Twenty-eight! What the hell was she thinking of to seduce a boy of fourteen?'

'She said she was in love with me. But I think even then, even while we were together, I knew there was something wrong with what she was saying. Something off about a woman so much older than me wanting to be my friend, to chat about things that fourteen-year-olds chatted about. Looking back, I think she was more in love with my youth than with me.'

He stared into the fire, watching the embers glow. If he poked it, flames would flare up. It was the same with memories; prodding them made them burn brightly so that for a few minutes, it was as if he was back over forty years and everything was as clear as if it happened only yesterday.

Once again, it was Lydia's voice that dragged him back.

'You were lucky you got out of it when you did,' she said. 'But I'm not sure why you kept it a secret; I would have understood.'

Lucky? But then, she didn't know the whole story yet. 'There's more to tell you,' he said. 'Ellie didn't give up. She waited for me on my way to school, walked alongside me, telling me how much she missed me. Some days, she'd be there on my way home. She'd wait outside my house at weekends and follow me if I was going out to meet mates. She wouldn't join us, but I'd see her hovering at the edge of my vision. If I left to walk home alone, she'd join me, telling me again how much she missed me, how much she loved me.

'It got to the point where I didn't want to leave the house at weekends. I wanted to tell my parents everything, but I was afraid to. Or maybe embarrassed is the better word. Too embarrassed to tell my parents what Ellie and I had been doing. Instead, I made up some story about there being some odd people hanging about to persuade my mother to drive me to school.'

'What a dreadful woman she was. It must have been terrifying for you. You were only a child.'

He knew Lydia would be sympathetic; he just hoped she'd stay that way when she heard the remainder of his story.

'I remember feeling scared the whole time. I suppose my parents must have realised something more was to blame, and had discussed what to do with me, because one evening, not long after, my father took me aside and asked me to tell him what was troubling me. He was a good man, big and gentle. And I suppose it was the opportunity I'd been waiting for.'

It had all come out then. Every sordid detail. He remembered his father dragging him into a hug, holding him so tightly, he could barely breathe, and telling him again and again that it wasn't his fault, that he'd done nothing wrong.

Lydia shuffled in her seat. 'What happened?'

'Ellie was arrested the following day and was eventually sentenced to fourteen years in prison. She was also put on the sex offender's register and banned from teaching for life.'

'That must have been a very difficult time for you.'

Difficult? She still didn't know the worst. 'The press got hold of the story and Ellie was only too happy to speak to them, telling them that her only crime had been to fall in love with me, insisting that I loved her too and it was my parents that were keeping us apart. I think she wanted to spin it as some kind of modern-day *Romeo and Juliet*.'

'She was off her trolley!'

'Probably, but she was also ridiculously believable. It helped her cause that she was small, slight, and very pretty. She couldn't name names, of course, but it didn't take long for people to realise that "the boy who loved the violin as much as me" she'd mentioned more than once was me.' I saw the horror on Lydia's face and smiled. 'Yes, you can imagine, can't you? The gossip, the press on our doorstep, the sideways glances from neighbours.' And he still hadn't told Lydia the worst. But it was time. 'The stress for all of us was unbelievable. Especially…' He took a deep breath. 'Especially when, by the time it came to trial, Ellie was heavily pregnant with my child.'

45

LYDIA

It's such a cliché to say you're lost for words, but I was. Completely. My mind simply couldn't process what I'd heard. The first part – the seduction of a child by someone in a position of trust, was a sad, but unfortunately too common story. Nor was it unheard of for a child to be the result of such a union. It was the hugeness of the secret Rich had kept from me that staggered me more than anything.

He was waiting for me to speak. I'm not sure what he wanted to hear. A sympathetic *you poor thing*, perhaps? But all I had were questions. I started with the first. 'Why didn't you tell me all this before? Perhaps not when we first met, but certainly before we married.'

He ran his fingers roughly through his hair, making it stand on end, then spent more time smoothing it down. 'It was a difficult time. For me, for my parents. When we were told she was pregnant and insisting that I was the father, it made things a million times worse. After the trial, when the scandal didn't seem to be dying down, they decided it would be better to get away.

Start somewhere fresh. When we moved to Sussex, my parents made me promise never to mention what had happened.'

His eyes slid away from mine and I knew he was struggling with the memories. Perhaps I should have been extending sympathy, like the good wife I'd always been, but I knew, I just *knew*, there was more to come.

When he spoke again, it was with the sad melancholy of an adult looking back on the child he had once been. 'To be honest, it was an easy promise to make. By then, I was exhausted with it all: the jeers and knowing looks of my peers, the whispers of the neighbours. I was glad to leave it all behind and to never speak of it again.'

'But what happened to the baby?'

A range of emotions flickered across Rich's face. It was unsettling to watch him struggle with them, as if he couldn't decide how he felt, then when he did, when he brushed aside regret and guilt, it was something else that remained, something I couldn't identify for a few seconds. Then I did, and it made my skin crawl. It was self-justification. I reminded myself that he'd been a child. One who'd been groomed and manipulated by an adult who should have known better. But he wasn't a child any longer, and he should be able to look back with different eyes.

'What happened to the baby?' I asked again.

'I didn't want to know,' he said with a dismissive shrug, as if it was perfectly acceptable. 'You have to understand, I wanted to forget all about it. To be a normal teenager, doing normal teenage things. I wanted to fit in with my schoolmates and not be known as the boy who'd been seduced by his teacher, a boy who'd fathered a child.'

I kept telling myself that it was perfectly understandable. He'd been so young. But shouldn't he have had some interest and concern for the life he'd inadvertently made?

'So you don't know what happened to it?' I frowned. Had the baby died? Was that it? Trauma upon trauma. 'Did she lose it?'

He looked at me, puzzled. 'Lose it?' When clarity dawned, he gave an embarrassed laugh. 'Oh right, no, she didn't; she had it okay, although, as I explained, I didn't know anything about it. Much later, I learnt that my parents had thought about looking after him while the mother was in prison, but thought better of it once they'd moved away. So the baby was fostered.'

Him. He'd had a son. An older half-sibling to the twins. I'd have to tell them. 'I'm your wife; you didn't think it was something you should have told me? Didn't I have a right to know that you had a child?'

'I didn't have a child.' He wiggled his index fingers in the air to make quotation marks around the word *child*, as if by doing so, he could further distance himself from it. 'Everyone involved, my parents, the social workers, even the damn counsellor I saw, agreed it was better for me to put it all behind me.'

And never to take any responsibility for the blameless, innocent child he'd fathered. I'd managed to scrape up some sympathy for the abused fourteen-year-old, but my heart ached for the poor, unwanted baby.

'Did the mother claim him when she was released?'

I wasn't surprised when Rich shook his head. Only in books and movies did such a sad, tragic story end happily. 'When I was older, I did ask about her and the baby,' he said. 'It was only then I learnt that she'd been attacked by a fellow inmate five years into her sentence. She'd died of her injuries a few days later.'

The woman had been a manipulative predator but it still shocked me to hear she'd died in such a brutal way. I was also stunned by Rich's cold detachment from what had happened and was almost afraid to push for an answer to my question. But I needed to know. 'And the baby? What happened to him?'

'He'd been in various foster homes. After her death, he was put up for adoption.'

I didn't need to ask if Rich had ever seen the child; it was obvious he hadn't in the dismissive way he spoke about him.

After the drama of my morning, Rich's revelations seemed all too much to take in. I stood, without a word, and crossed to the cabinet where we kept our modest supply of booze. Despite recent events, neither of us were big drinkers and there were bottles inside, brought from the duty free after various holidays, that had been lurking untouched for years. There was no whisky. Instead, I took out a virulently coloured liqueur and held it out. 'I think this conversation calls for something to oil its consumption, don't you?'

He looked surprised, and dubious, especially when I took out a tumbler and half-filled it before handing it to him.

I took another glass and poured a generous measure for myself. 'Cheers,' I said, waiting till he took a drink before lifting my glass and swallowing half the contents in two swallows. It didn't have the same delicious burn as the whisky, but I'd seen the alcohol percentage and guessed it'd do the job.

I needed something, because sad and awful as Rich's tale had been, stunned as I was that he'd never told me, I knew there was more to come. It would have been easy to have thought that he was telling me now to elicit my sympathy and to deflect attention from my accusation. But I wasn't having it. Something that had happened more than forty years before was hardly responsible for what was happening now, was it?

Or was it?

Rich's eyes slid away from mine. Had he always been so sly and shifty? I took another mouthful of the quite vile drink, then put the glass down before thumping his arm as hard as I could. With a grunt, he looked at me. Only then, when I had his undivided attention, did I ask, 'You've kept this a secret all these years, so why tell me now, and what's it got to do with that whore you've been shagging?'

46

LYDIA

It was Rich's turn to be lost for words. I could see him floundering. Perhaps I was wrong, and he had told me the sad story of his childhood abuse simply to garner some sympathy and make me forgive his adulterous behaviour. I reached for my glass again and took another mouthful of the liqueur. I was beginning to think that maybe things weren't all that bad. After all, if Rich had told his sad tale in order to get forgiveness, didn't that indicate the affair was over? That he wasn't thinking of leaving me?

The alcohol was blurring things but there was something fighting to get through, something important... Before his revelation, what was it he'd said? That he'd told me the truth about his relationship with the whore, but I struggled to remember the exact words he'd used, and suddenly, it was important that I did. Hadn't he said that *then,* it had been business. *Then* – didn't that mean it wasn't business any longer?

I drained my glass and reached for the bottle I'd left on the coffee table. 'Bloody awful stuff,' I said, filling my glass almost to the brim. 'It's making me a little numb though, so it's a good time for you to be brutally honest.' It was a lie. I wasn't feeling at all numb; I was feeling hard done by, and an angry bitterness was beginning to edge its way over me.

Rich swirled the drink in his glass, hard enough for it to lap over the edge and run down his hand. If it dripped to the floor; it would stain the carpet but I couldn't bring myself to care.

'I told you the truth,' he said. 'I didn't know anything about my son. Never asked for any details about him or his mother until I was almost twenty. That's when I learnt Ellie had died, and he'd been adopted.'

Twenty? We'd been together years by then. I thought I knew everything about him, that we'd shared everything. How could he have discovered such shocking information – and regardless of her crime, the death of the young woman was shocking – and not told me? How could he have married me without telling me about his past? My God, how had I never known he was such a liar? Because wasn't that what he was? Lying by omission.

He was still speaking, still explaining, as if his words hadn't already sliced through me. I tried to listen objectively and swallowed down the pain of his betrayal.

'It seemed a fitting end to their story, and I didn't think about it again,' Rich said.

A fitting end to their story? The child had already been more or less wiped from Rich's life. Did the knowledge of the adoption mean he could wipe him from his memories? As if the boy had never existed?

I slurped noisily from my over-filled glass and tried to put the child from my mind as Rich had done. I wanted to focus the conversation on what was happening now, not on his past, and certainly not on the pathetically sad story of an unwanted baby.

'You said your relationship with the woman *had* been business,' I said. 'What did you mean by that?'

His Other Woman

He swirled and sipped, swirled and sipped, until I wanted to get up, grab the glass and empty the contents into his face. I'd never have considered myself an angry, violent woman, but recently, it was as if a rage had been building inside me and was simply waiting for any opportunity to spew forth. It had driven me to daub those words on the walls of that woman's apartment, but there was more building as I stared at this man I thought I'd known so well, but who, it turned out, had lied to me from the very beginning.

Luckily, Rich stopped the swirling before I was driven to take action, although what I'd have done, I wasn't sure. After years of being the good wife, rage was new to me and still unfocused. I had to admit, I quite liked this new version of me. I didn't know for sure, but I was guessing I was learning to be more like *her*.

'Almost two months ago,' Rich said, 'I had a phone call. It was a voice I didn't recognise. A man who introduced himself as Phillip Coren. He said he had something important to discuss with me and asked if we could meet. In the business I'm in, it wasn't unusual to get such requests, so we arranged a get-together.'

It didn't take much imagination to speculate who the man might be. 'He was your son?'

Rich gave a slight smile. 'Not too hard to guess, was it?' He put the empty glass on the table and sat back with a weary groan. 'Perhaps I should have expected it to happen, but I never did, so it came as a shock when he told me.'

I thought of the poor, unwanted baby, grown-up now, but still needing to find his father. 'Was he angry?'

Rich looked at me in surprise, then smiled again. 'That's the way it would be in a movie, wouldn't it? He'd have been mistreated and was looking for revenge.' He huffed a laugh and shook his head. 'It wasn't quite like that. He was certainly shunted around a lot in the beginning, and I'm not sure he was that happy. But when he was almost five, the opportunity arose—'

The opportunity. How had I never noticed how callous Rich was? 'You mean when his mother died?'

'Exactly.' He nodded, as if pleased I understood. 'The foster family who were looking after him at the time jumped at the chance to adopt him. They were sensible parents but maybe a bit naïve. They believed in total honesty and when they thought he was old enough, they told him everything about the circumstances of his birth. He was only ten at the time, and I think he found it difficult to take in. It's probably not surprising that he went off the rails a bit for a few years and needed counselling, but he seemed to have pulled through okay. He did well at school, went to university, got a good job. He looked for information about me but never made any effort to get in contact.'

'But then he did,' I said, when the silence stretched too long.

'Yes, but only because he wanted something.'

'Money?' I was surprised.

'No.' Rich shuffled in his seat, sat forward, reached for the glass, then thought better of it and sat back again. 'It would have been better perhaps if it had been that easy.'

I was getting weary of this. 'So if it wasn't money, what did he want?'

'He was working as a financial consultant and had been recently promoted to a more senior position. A series of mistakes occurred. They were blamed on him, and he was fired. But he insisted he was innocent of any wrongdoing.'

Maybe drinking the liqueur had been a bad idea because this story wasn't making any sense. 'So what did he want you to do?'

'Get proof that someone else was to blame.' Rich did reach for his glass then. Finding it empty, he stretched a hand out to grab the bottle. 'When Phillip was fired, the woman who'd lost out to him for the promotion finally got it. He insisted she'd set him up. That she'd been responsible for the errors he was accused of, but he needed proof and that's why he wanted my help.'

'Your help?' I laughed, trying to see Rich as the James Bond type. 'What did he expect you to do?'

'The woman often worked from home. He thought that if he could get access to her laptop, he'd find something to exonerate him and incriminate her. Obviously, he didn't want to do anything illegal, like breaking into her apartment. He knew I was in a similar business, so I'd know what to look for, and that's why he came to me for help.'

'After all these years?' I was struggling to understand that Rich wasn't having an affair, that what I'd seen wasn't the whole truth. I'd been paranoid and had jumped to stupid conclusions.

Rich sighed. 'He was desperate; I don't think he'd have contacted me otherwise.'

'So...' I regretted the alcohol now; it was making it hard to think. 'So... what did you do?'

'We came up with a plan.'

A plan. I saw it then, in the flush that raced over his cheeks, in the way his eyes suddenly slid away from mine. Again. Had he always been so fucking shifty?

'Tell me.'

'I arranged to accidentally bump into the woman and it went from there.'

It went from there. I laughed at the euphemism. No, I hadn't been paranoid at all; I'd been right about what I'd seen, about everything. But if I understood what he was telling me, it was all so much worse. 'You had an affair with her.'

When he nodded, I laughed. I couldn't help it. It rang out,

loud, uproarious, slightly manic, because the truth was a staggering, unbelievable, heart-breaking, mind-fucking blow.

'Are you telling me, and you have to realise that I'm finding this hard to take in, but are you seriously telling me that you cheated on me, your wife of forty years, that you risked our marriage, all we'd been to each other, that you slept with that woman, to help a man – a son – you didn't know or care about, one you hadn't given a thought to in all of these years?'

'That's putting it rather bluntly—'

'But truthfully, yes?'

Irritation pushed his forehead up into tight lines. 'You don't understand!'

He was right; I didn't. How could there be anything that would justify what he'd done? 'How about you explain it to me then?'

'Guilt,' he said quietly. 'You're right, of course; I'd not given a thought to him in years, had barely thought of him *ever*, but then suddenly, I was sitting opposite a child I'd fathered, a man who looked like a younger version of me, and he was asking for my help. Regardless of the circumstances, I was filled with regret for never having reached out, for not having tried to find him. And for the first time, it hit me that it was thanks to me that his mother had died.' He held a hand up as if to stop me from contradicting him, thinking perhaps that I'd remind him that she'd brought it all upon herself. I hadn't planned to though, because despite what she had done, despite him being a child at the time, I thought it was wrong that he hadn't tried to contact his son. That didn't mean, however, that I agreed with what he was doing now: helping the son and destroying me and our marriage in the process.

When I stayed silent, he continued.

'Phillip asked me for help but it wasn't his idea for me to sleep with Fiona.'

The fire suddenly crackled loudly and burst into flame. It drew our attention and for a moment, that's all there was. An old married couple staring into the fire and watching their marriage go up in flames. Whatever had cause the sudden flare-up vanished, and the fire returned to barely glowing embers. I got up, took the poker, and stirred the coals.

'So it was your idea to sleep with her, was it?' Had he seen her, been instantly smitten, and justified it in the name of paternal care?

The silence dragged on. Was he thinking of how best to put it into words to make it all seem acceptable?

'It wasn't an easy decision,' he said.

I wanted to laugh. To turn and tell him that I'd seen her, had seen them together, that I'd seen how fucking easy it had been. I did turn to face him then but stayed silent.

He shook his head, a sombre expression on his face. 'It wasn't, but I didn't have a choice. Phillip's life had been devastated by her actions. He was broken by it all and I felt I owed it to him to help. Getting close to her seemed to be the only option available to me.'

When he gave a tired laugh, my fingers tightened on the poker I held. I had an unbelievable urge to swing it against his head. To hit him, to crack his skull wide open so that he'd never laugh again.

'I'm glad you find breaking our marriage vows to be so amusing.'

'It's not that,' he said, reaching up to loosen the knot of his tie. 'It was the whole Bondesque vibe to it all. The whole pretence thing. I was playing a part and it felt surreal.'

He was playing a part? Hadn't he been for all the years I'd known him? Did he really not understand the lie he'd lived?

'Did it work?' The question seemed to puzzle him, so I elaborated. 'Did you get what your son needed to clear his name?'

He looked away, but colour flushed his cheeks. 'It's complicated.'

It was my turn to be puzzled. 'Either you did, or you didn't. Seems simple to me.'

Instead of answering, he picked up his drink, swirled it and watched the liqueur lap the sides of the glass. He didn't look up from it as he spoke. 'I wasn't lying when I said it was business. That's all it was then.'

There it was again. *Then*. A simple four-letter word but I knew it was going to change everything.

'Go on,' I said.

'In the beginning, all I wanted to do was to get whatever was needed to exonerate Phillip. But before I knew what was happening... before I realised it... Fiona and I... well, I suppose you could say we just clicked. It was instant and mutual. And suddenly, I couldn't think of anyone else.' He looked at me. Met my gaze without wavering, as if to reinforce exactly how strongly he'd felt. 'Not of you, nor of Phillip. That's what I meant. It started as business, but I fell in love with Fiona and everything changed.'

47

RICH

Rich watched Lydia's expression change from sadness to derision. He wasn't surprised. Hadn't they both sat and watched in disgust when a politician had used the same line to excuse himself for breaking lockdown rules and betraying his wife? *Because he'd fallen in love.* It had been so easy to sneer, to dismiss him as a fool. And now here Rich was, in the same boat.

Worse.

Because not only was he betraying his wife, but also his newly found son.

Rich hadn't answered Lydia's question. How could he admit to her that yes, he had found sufficient information on Fiona's computer to show that she'd participated, perhaps even instigated, some of the issues that had been blamed on Phillip?

Rich couldn't admit it to Lydia, because he'd already made a decision.

He wasn't going to tell Phillip that he had found the proof he needed. Rich was going to lie to protect the woman he'd fallen in love with.

Lie to Phillip, and more importantly, he was going to lie to

Lydia. He had to; how could he tell her the truth: that he'd sacrificed her to save his son, but he wasn't willing to sacrifice Fiona? He couldn't do that to Lydia. They'd been together a long time. And they'd been happy once. Recently, it had been more of an easy acceptance that this was their life. Content, if not exactly happy.

Perhaps that was why he'd fallen so easily, so hard for Fiona. He'd discovered – or perhaps *remembered* was a better word – what happy felt like. And he didn't want to let it go.

He sounded just as pathetic as that almost-forgotten politician who'd ruined his career by declaring his love for another woman. But now that Rich knew there was something more for him – more than the slow decline into a slipper-wearing, threadbare kind of life, one that was comfortable but lacking in any excitement or any sense of a life still worth living – he knew he could never go back.

He didn't want to hurt Lydia. She was a good woman. She'd been a good wife, a brilliant mother, and maybe he was wrong, but fuck it, he wanted more. He wanted *happy*.

And if there was only one thing he was certain of in all this mess, it was that he loved Fiona.

With her, instead of feeling threadbare, his life seemed to be fizzing with possibilities.

There'd be regrets, there would certainly be recriminations, but most of all, there'd be that bright, glittering future.

And he'd get that *happy* he so desperately wanted.

48

LYDIA

Having caught Rich out in one lie seemed to make it easier to see the rest of them. Lies of omission were equally as bad as lies of commission. He probably thought I wouldn't notice that he hadn't answered my question. *Did you get what your son needed to clear his name?* It was the upside, or downside depending on your point of view, to having known someone forever: he didn't need to answer; I could see the truth in his eyes. Yes, he had found enough information in the whore's apartment to exonerate his precious, newly found son.

Knowing Rich forever, as I did, made it easy to see the quandary he was in.

If he admitted the truth to Phillip, he'd give him the ammunition to destroy the woman he blamed for his downfall.

The woman Rich was in love with.

But if he didn't tell Phillip the truth, if he was willing to sacrifice his son's future to save this new love, what did that say about me, the woman he was only too happy to cheat on to save that same son? What the fuck did it say about how little he thought of me? How very dispensable I had been.

I could have called him out on it. Told him that I knew exactly what he was doing, but I was afraid if I spoke right then, if I as much as opened my mouth, all that would come out was a stream of vile effluent which would give him reason to believe he'd made the right decision.

Because I could tell, right in that bitter, soul-destroying moment, that he had made that decision. He was going to leave me for the other woman.

I needed time to gather my scattered thoughts. Time to make a plan. The first step was easy: I needed to diffuse the current situation. 'It seems like you have your work cut out for you, doesn't it?' I was pleased how the words came out. Quiet, neutral, as if I were in control. 'I understand. You feel you owe your son. So until you get the information he needs, you're going to have to hang in there. Telling yourself you love her,' I resisted calling her the whore with great difficulty, 'seems to be the best option for the moment.'

I almost laughed as I watched a range of emotion sliding across Rich's face – mostly relief that I wasn't attacking him for being a cheating, lying bastard, but disbelief too that I was seemingly taking it so well. The stupid fuck really didn't have a clue that it was a game. I just needed to find my place in it and find a way to win.

I stood, too quickly, my head immediately spinning. There was a second when I wondered if the best play would be to collapse in a heap at his feet, maybe fake a health scare of some sort. I'd watched enough medical programmes over the years; I was sure I could pull off a mild stroke or heart attack to keep him by my side. One second for that thought, another second was spent hating him for making me so pathetic that I'd even consider doing something so desperate.

I reached for the arm of the sofa and held on to it until I got my alcohol legs. 'I need to get to bed. I'll see you in the morning.' I didn't look at him, but I knew he'd be sitting there with his mouth slightly agape as he wondered if he'd made it clear. That he was in love with another woman.

I moved away then, staggering slightly, feeling as if my world and everything in it was in a state of flux.

In our bedroom, I did something I hadn't done in a long time: I went to bed naked. It felt slightly daring to feel the soft cotton of the sheets against my skin. Even as I enjoyed the sensation, I wondered how sad and pathetic I'd become that I considered something so mundane to be daring. I brushed my hand over my skin. It wasn't bad for a woman of my age. Maybe a little too soft around the middle, but otherwise, I was in good shape. If Rich left me... when he left me... because I had to face it, he already had, maybe I could find someone new. Love wasn't exclusively for the young.

I tried to generate some excitement in the idea as I lay there staring at the ceiling. But I'd heard enough horror stories of dating in the twenty-first century for the idea to leave me shivering with dread. My marriage might not be scintillatingly exciting, but it was comfortable, known, safe. Dull – it was dull like me. I never used to be, nor had our marriage, just somewhere over the forty years we'd been together, things had got lost. All the excitement and romance had been worn away by familiarity and time.

I thought back over the evening, remembering Rich's expression when he'd mentioned Fiona. There had been a light in his eyes I hadn't seen for a long time. Perhaps that was it. It wasn't love, or not solely love, that he craved; it was the excitement of it all. What had he called his decision to help Phillip? I struggled to remember, then smiled. He'd called it *Bondesque*. He'd laughed, but I could see he was secretly enjoying it. It was probably every man's fantasy to play the James Bond role. Add in a beautiful woman – because I had to admit, she was that – and he had the whole package.

How could our comfortable, safe, dull marriage compare to that?

It was just bad luck for me that the woman who'd been responsible for Phillip's downfall had been both glamorous and beautiful, not someone who was best defined by the adjectives *motherly* and *housewifely*. Not someone who'd let herself go. Because I had, hadn't I? I ran a hand over my belly again, felt the roll of fat under my fingers, and sighed. Who was I kidding? I wasn't in good shape at all, and the thoughts of being naked with some strange man appalled me. I couldn't even remember the last time I was naked in front of Rich. Our lovemaking, the rare time we indulged these days, was performed in the darkness under the sheets. I could blame the children, the demands of motherhood, the passing years, but the truth was that I'd got lazy, and comfort had become my raison d'être.

Not so with Fiona obviously, although maybe in twenty years' time, she'd see the joy in flat shoes rather than the sky-high stilettos she favoured. I tried her name for size, rolling it around my tongue, but when I whispered it into the night, it came out differently: *whore*.

49

LYDIA

Thanks to alcohol's influence, I managed to get a few hours' sleep. When I woke, I was in the middle of a dream where I was wielding a pair of stilettos to chase Rich from the house. My first thought, that I'd have to buy a pair first, made me snort a laugh I quickly smothered with the duvet. Rich had spent the night in the spare bedroom and it was the creak of a floorboard in the landing outside our bedroom that had woken me. I didn't want him to know I was awake. Didn't want him to come in to speak to me until I had everything straight in my head.

It didn't take long. It was painfully clear. Rich had cheated on me to save a son he didn't know, but he'd fallen so madly in love with the woman he'd cheated on me with that he was now willing to sacrifice the son for her. And I – I was nothing, nobody, worthless and dispensable.

Did I stop loving him right at that moment? Or had the love been replaced by habit a long time ago? Perhaps it had and I'd simply been fooling myself these last few years.

If Rich had heard me, he didn't stop, and a moment later, I heard his heavy tread on the stairs.

The shadow of the dream I'd had stayed with me as I threw back the duvet. Chasing Rich from our home was an option. But it wouldn't be a permanent solution. If he was leaving me for her, the house would need to be sold and I would need to consider where to go and what I could buy with my share of the proceeds. Something small and boxy with little personality. And no memories. Perhaps I should look on it as a good thing. A fresh start and all that crap.

But as I went down the stairs, my hand sliding over the oak banister, the memories I'd made in the house worked like a balm on my pain. And as the pain of rejection eased, something inside me reignited. A feeling of self-worth that had been bashed and broken but thankfully, hadn't died.

I couldn't save our marriage, but suddenly, that seemed unimportant, and it was saving my home that became my priority. Rich was to blame for this change. He'd shattered everything I'd believed in, and now it seemed the pieces of me, and of my life, had realigned themselves. It was different; now I just had to make it work.

And that meant finding a way to chase him from our home.

'Good morning,' I said as I pushed open the kitchen door. 'Coffee! Just what I need.' I took a mug from the cupboard and filled it from the cafetière. 'I shouldn't drink so much.' I wagged my head. 'Or maybe mixing whisky and liqueur was a bad idea.' I was trying for light-hearted cheerfulness but I think by his bemused expression, I might have crossed over the line into slightly manic. Or perhaps he was still expecting to see me devastated by the previous evening's admission of love for another woman.

I didn't give him a chance to speak. 'I'm expecting delivery of our fancy-dress costumes today.' It looked as if he was going to speak so I hurried to add, 'You haven't forgotten, have you? The charity event on Saturday?' My laugh was definitely over the top. I reined it in and settled on a smile. 'Of course you haven't forgotten. You're on the board. I'm sure you've had a million emails about the plans.' I wondered if she was going. It was a big event in the London social scene and various institutions, including financial ones, were always well represented. 'I hope you like the costumes. I'm sure we won't be the only couple going as Mr and Mrs Claus, but I promise you, our costumes are going to be amazing.' They should be; they'd cost a ridiculous amount of money. I'd justified it by thinking we could use them again, perhaps to whatever party we'd be invited to on Christmas Eve. Maybe I'd gift them to Rich when we got around to talking about a divorce settlement.

My snort of amusement made Rich raise an eyebrow in question. I smiled, reached for the cafetière and held it towards him, like the good attentive wife I was. When he shook his head, I put it down, and indicated the kitchen clock with a tilt of my head. 'You're going to be late.'

'Yes,' he said. He lifted the mug he was holding to his mouth, then put it down without drinking. 'I...' But that's as far as he got. With a sigh, he eyed the clock again, then, without another word, he left the room.

Perhaps he knew there was nothing left to say that hadn't already been said. What could there be after his admission that he loved someone else? Maybe those words he'd said, *I fell in love with Fiona,* had drawn a heavy, bold line through our marriage. There was time enough to dot the i's and cross the t's. It was over. Even the sound of the fat woman singing had faded. Bitterness shot through me. The pain of being discarded for a newer, shinier model. A story as old as time.

Rich returned a few minutes later, dressed for the outdoors, his briefcase hanging from one hand. I recognised the scarf that was wound around his neck. A cashmere one I'd bought him for his birthday the previous month. It was a shade of blue that matched his eyes. I wanted to reach out and pull it from his neck. Worse, I wanted to reach for the two ends and pull them tight.

Usually, he'd kiss me on the lips or the cheek as a farewell gesture. That morning, he hesitated in the doorway, as if he was suddenly unsure how to behave in this new world he'd carved for us.

I guess he'd have been happier if I had screamed and berated him. He probably could have coped with that, but I could see by the tight line of his mouth, he didn't know how to handle my unexpected reasonableness. I was suddenly weary of it all.

'You'd better get going.' I lifted my hand and gave him a wave. Not precisely chasing him from the house but wishing him gone.

'Right.' He waited a moment more, then raised his hand and mirrored my wave.

For a long time after he left, I sat sipping my coffee. It was cold and bitter, much like the thoughts spinning through my head.

Had I been fooling myself these last few years? Had I layered contentment thickly over my marriage so I wouldn't have to face the reality that it had begun to rot and fall apart? The same rot that had made it so easy for Rich to break away.

The truth was painful, and strangely freeing. Because if I didn't have to focus on saving my marriage, I could concentrate on saving something more important to me: my home. I wasn't giving it up without a fight so that he could buy something with the whore. But as that thought crossed my mind, I knew fighting wasn't going to get it for me. More drastic action was required.

I couldn't chase him from the house, but there had to be something I could do.

Or maybe it wasn't me that needed to do it.

I thought about our conversation of the previous night.

It was all very interesting, and I thought... no, I knew... there was something there I could use.

What was that old expression – you couldn't make an omelette without breaking eggs – well, nobody said you had to break them yourself, did they?

50

RICH

Rich walked to the station in a daze. He'd barely slept, which accounted for some of his confusion, but it was Lydia's reaction to his announcement that accounted for the rest. He'd told her he was in love with someone else, hadn't he? He hadn't imagined saying those words. He was almost sure. Almost. He'd drank some of that foul liqueur. How long had that bottle been in the cabinet? Ten years, perhaps more.

Maybe he hadn't told Lydia the truth, after all.

He couldn't have done. If he had, she wouldn't have been smiling so carelessly at him, wouldn't be wittering on about the damn charity ball. And talking about the Mr and Mrs Claus costumes she wanted them to wear. Fuck, they were going to look ridiculous. He was going to look like an idiot.

He tried to remember the previous night's conversation. That damn liqueur had made everything hazy. He definitely remembered telling Lydia about Ellie and Phillip, but that was all. He hadn't been stupid, or crazy enough to tell her about Fiona, had he? He'd need to be stone-cold sober to tackle that conversation. But it would have to happen soon. Fiona wasn't going to play the other woman forever. He brushed a hand over his forehead and loosened the too-warm scarf from its chokehold on his neck. Lydia had been behaving a little strangely, though. That laugh, she sounded manic. Fuck, maybe he had told her.

When his mobile buzzed, he pulled it from his pocket and looked at the screen. *Phillip*. Rich sighed, shook his head and put the buzzing mobile back into his pocket. It was cowardice, pure and simple. He'd found the proof needed to exonerate Phillip, but wasn't willing to pass it over. Rich would have to lie and tell him he'd found no evidence that Fiona was to blame for his fall from grace. But he wasn't ready for that conversation yet.

He'd told Lydia the truth. He *had* felt guilty when he'd met Phillip. For the part Rich had played in his conception, the role he'd played in his mother's death, and mostly for never having cared enough to have found out what had happened to his son. The promise to help him had been made in good faith and in all sincerity.

There hadn't been a lot of information on Fiona's computer, but there was sufficient to have implicated her in some underhand dealings. But he'd also seen enough to suggest his son wasn't totally blameless. Had he been more efficient and more competent, he would have noticed the errors and been able to address them before they became disasters. It was clear to Rich that Fiona had been correct in her assertion that Phillip had been promoted over her, not because he was better at the job, but because of connections.

So wasn't it fair to let things stand as they were? Because if Rich passed on what he'd found, Fiona would be destroyed. She might even face criminal charges. If things stayed as they were, Phillip would get another job. Perhaps not with quite such a prestigious firm, but one possibly more suited to his skill set.

Wouldn't it all be for the best to leave well-enough alone?

Rich shuffled off the thought that he was lying to everyone. With more difficulty, he ignored the little voice in his head that told him the web of lies he was spinning might turn into a noose to strangle him.

He'd ignore all the doubts and would continue to lie without compunction, because although blood might very well be thicker than water, love was thicker than both.

51

LYDIA

The idea that had come to me was so twisted, it made me gasp. The woman I had been, the one I'd left behind to crumble in the rot of our marriage, would never have come up with such a cunningly warped, *evil* plan.

But this was the new me, born of betrayal, and if it worked, it would be the answer to my problems.

A glance at the clock told me I needed to hurry. I'd pulled on a worn pair of jeans and a brown sweater chosen for warmth rather than any attempt at style. There didn't seem to be any point in changing. No matter what I wore, I could never compete with *her*.

I needed a few minutes in Rich's office, then I was ready to go.

With speed being necessary, I pulled on my warmest coat and a beanie hat that didn't match. Nor did it flatter. I hadn't bothered with make-up either and when I checked in the hall mirror, it told me the inescapable truth: I looked every minute of my age, if not several years older.

For what I planned to do though, looking like a worn-out bag lady might work in my favour. The idea made me smile and sent me out the door with a spring in my step. I was down, but I wasn't fucking-well out.

I made the journey far quicker than I'd expected and was outside the apartment block by eight. I might have been wrong, of course, but I was convinced that Fiona – I had to remember to call her that and not the derogatory term I'd been using, not if I wanted her to fall in with my plan – wouldn't leave for work before eight.

I looked at the keypad, wondering if using it to enter would remind her that I'd been responsible for the graffiti. She had to have known it was me, but perhaps it was wiser not to confirm her suspicions. I pressed the bell by her apartment number.

When it wasn't answered, I swore softly, then pressed it again, holding my finger on it for longer. This time, I had a response.

'Yes?'

The irritation in her voice was obvious. It wasn't going to improve. 'It's Lydia. I need to speak with you.'

She didn't answer, and I imagined her in her apartment, mouth agape, wondering what the fuck I was doing there. I half-thought she'd ignore me and was relieved to be wrong. Without her saying a word, the door buzzed to allow me to push it open.

I wasn't surprised to see that my handiwork had already been removed, but hoped it had been there long enough to cause a sufficient amount of embarrassment.

A few minutes later, I was in front of her door, ready to knock. It opened before I had the chance, and finally, there I was, standing face to face with the woman my husband was in love with.

'Fiona.' I had to swallow the word that would always be associated with her in my head.

'Lydia.' She raised an eyebrow and looked pointedly at my hands. 'No red paint today?'

'I wouldn't want to be guilty of overkill.'

Unexpectedly, she laughed, then with a shake of her head, she stood back and waved me in. 'I've given the neighbours enough to talk about for a while.'

I followed her into a spacious room. Expecting it to be furnished with garish opulence as befitting a woman of her morals, and fully prepared to sneer at it, I was surprised at the restrained colour palette and minimalist furniture. I wanted to ask her if it was rented, and therefore supplied furnished and decorated, or if this was her style. I wanted to, but I didn't. We weren't friends. So I neither sneered nor admired. Instead, I crossed the room and, uninvited, sat on the sofa.

She was looking relaxed. Either she was a very good actress, or she was finding my presence amusing and not in the least threatening. I mustn't have looked like the kind of woman who could offer violence. She was right, I suppose; I couldn't offer it, but I was damn sure I could arrange it.

'I suppose you're wondering why I'm here?'

'I think I can guess.' She checked her watch. 'I hate to rush you, of course, but I'd appreciate if you'd say what you've come to say, then leave. Some of us,' she added, with the trace of a sneer in her voice, 'have jobs to go to.'

I shuffled in the seat and rested my arms along the back of the sofa. As if I was settling in for the long haul. 'Oh, I don't think you'll be rushing to work after I'm done talking to you.'

I thought I saw a flicker of nervousness cross her face, and she definitely looked behind her to the door as if estimating how long it would take her to reach it if I suddenly attacked her.

'Don't worry,' I said with a smile. 'I don't plan to harm you.' *Not physically anyway.*

She didn't look reassured, but she sat. Just on the edge of the seat, though, as if prepared to jump up and run at the slightest provocation. I wondered if she was always so nervous, or if I frightened her.

'What do you want?' she said, checking her watch again and sighing loudly.

It's odd how what we want can change in the blink of an eye. Had she asked me this question a day before, I'd have stated that I wanted my husband back. It was no longer the case, but it didn't mean I was willing to hand him over to her.

'Are you in love with Rich?'

If she was surprised by the question, she didn't show it. I imagined she'd be an excellent negotiator. It was the slight softening in her eyes that gave her away.

I sniffed. 'You don't need to answer. I think you are. And you think he loves you, don't you?' I reached into my pocket for my mobile. Switching it on, I found what I wanted, then handed it to her.

She hesitated a moment before taking it from me. As she read what was on the screen, a puzzled frown appeared and the colour faded from her cheeks to leave her make-up looking stark and clownish. 'I don't understand,' she said, looking from the screen to my face and back. 'Where did you get this?'

It had only taken me a couple of minutes to find it on Rich's computer. He'd never learnt the wisdom of changing passwords and had used the same one for as long as I could remember. 'You thought it was pure chance that Rich bumped into you that day? It wasn't.' I folded my arms, enjoying myself. 'Let me tell you a story.'

It didn't take me long to tell an edited, slightly skewed version of what had been going on. She listened without comment or interruption. Initially, she looked stricken, there was a definite tremble in her lower lip and the shimmer of tears in her eyes, but by the time I'd finished, her expression had hardened.

'So there you have it. Rich had it all planned.'

'Phillip is his son?' Fiona shook her head. 'That can't be right; he's not old enough.'

It wasn't surprising that she was absorbing my tale in bite-sized portions. 'Rich was young when he fathered him.' She didn't need to know the details. 'As I explained, they hadn't been in contact until recently. It was only because Phillip wanted help that he sought him out.'

'And Rich agreed.' She got to her feet and crossed to the window to stare out across the city. 'He used me.'

There was such sorrow, such disbelief in her words, that I'd have to have been made of wood not to feel a smidgeon of sympathy. 'He used you, and was willing to cheat on me, all to help a man he didn't know.' I let anger bleed into my words, doing a sufficiently good job to make her turn to look at me. 'We've been married forty years, so how do you think I felt?'

'Pretty pissed, I'd say.'

'To put it mildly.'

She held up my mobile. 'So he intends to give this information to Phillip.'

I didn't know. If I was right, if I'd read the situation correctly, Rich was caught in a dilemma. If he handed over the information he'd found, it would destroy this woman's career. Not to give it would damage his budding relationship with his son. Since Rich had proven himself to be such a good liar, I'm guessing he planned to tell Phillip that he'd been unable to find anything to prove Fiona was involved. If Rich really was in love with her, it would be the best path for him to take. But it suited my plan for the whore to believe he intended to hand the information over to Phillip.

'Yes,' I said. 'He does.'

'I'll be fired. My reputation will be destroyed.'

Did she really expect my sympathy? 'Yes, I'd say you will be.' I waved a hand around the room. 'I'm guessing rent is high; you'll have to move.'

'I don't rent,' she said, lifting her chin. 'It's my apartment.'

But I saw the fear that glimmered in her eyes and guessed it was mostly owned by the bank.

'The bastard,' she said, as the shock of discovery eased, and anger at the reality of her situation grew. 'He had me completely fooled. I really thought that he...' She didn't finish the sentence. Perhaps she realised that telling Rich's wife that she'd believed her husband was in love with her was a bad idea.

'He fooled you, used you, and cheated on me.' I waited for my words to sink in before adding, 'I'm not planning to let him get away with it. Are you?'

I'll give her one thing: the whore wasn't stupid. She raised an eyebrow, then returned to sit on the sofa opposite me. 'I wondered why you'd come; now I understand. You think we cheated women should gang up to get our revenge, do you?'

There didn't seem to be any point in sugar-coating it. 'Revenge is such a bitter-sounding word; I'd prefer to think of it as Rich getting his just deserts.'

Fiona smiled. 'What did you have in mind?'

Perhaps she could see the truth in my eyes, because as she continued to stare at me, her smile faded. I was determined to carry on, because every time I weakened, every time I thought I couldn't go ahead with what I'd planned, the new tough woman who'd taken up residence in my head reminded me that Rich had chosen some strange man and this woman over me, and he deserved what was coming his way.

This way, my marriage would still end, but on my terms, plus I'd get to keep the house. It was time I learnt to be selfish.

'I want you to kill him.'

52

FIONA

Fiona laughed. This strange woman was joking, wasn't she? Fuck, wasn't she? Granted, right at that moment, she'd have happily killed Rich. He'd fooled her. Completely. All her dreams, her hopes, she could feel them shattering, the shards falling and slicing her on their way to the bottom.

The bottom. It was exactly where she'd be if Matt Donaldson discovered how she'd set Phillip up. She'd be out. Without a reference and blackballed in the industry. She'd no savings. Her credit cards would keep her going for a while. She might be able to swing the next month's mortgage repayment, but that would be it. She'd lose everything.

Rich, the bastard. She shut her eyes, cringing to realise how stupid she'd been. How gullible. She'd been willing to believe every blasted lie he'd fed her. Of course she hadn't given him permission to use her computer or given him the password. She gave herself a little credit, she had been suspicious, just not enough. But seriously, how could she have known he was Phillip's father?

Yes, she'd liked to have killed Rich for what he'd done. But she didn't mean it literally, did she? She looked at Lydia and tried to laugh again. But this time, the sound was a strangled yelp. 'You are joking, aren't you?'

'No.'

It was so blunt that it made Fiona shake her head in disbelief. 'No? You're seriously asking me to kill Rich?'

'Don't you want to?'

This time, Fiona's laugh was more successful, but it was a slightly hysterical sound that worried her. What worried her even more was that Lydia was right; now that the initial shocked numbness was beginning to wear off, she realised she did want to kill Rich. She'd like to tear the bastard to pieces. Feed him to the pigs she'd seen snuffling around in a field near a farm shop she'd visited a few weeks before. According to something she'd read, they could be depended upon to eat anything. Even lying bastards.

She wanted to push her hands into her hair and pull it out, cause herself pain for a change rather than allowing someone else to hurt her. Some fucking idiot like Rich. How could she have been so stupid? How? She was an intelligent woman; how could she have allowed herself to be treated so badly? How could she, at her age, believe that dreams came true, that she'd found the perfect man? He'd made her love him so desperately that even when she knew he wasn't perfect, she'd still wanted him.

He'd done this to her. Made her weak.

For that alone, she could kill him.

But could she really? It was a huge step up from destroying a man's reputation to destroying a man. She saw a strange smile twist Lydia's mouth and wondered what she was thinking. Did she really believe Fiona would agree to kill Rich? How did she know she was capable of such violence? Fiona was, of course. All those men in laneways who'd become victims of the self-defence course she'd taken in her twenties. She'd perfected the skill of the heel of her hand to a nose, her knee to a groin. True, no man had ever died from their injuries, nor, as far as she was aware, had any ever reported the attack. Their shame and guilt had silenced them.

But Lydia didn't know about any of that, so how did she know that Fiona might be willing to kill, and was definitely able? Sometimes, it was wiser to keep silent and let your opponent do the talking, so Fiona waited.

'Rich told me what you'd done to his son. How you'd managed to get him fired. Then you got the promotion you wanted. A woman like you will always find a way to succeed.' Lydia indicated the mobile phone that Fiona still held. 'That information is on Rich's computer. It'd be a shame if it found its way to the CEO of Donaldson and Partners, wouldn't it? After all your trouble.'

Fiona had underestimated the wife. The bitch was right. It would be a disaster if Fiona lost her job now that she'd lost her future with Rich. She shut her eyes, refusing to cry. Refusing to let the wife know how badly his betrayal had affected her. She loved him, had really believed he loved her. How terribly pathetic she was. 'If I kill Rich, you'll delete all that information; is that the way it goes?'

'That's exactly the way it goes.'

Fiona had destroyed the son; now she'd destroy the father. They both deserved it. 'Okay, I'm in. Assuming you have a plan, that is; I have no fancy for prison life.' She glanced around the apartment. 'Plus, as well as your assurance that the information will be destroyed, I'll need payment for being the instrument of death.' Financial compensation for having her heart broken and her dreams trashed.

'Money, eh?' Lydia rubbed her nose, as if the idea had a bad smell to it. 'You don't think getting revenge is enough?'

'It doesn't pay my mortgage. I'm thinking a million pounds might.' Having no idea how their finances stood, Fiona had plucked the figure from the air. The art of negotiation meant she had to start somewhere. And why not at the top?

But it seemed they were well matched in dramatics as Lydia cackled and slapped her hands on her knees. 'A million! If Rich gave you the impression we had that kind of money, he was a bigger liar than I gave him credit for.'

'I've seen the house you live in.' Fiona deliberately allowed her eyes to sweep over Lydia. 'But I'll admit, I've also seen the clothes you wear, so okay, you're not filthy rich; I'll settle for three hundred k.'

'I've seen the clothes you wear too. I'm guessing it costs a lot to look that tarty, but three hundred is still beyond my reach.' Lydia sighed as if coming to a decision. 'We're in this together. Fifty thousand is the best I can do.'

'We might be in it together,' Fiona said, 'but if I'm the one doing the deed; the risk is higher for me. One hundred thousand or I'm out.'

It wouldn't come close to clearing her mortgage but it would give her a safety net if she lost her job. Phillip had gone to a lot of trouble to get information to prove his case. It seems she wasn't done with him yet and her destruction of him might need to be more permanent. Like father, like son. She'd have to come up with a plan. It looked as if she wasn't the only one making them, though. She watched Lydia frown and blink rapidly, as if the little cogs in her head were spinning.

'One hundred k. Is it a deal?'

'Yes, but it's going to take me a while to get that amount together.'

'That's okay,' Fiona said, 'I'm not in a hurry. It's better to be careful anyway; we don't want to arouse any suspicion by moving money around too quickly. Let's settle on a month after the deed is done.'

Lydia hesitated before nodding slowly. 'I should manage that. Right, let's get down to the nitty-gritty then, shall we?'

The nitty-gritty? It made the idea of killing Rich seem so normal: an everyday occurrence on a list they could cross out when done.

'What do you have in mind?' Fiona held up a hand. 'Before we start discussing details, I'd better give my office a call. It seems you were right; I don't feel like going in today.' She could have said she was working from home or perhaps dragged that Japanese investor back into the limelight, but she didn't have the energy for more lies. Instead, she told a version of the truth. 'I've come down with something, Trish, so I'm staying home today. Later, if I'm feeling up to it, I'll check my emails so if anything comes up, just email me, okay?'

Trish sounded as bored, as usual. 'No problem, feel better soon.'

It hadn't been a lie. Fiona did feel sick. Betrayal had a bitter taste. It was corrosive too. She could feel it burning away hope and dreams. The pain of it all was unbelievable. If there had been any doubt, there wasn't any longer. She'd have killed him without Lydia's blackmail, without the added incentive of money. She'd kill him because the bastard didn't deserve to live.

'Right,' she said, getting to her feet, 'let me make some coffee and we can get down to it.'

They could sit, like two old friends, and plot how to kill Fiona's lover and Lydia's husband.

53

LYDIA

I wasn't surprised when Fiona fell in easily with my plan to kill Rich after I'd spun my tale about his treachery, but I was amused she believed every word I'd said so easily. Poor Fiona. She might be a canny businessperson, but like most women, she was an idiot when it came to love.

Or perhaps she'd known from the beginning that it was too good to be true. She was lucky. It took me over forty years to learn the same thing.

'My plan is simple,' I said when she'd handed me a mug of coffee. Of course she had one of those monstrous machines that grizzled and spat as it made it. I wanted to hate it, but it was the best coffee I'd tasted in a while. Had we been friends, I'd be begging her to know what brand it was. After a second sip, I put it down. 'May I assume you're going to the charity ball on Saturday?'

She had a face for poker. Not a glimmer of surprise at my question.

'Yes, I am.'

'I thought you might be.' My plan depended on it. 'Rich and I are staying overnight. Everyone is going to be out to impress, wearing all their finery, and that's my plan. A burglary-gone-wrong scenario.'

She looked decidedly unimpressed and I didn't have to have mind-reading abilities to know she was thinking *is that it?* What had she wanted? Some mundane plan to push Rich under a train, or bus, or to shoot him in a dark alley? I'd considered and discounted them all. CCTV in London made the first two almost impossible to get away with, and the latter required purchasing a gun, thereby involving a third party in our plan. And the more people involved, the more chance of mistakes. Anyway, I had no idea how to use a gun, and I doubted if she had either. My plan was simpler. 'When we return to our room after the event, you'll be waiting. You attack us both, steal our jewellery and escape the way you came in.'

Fiona laughed and shook her head in obvious disbelief. 'That's your plan? Fuck's sake, that's got failure stamped all over it! First of all, how do you think I'm going to break into your room? Climb up the bloody walls of the hotel like Spiderman? And even if I managed such a gravity-defying feat, what would I attack you with? My purse?'

She had no imagination. I could have found a weapon in her apartment. Could have killed her with the ugly lamp that sat on a side table. One swing of it against her head would have smashed her skull in. I could have done – maybe even would have done – if her death had served my purpose. It would have done a week ago, but now my objective was to get rid of Rich, not her.

'First of all, you don't need to scale any walls. These damn parties always go on far longer than they should so I checked the rooms to find one the furthest from the hall where it's being held. As it happens, it's their ground-floor room so I booked that.'

'Right, a ground-floor room. Unless they're the stupidest hotel owners in existence, that window will be alarmed.'

'It's an old hotel, and I've checked, it doesn't have air conditioning.' I reached for my phone and brought up photographs of the hotel. 'Here's one of the room we'll be in. With no air con, we'll have to be able to open the windows, therefore they won't be alarmed.'

'You think!'

I ignored her sarcasm. 'We're going down early. Rich is planning to play a round of golf that afternoon. We've asked for an early check in, so there'll be plenty of time to examine them.'

Fiona still didn't look convinced. 'If you're right, there's still the problem of how I get in. I'll be wearing fancy dress; it's not conducive to climbing in through windows.'

'If you're going to be difficult about every—'

'I'm not being difficult,' Fiona interrupted. 'I'm being practical.' She pointed to the photograph of the hotel room that was still displayed on my phone. 'If there's no alarm, then I bet there's a big drop on the outside. A professional burglar might very well be able to gain access but I'm not one, remember.'

There was silence as we glared at one another.

'Of course, I don't actually need to break in through the window,' Fiona said. 'It just needs to appear that someone did. I could get in through the door.'

The bitch was right. 'Okay, good. Yes, I'll keep the key or key card, whatever they use, and slip it to you during the night.' I nodded. Yes, that would work. 'When you get in, you could open the window, maybe break the glass.' I held up a hand. 'Actually, a better idea: I'll leave the window a little ajar so you could simply open it wide. Later, when the police ask, I'll play the grief-stricken wife who did such a foolish thing as to forget to shut the window properly.' I grinned. It would work perfectly.

'And the weapon?'

I indicated the picture of the hotel room on my mobile, but it was too late; the screen was blank. It didn't matter; the stupid cow obviously needed everything spelt out for her. 'There are lots of things in the room you could use, but even better, Rich always brings his golf clubs inside in case they're stolen from the car. The driver would be the best bet.'

Fiona's blank look irritated me and I was beginning to wonder if this was a really bad idea. How could a successful businesswoman have so little imagination?

'The driver is the golf club with the biggest head. You couldn't miss the target using it.' The target: my lying, cheating husband's head. I refused to let the reality of it deter me.

Fiona was still regarding me with a dull, vacant expression. I could laugh, tell her I was having her on, that I wanted to see how far I could go with her, then make my escape. Perhaps I would have done, if she hadn't suddenly said, 'Yes, that'd work. I could wait inside the door and as soon as I heard the door opening, I'd lift it and bring it down on his lying head.'

'Yes,' I sat forward. 'Then you'd need to hit me hard enough to leave bruising. It doesn't have to be hard enough to knock me unconscious. I can pretend I was. We just need to make sure Rich is dead before you leave.'

'I'll need to get some disposable gloves.'

'Yes, and make sure you take them with you when you leave and dispose of them carefully. We don't want to be caught by something stupid.'

'Right. And you need to get rid of anything dodgy from his computer beforehand, just in case.'

I knew what she meant. She wanted anything deleted that might implicate her if we were caught. I didn't blame her for asking, but despite my promises I wasn't planning to destroy anything. After all, I might need it.

But she wasn't stupid. I had to stop underestimating her.

She reached for her mobile, and a few seconds later my voice filled the silence. The bitch had been recording us since I arrived.

'I want you to kill him.'

When the six words rang out, she switched it off. 'Now we understand each other,' Fiona said. 'Now we both have information that would prove, how do I phrase it... let's go with *detrimental*. A nice word. Information that would prove *detrimental* to our future. So get rid of anything dodgy on his computer, okay?'

The bitch! My eyes flicked to that ugly lamp. But if I could kill, I wouldn't have needed her in the first place. 'Rich may have already handed over that information.' Of course he hadn't, and probably never intended to. I had thought about getting revenge on her for her part in the messy end of my marriage, by passing on all the details of her involvement in Phillip's downfall to her boss. Then I reminded myself that my priority was to get rid of Rich. Revenge could wait. For the moment, I needed her. 'If he has passed it on to his darling son,' I said, 'that's nothing to do with me.'

'He might have done, but I'm guessing he hasn't,' Fiona said calmly. 'Not yet. So you leave that to me. If he hasn't passed the information on by Saturday, he's not going to get the opportunity to, is he? Then it'll be up to you to destroy it. Once it's all over, and I get my money, then I'll delete this recording.'

She thought she was so damn clever. 'You seem to forget that you're on that recording too, agreeing to kill him.'

'Am I?' She pressed the recording to play again. After my words, it stopped. 'Oops,' she said. 'I must have shut it off early.'

'You...' I was so angry, that for a change I couldn't think of anything bad enough to call her. 'How can I trust you to delete that afterwards?'

She smiled. I imagined she used the same one in business when she'd done a deal. It held a hint of smugness, a touch of *I'm better than you*. I'm sure I wasn't the first who wanted to wipe it off her face with a hard swung slap. I couldn't. Not then when I needed her. But I'd remember it.

'I suppose you'll just have to take it on faith,' she said finally.

The bitch was right. I'd started this ball rolling; now I'd have to try to keep up with it, and at the same time, make sure it didn't flatten me on the way.

54

FIONA

For two women plotting to kill a man, they were extremely calm about it. They were sitting drinking freshly made coffee and going over the details. Or maybe it was like that old saying about swans – calm on top, paddling furiously below.

Fiona certainly was. She was sure Rich hadn't passed the information on to his son, because if he had done, Phillip would have gone straight to Matt. And *he* wouldn't have wasted time wondering where the information had come from before cutting her loose. She thought he'd take great pleasure in doing so; they'd never really gelled.

No, she didn't believe Rich had given his son the ammunition he'd been looking for as yet, and it was up to Fiona to make sure he didn't. *His son* – she was still shocked by that. The rest – the betrayal, the shattering of her dreams, the sheer cruelty of what he'd done – it was all smothered in layers of grief so deep, she was numb.

She forced herself to concentrate on the details of their plan. There weren't many. It was, as Lydia kept insisting, straightforward and simple.

'Yes, but I'm the one actually doing the evil deed,' Fiona pointed out. 'And there are far too many "if this happens, we do that" for my liking.' They had to wait until Lydia had access to the room early Saturday afternoon. Only then could she review the windows and finalise how Fiona was going to make it look like a break-in.

'I think, rather than you trying to find an opportunity to slip me the key to your room during the evening, you should make some excuse to return to unlock the door, then I could let myself in and open the window wide as if I'd come in that way.'

'Right, but what if it's a key card, not a key? It will simply lock itself again.'

Fiona gritted her teeth. Working with this stupid, unimaginative woman was a mistake. She could have handled Rich herself, could have made him suffer. If it wasn't for the information on his computer, she'd tell the wife she was pulling out, that it had been a crazy idea from the start. But that information was there, like an evil monster waiting to destroy her.

'If it's a key card, we go back to plan A, and you'll have to find a way to slip it to me during the evening.'

'Okay,' Lydia said slowly. 'Then you'll go in, open the window wide as if you'd come in that way, maybe knock over something as if you had.'

'What if the bigger windows can't be opened? It's a ground-floor room; the hotel has to be taking some precautions. There are smaller windows. They may only allow those to be opened and they'll be no bloody good to us.'

'As soon as we arrive, I'll check that out.' Lydia tapped her fingers on the side of the mug she was holding.

'And if there is no way I could get in through them?' Fiona asked when the minutes stretched out.

'If they don't, you'll have to jimmy the door to make it look as if you broke in that way.'

Fiona had to laugh. 'Jimmy the door. Do you even know what that means?'

'Force it open somehow.'

Fiona wasn't 100 hundred per cent sure what it meant but she guessed that was close. She also guessed Lydia had no more idea than she did on how to make a door that was supposed to be locked appear to have been forced open.

'Run at it, break it down with a blow from my muscular shoulder.' The words were heavily laced with sarcasm. Why had she agreed to get involved with this nonsense? Her eyes drifted around the apartment again. If the information Rich had got out, she'd lose her job, and she'd have to sell up. Probably at a loss.

'I think breaking it down would make too much noise. You need to have some kind of lever.'

Fiona looked back to Lydia and shook her head. 'Fuck's sake, I was being sarcastic! I'm not super-bloody-woman!' She held up a hand appeasingly. 'Listen, it looks as if we're just going to have to wait to see what we're dealing with. If the windows open, if I can make it look as if I got in that way, then we'll be okay, and I'll be waiting for you when you return.' She smiled, a wicked tilt of her lips that she saw made Lydia nervously lick hers. 'After all, it'd be better if I took you both by surprise, wouldn't it?'

There seemed to be nothing left to say and Fiona was relieved when Lydia stood to leave.

At the doorway, there was a moment of uncertainty. They weren't friends, but they were co-conspirators. How did they say goodbye?

It was Lydia who broke the uncomfortable silence. 'As soon as I check in, I'll be in touch. It should be shortly after midday.

I'm going to buy a pay-as-you-go phone to use so you won't recognise the number, okay?'

It was odd that it was something mundane that hammered the reality home. They were really going to do this. 'Yes, right,' Fiona said. 'Good plan.' It seemed the right thing to say, although she'd no idea why the wife had thought it was a necessary step.

When she was gone and the door shut, Fiona leant against it. Could she really do this? But all it took was the memory of the hope that Rich had stirred in her heart, the dreams that he'd made her believe could come true, the absolute fool he'd made of her, and the stinging grief that was oozing from beneath that layer of numbness, to harden her resolve. Yes, she could.

He'd used her; now it was her turn.

She didn't get to where she was by sitting back, waiting for things to happen. She wouldn't now.

First, she rang her office.

'Just checking in, Trish. No problems?'

'Nothing out of the ordinary. A few emails, but nothing that can't wait till you're back.'

Fiona heard the note of surprise in her secretary's voice at her call, at diligence Fiona used to think of as the norm. She'd been letting things slip. Worse, if Trish was noticing it, so would others. Something else Fiona could blame on Rich.

'Excellent. I'm already feeling a little better so I'm planning to be in after lunch. I'll deal with them then.'

She hung up and took a breath. Things may have slipped a little, but knowledge was power. She could fix things. Starting with Rich.

'Hi,' she said, when he answered her call almost immediately. 'Can you talk?'

'It's a bit manic this morning; can I get back to you later?'

Her fingers tightened on the phone. 'This can't wait. It'll just take a minute.' She was irritated to hear the pleading tone to her words. A few days ago, he'd have been begging to speak to her. Things had changed, and she knew why. The phone was pressed so tightly to her ear, she heard the sigh he tried to hide. If she hadn't already planned to kill him, she would have done then.

With another sigh, he said, 'Right, okay.'

She gritted her teeth, then choosing her words carefully, said, 'I know you accessed some private papers on my computer, Rich. I'm not sure why you felt the need to, and I guess you might have been horrified by what you read, so I thought I'd tell you that I'd already decided to do something about it.' She sniffed. Loudly. As if she was crying. 'What I did, my part in Phillip's dismissal, has been weighing on my mind so I've decided to put things right. I plan to go to the CEO and tell him everything.'

'Wow, well, okay, that's amazing.' There was silence for a few seconds and when he spoke again, his voice was more subdued. 'I did accidentally access some stuff and I'm really sorry about that, but wow, I'm so proud of you for sorting it all out.'

The hardest thing she'd ever done was to stop herself screaming at him that he was a bastard, that she'd loved him and he'd destroyed her. She was damned if she was going to give him the power of knowing that. His downfall was in her hands, she'd enjoy making sure it was complete. Meanwhile, she needed to protect her future and if that meant playing the helpless female for a bit longer, so be it.

'Thank you, that means so much. Matt, the CEO, is involved with the charity ball on Saturday. I think it's important not to throw a cloud over that so I'm going to wait till Monday before going to him and telling him everything. It probably means I'll be fired, but Phillip Coren will be where he deserves to be.' *At the bottom of the shit pile where I hope he drowns, the bastard.* 'I know you wouldn't say anything to anybody about what you saw on my computer...' Fiona drew a loud, ragged breath in what she considered to be an Oscar-worthy performance. 'You haven't, have you? I'd hate anyone else to know what a cow I've been. I'm really hoping to be able to get it sorted and put it behind me.' When there was silence, she added, 'I hope you don't think too badly of me either.'

'I don't think badly of you, and of course I haven't mentioned it to anybody.'

Fiona heard the ring of truth in his words and punched the air in satisfaction. He hadn't told Phillip, and if things went to plan, he never would.

55

RICH

Rich sat back in his chair and smiled. It was all going to be okay. Fiona would set the record straight; Phillip would go back to his role in Donaldson and Partners – and probably make a mess of it. Rich wasn't a fool, his son wasn't up to the position and it should have gone to Fiona in the first place.

Unfortunately, the CEO wouldn't be left with any option and she'd be fired.

She was going to need support. Rich rocked gently in his seat. He'd be there for her every day. He'd gone over and over the previous night's conversation and had finally concluded that he had indeed told Lydia that he was in love with Fiona. Lydia's response had been odd. He guessed she was in denial but he had no doubt that she'd come around eventually. She had to be aware as much as he that their relationship had reached the end of the line months, if not years, before.

He'd move into Fiona's apartment. It'd be nice to live in a modern, purpose-built place after living in the money pit he'd called home for so many years. More than nice to be with the woman he loved.

Phillip had been wrong about her. He'd called her 'a woman, morally corrupt, with no conscience'. Rich would take pleasure in telling him the truth.

He frowned when he saw the time. There was a meeting he needed to attend, but later, he'd make the call he'd been avoiding making all week.

It was several hours later before he had time to ring. 'Hi, it's...' He wondered about using *your father*, or *Dad*, but settled in the end for his name. 'Rich.'

'You've taken your time getting back to me, haven't you?'

It was guilt that made Rich hold his tongue. The intense, gut-rotting guilt that he'd sacrificed his marriage with little thought but hadn't been willing to sacrifice his second chance at happiness by giving Phillip the information he'd found on Fiona's computer. Now, thanks to her sense of what was right, her innate decency, Phillip would get what he wanted and never need to know the truth. 'I'm sorry. It took longer than I'd expected, but I have good news for you.'

'Good news, well, that'd be something. Tell me.'

No *thank you*, or *please*. Rich shook his head. Phillip might have had a happy childhood, but his parents missed out teaching him manners. Or was Rich just getting old?

'Fiona is going to confess her part in what happened. She's going to the CEO—'

'Matt Donaldson?'

'Yes. She's planning to go to him on Monday and tell him everything.'

'Monday! Why wait? Fuck's sake! Why isn't she going today?'

'There's that charity ball on Saturday. Donaldson's very involved with it, so he's tied up in meetings.'

'That's the ball where I'd hoped to be able to make an announcement. Everyone who is anyone will be there. I was going to tell them I had proof that bitch conspired to get rid of me. It'd have been the ideal opportunity.' He groaned loudly. 'Did you manage to get any proof of what she did, anything I can use? I don't have to bloody-well wait for her to decide to put things right.'

'I'm afraid not. You're just going to have to sit tight, I'm afraid.'

Rich had done enough. He wasn't sacrificing Fiona for a man he didn't know, a son he should never have had, the by-product of an illegal liaison. Rich didn't owe him anything and on that thought, he brushed the last of the guilt away. It wasn't his place to offer advice either, so he wasn't going to point out that hijacking a charity ball for his own ends was a bad, shoot-yourself-in-the-foot kind of idea that would have endeared Phillip to nobody.

'I'm sorry, but I have to go. When you're back in Donaldson's, give me a shout and we'll meet for lunch.'

'Sure, I'll do that.'

Rich knew he wouldn't. And he couldn't bring himself to care.

56

LYDIA

Cranford Castle, built in the sixteenth century, had been sympathetically converted to a twenty-five-bedroomed luxury hotel. As the venue for the Art United Christmas Charity Ball, it was perfectly situated just an hour's drive from the city. Those lucky enough to have thought far ahead, or to have been in the know, had booked a room to stay overnight. The rest either did the long drive home or stayed in other local hotels a taxi ride away.

The castle's demesne incorporated an eighteen-hole golf course which many of the attendees were hoping to avail of, and a walled garden which held little of interest so late in the year.

I would normally have been entranced by the view of the castle as we drove through the gates just before midday. Perhaps I should have made an effort, oohed and aahed at the view, as if everything was normal. Instead, I sat and silently stared at the place I'd chosen for Rich's demise.

'You okay?'

I kept my eyes fixed on the castle. How many times had he asked me the same thing in the past few days? He was puzzled by my lack of reaction to his announcement that he was in love with another woman. It was almost amusing. He probably thought I was in denial. Maybe he thought I was accompanying him to this ball to remind him what a good wife I was. The thought made me snort a laugh that I quickly converted into a cough. Rich had no idea what I was capable of. It wasn't surprising; I'd only discovered the presence of my inner monster recently.

'I'm fine,' I said, turning to look at him. 'It's a good day to play golf.'

It was. The sun had been shining since they left the city. There'd be no reason for him not to play. I'd be free to check out the room and that window situation and be able to breathe more freely when it was done. Once Fiona was in receipt of the information, the plan would be set in motion and there'd be no going back.

* * *

'Welcome to Cranford Castle,' the receptionist said.

'Thank you. Richard and Lydia Pickering-Davis,' Rich said. 'We have a reservation.'

The receptionist's fingers tapped a few keys on her keyboard. 'And you requested early check in,' she said, looking up with the smile still in place. 'So the room is all ready for you.' She reached behind for a large, ornate key and handed it to him. 'Would you like assistance with your luggage?'

'No, thanks, we're good,' Rich said. He handed me the key and picked up our cases.

A proper key. It was a good first step. An omen. Everything was going to work out just as we'd planned.

The receptionist pointed a manicured finger. 'If you head that way, follow the corridor as it turns left, your room is the last door. If there's anything you need, or anything we can do to make your stay more enjoyable, please let us know.'

We followed the directions to the room, where I slotted the key into the lock. It turned easily. Removing the key, I reached for the doorknob. It wasn't so obliging. It took a few seconds of twisting and rattling before I managed to push open the door. I'd have to warn Fiona; that rattling would sound louder at night.

The bedroom was large, with windows on two sides. In pride of place was a massive half-tester bed draped in a jewel-coloured throw. Matching heavy curtains hugged each side of the windows.

'Very nice,' Rich said, lifting my case onto the luggage rack. He walked to the door of the en suite and peered inside. 'Modern facilities, thank goodness.'

'It's a five-star hotel; what were you expecting, a bucket and ladle?'

From the corner of my eye, I saw him look up to the ceiling and sigh. He never could handle sarcasm.

'Are you going to play golf straight away?' I wanted him to go so I could get on with my plan.

'As soon as I change, if that's okay with you?'

I turned to him with a sweet smile that confused him. 'Of course, darling, take your time. There's no rush.' I nodded to the generously laid hospitality tray in the corner. 'I could make us a cup of tea, if you'd like.'

He shook his head as I knew he would. 'I'll change and be off.'

And five minutes later, he was true to his word. I waited till the door shut behind him before sitting on the bed and collapsing backward. Maybe I should stay there. Fall asleep. Forget about our stupid idea.

There was a small part of me that wished I could. If it had

been as simple as Rich falling in love with someone else, I might have eventually forgiven him. But it wasn't. He hadn't *simply* fallen in love with Fiona. He'd planned to use her to help a son he'd never known. A son he'd so little interest in that he was happy to forget about helping him when he had decided he was in love with Fiona. Choosing the son over me, then his mistress over his son, leaving me firmly at the bottom of the pile wallowing in the shit of rejection.

The small part of me that wished I could forget shrivelled and died. I could never forgive his betrayal. I was going to do this.

If Fiona knew that Rich really loved her and planned to leave me for her, would she forgive his initial deception? I wasn't sure. She struck me as being as tough as old boots, but love did strange things to people. It didn't matter; she wasn't going to find out the truth. I smiled. Not before she killed him anyway.

I sat up. Time to get working. The windows, as befitting a sixteenth-century castle, were mullioned. Keeping mental fingers crossed, I pushed down the lever on one of the windows and pushed. It didn't open. Peering through the small panes of glass, I could see why. It was too easily accessible. There were small windows near the top that did open, but skinny as the cow was, unless Fiona developed the power to miniaturise, she wasn't getting through them.

That was it. Fiona couldn't enter through the window, and the old and very solid bedroom door would be impossible to force open. Our plan had been childish and impractical. What had I been thinking? Relief made me sway and I reached out for support. One hand leant heavily on the glass as relief was swamped by a rising anger that Rich was going to get away with everything. That he might even get his happy ever bloody after. And me... I'd be the sad reject living in a soulless box.

Lost in my misery, it took a few minutes before I realised that my weight was making the mullioned panels of glass move. I stood back, then leant forward and gently pressed one of the smaller panes. As eureka moments go, it was pretty amazing. I went from the pit of despair to the giddy heights of impending success in seconds, because it only took that long to see that it'd be easy to push out enough glass and bend the aluminium frame to enable someone – AKA our imaginary burglar – to slip through.

I opened my case and dug amongst my clothes for the mobile I'd bought during the week. There was only one number on it and I pressed to ring.

'It's doable,' I said when it was answered. I quickly explained what she'd need to do. 'It'll just take a few minutes.' When there was no answer, I snapped an irritated, 'Fiona, are you listening?'

Was she getting second thoughts? I couldn't do this alone. Maybe it was for the best. It *was* a crazy idea. I was exhausted from the rollercoaster of emotion I'd been on for what felt like weeks. No wonder I felt sick. I was about to tell her it was over – everything – that I'd send the information to her boss and she could fuck the hell off, when she spoke again.

'Yes, I'm listening, but your idea has a huge problem. If I push the glass from the frame, it'll land outside, and I'm supposed to have broken in.'

Thinking of practicalities focused me and brought me back from the brink of giving up. Because the bitch was right. 'Okay,' I said, thinking on my feet. 'In that case, you'll have to go outside first and push the glass in.'

'You can do that, Lydia, because it seems like I'm the one taking all the risks!'

It might work better. I looked at the window. I could do it early in the evening. Rich would insist on going down in advance to make sure everything was going as expected. He'd be so busy glad-handing people he wouldn't notice if I disappeared for a few minutes.

'Yes, that'd work. Okay, leave that with me then.'

'Right, if that's it, I have to get ready.'

Suddenly, oddly, I didn't want her to go. 'You're okay with the rest of the plan, yes? You remember what to do?'

There was silence, then a loud, exaggerated sigh. 'Of course I remember. It's not rocket science. You're going to unlock your door during the evening. Once you begin saying goodbye to people, that's my signal to head to your room, where I'll have fifteen minutes to get ready for your arrival.'

'Watch the doorknob, by the way; it rattles,' I warned her. 'It'll be at least fifteen minutes. There's always someone who'll have had too much to drink and doesn't know when to shut up.'

'As long as it's not *less* than fifteen minutes, I'll be okay.'

'No, I'll make sure it's not. Right, I suppose that's it. We won't acknowledge each other tonight, okay?'

'The wife and the mistress huddled together.' Fiona laughed. 'Wouldn't that give them all something to talk about?'

'Nobody knows about you!' I was instantly annoyed with myself for reacting, for rising to the bait.

'You want to bet?' She laughed again. A cruel, mean sound. Then, just as I was about to hang up, I heard her sigh again. 'No, you're right. Rich was always very discreet. I was his guilty little secret.'

I almost felt sorry for her. But only almost. 'Right. I'll see you tonight.'

She hung up without answering.

57

FIONA

Fiona had debated finding someone drop-dead gorgeous to take with her to the ball, but she'd shelved the idea when she'd stupidly fallen in love with Rich. She hadn't wanted him to be jealous. Those kind of games were for insecure women and she hadn't classified herself among them. How smug she'd been. How stupid. So here she was, going to the ball with her friend and her friend's wife.

She wondered what they'd think if they knew what she'd planned to do that evening. It made her smile. They lived such a rarified existence, they'd never have believed she was capable of such an act. She hadn't told them Rich was going to be there, but since the world of finance was always well-represented at the ball, she guessed they'd know. Fiona wondered how many of the finance people who'd be present knew about her and Rich. Because she'd lied to Lydia; Fiona was fairly sure quite a few people knew about their relationship.

Both she and Rich knew so many people, discreet as they'd tried to be, it was hard to avoid seeing someone one or the other of them knew. Someone had honked a horn and waved at her while they were walking hand in hand back to her apartment one evening, and on another, someone had shouted a hello across the street to Rich. They were the people she knew who'd seen them; there were likely to be others. London could be annoyingly small when you didn't want it to be.

So no doubt, there'd be a few raised eyebrows seeing her and the wife at the same event. Those brows would rise higher if they knew what she and the wife had planned.

Fiona and her friends arrived on time and joined the throng of people entering the castle. Everyone was in fancy dress, which gave rise to much laughter and ribald comments. To Fiona's surprise, Jocelyn had given up on the idea of the drummer boy and drum costumes. 'It didn't seem fair to Kate.' Instead, the two women were dressed as fairies. 'It seemed appropriate,' Jocelyn said with a giggle.

'What are you supposed to be?' Kate asked, looking at Fiona so admiringly that Jocelyn punched her arm.

Fiona, making the most of her figure, had chosen a tight-fitting sequinned, ankle-length sheath dress. She raised both arms over her head and gave a wiggle. 'I'm tinsel.'

Jocelyn punched Kate again. 'Not for your Christmas tree, darling!'

Kate pulled her into a hug and kissed her cheek. 'She glitters, but you're my gold.'

Fiona gave another wiggle before dropping her arms. That was what she'd wanted. To be someone's gold. As she watched her friends saunter ahead of her, their arms wrapped around one another, hatred for Rich shot through her. He'd made her believe in the dream that she could have it all, had made her fall in love with him, had lied to her, used her. He deserved everything he had coming.

Forcing a smile, she joined her friends as they entered the function room.

'There's a surfeit of Santas,' Jocelyn said looking around. 'Honestly, have people no imagination?' She pointed to the bar. 'I spy champagne.'

A few minutes later, glasses of bubbly in hand, they were absorbed into a group of people. Fiona joined in with the conversation, the usual superficial chat she was used to on these occasions. Pretending to be interested in what people were saying but not giving a fuck. Especially that night, when she dropped in and out of the banter to scan the room for Rich and Lydia. Fiona needed to see them. To see him. Needed to keep that hatred for him on the boil. Otherwise, she wasn't sure she'd be able to go through with this crazy plan. Her life seemed to have taken on a surreal quality, as if she was a bit player in a bad play who wasn't quite sure of her lines or how the play was going to end.

It took a while to spot either Rich or Lydia. Almost every male, with a sad lack of imagination, was dressed as Santa. It was the wife she found first. She stood out for all the wrong reasons. Her Mrs Claus costume was cut too low over her ample bosom, and the wide, black belt encircling where her waist should be made her look as if she'd been cut into two parts. The thought made Fiona splutter a laugh. It surprised the man who was speaking to her in an earnest way that was out of place at a fancy-dress ball. 'Derivatives,' she murmured. 'I always find them amusing.' With a wave, she left him and headed to the bar. It probably wasn't wise to drink any more, but a second glass of champagne would help to steady her nerves. She stood sipping it and stared across the room. Rich was standing beside Lydia, barely recognisable in his Santa outfit, his belly grossly over-exaggerated, a fake beard almost obscuring his face.

He'd been surprised when she'd messaged him on

Wednesday morning to cancel their usual arrangement. 'I'm so caught up in planning what to say when I face the CEO on Monday that honestly, I don't have time for anything else right now.' It had been another Oscar-worthy performance.

'Yes, my goodness, of course. I'm really so proud of you. Next week, we can celebrate.'

'Next week, yes, that'd be good.' There didn't seem to be any point in telling him she'd see him at the ball. Let it be a surprise.

More a shock, Fiona thought, seeing Rich's eyes widen when he noticed her. How could he not, when she sashayed across the floor to greet an acquaintance standing only a few feet from him. Did Rich think she'd be at home, practising her lines for Monday? The idiot. She resisted the temptation to give him a little wave as she passed by, throwing him one of her favourite come-hither looks instead, pleased to see the quick colour race over his cheeks.

The bastard. She'd like to have run from the room, locked herself into a toilet cubicle, and given way to the tears that always seemed to be waiting. They filled her eyes and made her throat thick. 'A touch of hay fever,' she'd told Jocelyn earlier when Fiona had blown her nose for the umpteenth time.

She must have given a good performance, because her friend had appeared with a packet of antihistamine pills she'd sworn would help and insisted Fiona take one.

It didn't help, of course. There was no pill for heartache. She wasn't sure what she and Lydia had planned to do was going to help either. Was killing Rich really the answer? It wouldn't make the heartache or the sense of betrayal any easier. But if Fiona didn't kill him, that bitch of a wife would send the information to Matt, and Fiona's career would be over. It was all she had left; she couldn't see it destroyed. So it seemed she'd been left with little choice.

At the sit-down dinner, she was at a table of twelve people she knew well, making it a relaxing, convivial meal. The waiters were attentive and she noticed her wine glass never appeared to empty. And she was pretty sure she was drinking.

The after-dinner speeches seemed to drone on and on. The only one she gave any attention to was Rich's. For a manipulative, cheating bastard, he spoke well.

Then, with the food cleared and the lights dimmed, the real party began. A band began to play a series of upbeat, rhythmic tunes that had most people up dancing within minutes. Because it seemed churlish not to, Fiona danced with anybody who asked her. She'd never been a wallflower and it wasn't the time to start. Anyway, it was good to show Rich what he was missing.

When she wasn't dancing, drinks kept appearing in her hand and by some magic, the contents of each vanished.

She was taking a breather after a particularly energetic number when a voice hissed in her ear. 'For fuck's sake, I hope you're not drinking too much.'

Fiona turned to stare at Lydia. 'Relax, I'm fine. I'm dancing it off.'

'I've been watching you. You've been knocking them back like you've hollow legs.'

'Fuck off back to your husband, Lydia. As long as you've done your bit with the window, all will go as planned.'

'I've done my bit; now don't you mess it up.'

'I don't intend to.' Fiona held a hand up to a passing waiter and took a glass of champagne from his tray. 'Cheers!' She downed the contents in a couple of mouthfuls, handed the empty glass to a hatchet-faced Lydia, then rejoined the crowd on the dance floor.

As the night wore on, as the alcohol mellowed the anger and eased the pain, she wondered if it was all a crazy, bad idea. There was still time to get out of it. Time to call a halt to the madness. It was only when the music slowed, and she saw Rich and his wife dancing together, that the alcohol fog cleared and she remembered exactly why she was going to murder the bastard.

'No, thank you,' she said, when yet another Santa doppelganger asked to dance. 'I think I need a break.'

'I think you owe me a dance, at least.'

The voice sounded vaguely familiar, but it was impossible to identify the person behind the costume. 'I don't owe you anything,' she said. When the man grabbed her arm, she pulled away. He might have tried his luck again but she was saved by a conga line of Santas coming between them. When they were gone, so was she, leaving whoever it was behind to annoy somebody else.

The last energetic dance had left her feeling a little dizzy, but when she sat, the room continued to spin around her. She glanced at her watch but it took several seconds before she was able to focus enough to see the time. Almost midnight. Lydia had said they wouldn't leave the ball till one. Fiona had time to sober up. Maybe she'd have a lie-down somewhere. Yes, a lie-down. The idea seemed to take on epic proportions and it made complete sense that she'd avail of Lydia and Rich's room to have a little pre-murder rest.

She was almost giggling as she slipped from the function room, the noise and music fading as she followed the corridor around reception to where the bedroom was situated. When she reached the door, she stopped and glanced behind her before reaching for the doorknob. Was it going to open? Perhaps, like her, Lydia had had second thoughts. The doorknob didn't turn, and for a second, Fiona thought the door was still locked, but then she remembered Lydia's warning and twisted the knob again. With an ominous rattle, it turned and she pushed the door open.

It was a lovely room, even if the furnishing wasn't to her taste. After a cursory glance around, and noting the golf bag sitting in the corner, she crossed to the window and pulled back the curtain. Lydia had done her job well. The glass of one of the windows had been pushed through, the frame bent out of shape. She doubted very much if Lydia could have squeezed her rotund body through the gap but Fiona thought she could have done. The glass panes lay unbroken on the carpet. She walked on a few, the crack of breaking glass louder than she'd expected. Did it look like a believable scene? What about outside? Had Lydia thought to leave large footprints in the soil? Probably – she seemed to be a woman who thought of most things.

Fiona eyed the half-tester bed. It definitely wasn't her style. She sat on it, surprised to find it more comfortable than she'd expected. There was an hour to spare. It wouldn't do any harm to rest for a while. She sank back, shut her eyes, and thought about the man who'd abused her trust. He deserved to die.

A rest would do her good. She'd need energy to swing that club. The thought of bashing Rich's head in would keep her from falling asleep.

But of course, it didn't.

58

FIONA

It was the rattle of the doorknob that woke Fiona. Disorientated, she sat up abruptly and set her head spinning. Fuck! She looked around, trying to figure out where she was. There was a vague memory of dancing, and a clearer memory of drinking. Fuck, how much had she drunk? And where the hell was she? It was another rattle of the doorknob that cleared her thoughts a little. She was in Rich and Lydia's room. Shit, she'd fallen asleep.

The doorknob was still rattling. Good old Lydia, she was giving Fiona plenty of warning. The plan? What the hell was the plan? Focus, focus... Hadn't she promised to kill Rich? Yes, that was it, the bastard had lied to her. Lied to her, made her fall in love with him. All a great big lie. He deserved to die. Shit, she was supposed to have a golf club.

It took only seconds to slide from the bed and dash across to the corner where the golf bag's silhouette stood out in the hazy light that squeezed through a gap in the curtains.

Of course, she'd planned to have time to choose the correct club – the one with the biggest head – but that choice was gone and she felt for the first one, the metal cold in her hand. She pulled it free just as the door opened and Rich stepped inside, turning to look behind. He was highlighted in the light from the corridor behind, making him the perfect target. Before she could reconsider, before she could think that this was a very bad idea, before she weighed up the morality of taking a life, she swung the club high and aimed for his head.

The thwack as it connected with Rich's skull was loud and sickening.

Fiona stood with the club clenched between her two hands, then took a step backwards as Rich stumbled forward and fell heavily to the floor. She waited with the club raised, prepared to strike again, because when you've come this far, there's no going back, but he didn't stir. They needed to make sure he was dead, but she couldn't move. Her breath was coming in frantic gusts, as if she'd been running for her life, not taking one.

'Lydia, close the damn door before someone comes.'

But all that greeted her request was silence. 'Lydia,' Fiona hissed, afraid to move. What if he got up? She might simply have knocked him out. 'Lydia?' This time, the word quavered with uncertainty. Maybe the reality of what they'd done had been too much for the silly cow and she'd passed out in shock.

Rich hadn't moved. Keeping an eye on him, Fiona skirted around his body towards the open door. There was no sign of Lydia appearing. Nor, when Fiona peered around the edge of the doorway to look down the corridor, was there any sign of her. 'Fuck!' She had no choice but to shut the door and hope the wife would return.

A horrible thought struck Fiona. Had she been set up? Was Lydia at that very moment screaming for help in the function room? Was there someone already ringing for the police?

'Shit, shit, shit!' Fiona dropped the golf club and rushed into the en suite to grab a towel. She wiped the shaft of the club with it. Of course she'd brought gloves. They were rolled up in the bottom of her clutch bag because she'd stupidly fallen asleep and her careful plans had gone to shit. Replacing the towel, she hovered in the doorway of the bathroom before returning to Rich's side. He was still wearing that ridiculous Santa costume. Bizarrely, she thought it looked even more stupid now that he was laid out on the floor.

She needed to check he was dead. With no sign of Lydia returning, it seemed it was up to Fiona. It was impossible to do anything in the dark. Using her elbow, she switched on the light, then, taking a deep breath to calm her nerves, she hunkered down beside the body and reached for his wrist.

She'd done a first-aid course in her day and knew how to feel for a pulse. His skin was still warm. She couldn't feel a thing, but wasn't there something about peripheral circulation shutting down first? She couldn't really remember the details, but did remember being taught how to find the carotid pulse.

It meant moving to face him. Somewhere in the preceding hours, he'd lost his Santa hat, but he was still wearing that crazy white beard. She pushed it out of the way and slid two fingers along his neck. Nothing, not the merest quiver. Rich was definitely dead.

Should she have felt happy? Satisfied? At that moment, she felt nothing apart from the lingering worry that Lydia had set her up. It was time for Fiona to get out of there.

Her fingers were still on Rich's neck. It was probably her imagination, but his skin was already feeling cooler. She pulled her hand away. Too quickly, it dragged the beard with it. With a grunt, she leant closer to replace it and looked directly into the face of the man she'd murdered.

The man she'd murdered.
What an awful thing to have done.
Much, much worse, in fact, because when she looked into his face, she knew for certain it wasn't Rich.

59

LYDIA

I checked my watch for the thousandth time. It was ten minutes to one. We'd already said goodbye to most people, just a couple more that Rich was insisting he needed to have a word with before we left the party.

I saw Alice and Gerald heading towards us and wanted to cry. Once they started to talk, we could be there for an hour. But I was in luck.

'We're melting in these costumes,' Alice said, 'so we're going to head to our rooms. We'll see you for breakfast in the morning.' And with that, Tweedledee and Tweedledum waddled away.

'Give me our Santa costumes any day,' Rich said, smiling at me.

'Right.' I tried not to let my agitation show. 'Are you ready to go?'

'Relax, will you? It's not like we have to do the drive back to London.'

'Thank goodness.' I managed to smile while I was frantically scanning the room. It had been a while since I'd seen Fiona in that perfectly obscene dress. It was obvious to every woman in the room that she was wearing nothing under it. Absolutely nothing.

She'd been drinking far too much. I tried to warn her to take it easy, but she hadn't listened. She'd made a spectacle of herself on the dance floor too. Gyrating, twitching and twisting like the whore she was. But that had been an hour or two earlier. I couldn't remember having seen her recently. Hopefully, she'd seen us starting our round of goodbyes and had headed to our room as planned. They only had one chance; she'd better not mess it up.

'That was a good night,' Rich said when they were finally making their way to their room. 'Did you enjoy it?'

'Yes, it was very good. Best night ever.' I wanted to say that the best was yet to come, but I didn't want to tempt fate. A lot was depending on a woman I didn't trust.

'I think I might have had just a little bit too much to drink.'

He'd had more than a little. I didn't remonstrate; every man on death row was allowed a final meal.

I took the key from my bag and pushed his hand away when he reached for it. 'I think I can manage to open the door.' It wasn't locked and I didn't want to forewarn him. Didn't want him to run to reception to say our room had been broken into.

I made a big to-do of putting the key into the lock and I rattled the doorknob noisily to alert Fiona to our arrival. Luckily, drunk as he was, Rich was oblivious to my shenanigans.

'Finally,' I said loudly. I pushed the door open, then indicated that Rich go through before me. 'Before you fall down,' I said, then had to swallow the guffaw.

'You're in a strange mood,' he said, then did as he was told.

I stood in the corridor and saw the swish of the club as it sailed through the air. There was an audible thunk as it connected with Rich's hard head. For a few seconds, I thought it hadn't been a good enough strike and he was okay, then, with a strange cry, he fell over and hit the ground with a thump.

Reality is always more shocking than you expect, and so it was I was frozen in place for a few seconds before I hurriedly went into the room and shut the door behind me. I could see Fiona silhouetted against the glimmer of light coming through the window. She was standing still with the golf club gripped between her two hands.

'You did it!'

'Twice.'

With no idea what she meant, I reached for the light switch. 'That was some whack you gave him. I can't imagine he survived it.' I needed to make sure, but I had a strange reluctance to touch this man I had known for so long. 'I suppose we should be certain before we get on with things.' I wasn't looking forward to being belted with the club, but I had to suck it up. It was necessary if we wanted our plan to work.

Perhaps Fiona sensed my reluctance to be the one to check Rich, because she dropped the club and leant down to pick up his wrist. I noticed she'd been sensible and was wearing disposable gloves. After a few seconds, she placed his hand back where it had been and took a step towards his head. 'The carotid artery is the best indicator,' she said, placing a finger on his neck. She waited longer this time before getting to her feet. 'He's dead.' She looked me straight in the eye, a strange expression on her face. 'They're both dead.'

My husband and her lover. I thought that's what she was getting at, and still thought it as she pointed further into the room. Then I realised exactly what she meant.

'Wh...' I couldn't finish a word. Couldn't think whether to say who, what, or how. I simply stood with my mouth open, wondering how the hell we were going to deal with this.

'I thought it was Rich.'

I turned to her with a growl. 'You thought it was Rich? How the hell...' I held a hand up. 'No, don't bother trying to explain.' I ran the hand over my face. I swear I'd aged ten years in the last minute. 'Hang on, are you telling me we really were being burgled?'

'No, I'm not.' She shrugged. 'At least, I don't think so. He tried the door, then just came in. I'd fallen asleep and the rattle of the doorknob woke me. I thought it was you so I did what I was supposed to do.'

What she was supposed to do! 'You weren't *supposed* to kill a total stranger!'

'He isn't.'

'What?'

She pointed to the body. 'He isn't a stranger. It's Phillip Coren.'

I glared at her in disbelief. 'You're telling me that you accidentally happened to kill the man you got fired? A man who was trying to gather information from Rich to prove you were involved?'

'That's exactly what I'm saying!' She pointed to him again. 'What was he doing coming in here? I was expecting you and Rich. You know that. It's what we'd planned. When he came through the door, he was wearing the same shit-stupid costume Rich had been wearing, down to the same crappy beard. I didn't say, "Hang on, stop a minute, are you Rich, cos if so I need to kill you," I just swung the fucking club and clobbered him.' She heaved a breath. 'It wasn't until I was checking to make sure he was dead that I realised my error.'

'Your error!' This was a disaster. I needed to stay calm if there was any hope of finding a way out of this mess.

'Of course it was a fucking error! You don't think I lured him in to kill him, do you? Him first, then his father.' Her voice rose till she was almost shrieking. 'Fuck's sake I'm not a bloody monster!'

I glanced nervously towards the door. 'For goodness' sake, keep your voice down.'

Fiona rubbed a hand over her face and took a shuddering breath. 'Right,' she said. 'It's a done deal, but what the hell was he doing sneaking in here?'

It didn't matter but I thought I knew. 'He was talking to Rich earlier. Neither of them cared that I was listening.' As if I didn't exist, didn't matter. I'd stood there in that fucking expensive stupid costume and felt invisible. If there had been any doubt in my mind about what we were doing, it vanished in that moment. 'It seems that Phillip had wanted to do a big reveal tonight.' Despite everything, Fiona's startled expression made me smile. 'Yes, that had been his plan. Rich was supposed to get the proof that you'd set Phillip up, and he was going to expose you during the after-dinner speeches.' I looked at the body of my late husband's son and struggled to find any sympathy for him. 'He was being quite aggressive and drawing too much attention. To shut him up, I told him Rich had saved something on his phone that might help him.' I held up a hand to stop whatever it was Fiona was going to say. 'Relax, it was simply to shut him up and get him to go away. Rich never brings his phone to social events, so he told Phillip he'd have to wait until tomorrow.'

The band had begun to play a song I liked. I dragged Rich away to dance so he'd never had the opportunity to ask how I knew he'd anything incriminating on his phone. I hadn't seen Phillip again. How could I have anticipated his next move?

Hearing that he'd planned to expose her in front of everyone, had helped Fiona to regain her composure. She turned to stare at the dead man's body with obvious dislike. 'It looks like he wasn't happy to be kept waiting.'

'Impatience can be a killer,' I said. 'The stupid bastard has left us with a major headache though, hasn't he? What the hell are we going to do now?' What I'd liked to have done was to lie down on the bed, go to sleep, then wake up and discover it had all been a dream.

'We go on as planned.'

Fiona's voice was surprisingly firm for someone who had just murdered two people. I had to remind myself what she was capable of. I didn't want to be her third time lucky.

Since I couldn't think of anything to say, I waited for her to continue.

'I had time to think after killing him.' She nodded towards Phillip. 'Going on as planned seems to be the only thing to do. Did anyone see you on the way here?'

'No, we said our goodbyes and came straight. There's a different exit to the car park from the function room so reception was unmanned when we passed by.'

'Good. Right, then that's your story. Rich wanted to give Phillip something, so he came back with you.'

I was beginning to feel dizzy as I tried to incorporate this new plan into the old one. 'Give him what?'

She paced the room, muttering, before turning to me with a grin. 'A present. A posh watch. He'd bought it for his son, had it engraved.'

I saw where she was coming from. 'And of course the burglar stole it.'

'Exactly!'

'It could work.' Actually, we didn't have any choice. It had to work. 'I could say they were both very drunk, which made them easier to overpower.'

'Yes. That's it. But don't over-embellish.' Fiona bent to pick up the golf club. 'Don't forget, you're going to be a victim too. Your memory of events may very well be affected.'

I watched her, saw the streak of cruelty in her eyes, the nasty tilt of her lips, and held my hand up to stop her. This was a very bad idea. 'I...'

And that was all I remembered for some time.

60

LYDIA

A Month Later

Although Christmas was over and a new year already ticking on, there were still festive lights strung on the canal boats docked along the Thames. I leant on the rail and stared at their refection in the water. But if there had been any cheer in their glow, it had already dispersed.

With a sigh, I pushed away from the rail, shoved my hands into my pockets and wished I'd dressed for the cold weather, rather than trying to make a fashion statement by wearing a coat designed for more springlike days. I hoped I wouldn't be waiting long but even as I finished that thought, I became aware of a presence behind me.

This was London; it was always sensible to be alert. I'd been on edge all day at the prospect of meeting Fiona after so long. It was sensible to be wary of her, but then, she'd reason to be wary of me too.

'You're late,' I said, finally turning around to face her. It was irritating to see she was dressed for the cold night in a thick, padded coat, a wool scarf wrapped around her neck, a hat with a ridiculously large pompom pulled down almost to her eyebrows. Dressed for the weather, she still looking stunning and I remembered how much I hated her.

'I was being careful.'

I dragged my attention from her clothes to her face and laughed at her worried expression. 'What? You afraid I'm being followed by the police? That maybe I'm wearing a wire so they can catch you saying you murdered Rich and Phillip?'

She stepped to the rail and gripped it with her sensible, leather-gloved hands. 'You were so insistent that we meet up—'

'It was what we agreed, remember?' I interrupted, surprised by the tremble in her voice. Was she haunted by the memories of killing the two men? Did she wake every night with the feel of the golf club between her hands? Did the echo of the sound as she smashed in their skulls fill the darkness? Did she lie there, on her own, and wonder how she could have done such a thing?

I hoped so, because I did. I woke in my empty home to the sound of Rich's skull being crushed. I walked around the rooms during the day, trying to find the memories, but they were gone, painted over by what we'd done – what *I'd* done.

I joined Fiona at the rail, staring straight ahead rather than looking at her face. Our arms were brushing and it would have been nice to think there was some kind of camaraderie between us, but I'd stopped fooling myself. Murder will do that to you. It makes you see things in blunt black and white.

I opened my bag, took out a parcel wrapped in festive paper and nudged her arm with it. 'Here, Happy New Year.'

She took it without a word of thanks. Without opening it, she shoved it into the leather satchel that hung from her shoulder. 'I assume it's as we agreed?'

'Of course.' I waited patiently, refusing to give her the satisfaction of asking for the items I knew she'd be carrying. My fingers were starting to feel numb. I envied her the leather gloves, the scarf, even that bloody ridiculous hat. I took my cold hand from my pocket and rested it palm up on the rail without a word.

'Right,' she said, as if all of this was just the same old same old to her. She reached into the pocket of her jacket, then there they were, in the palm of my hand.

I looked at them for a few seconds, then picked them up, one after the other, and threw them into the water. Rich's wedding ring, mine, my engagement ring. I wanted to believe I heard the plink as they hit the water, but of course I didn't. 'What about the watch?'

She sighed but handed it over. 'It's worth twenty grand, you know, maybe more.'

I knew; I'd bought it for Rich's fiftieth birthday. 'Safer to get rid of it.' I threw it, and this time, I was sure I heard the splash as it hit the water and sank from sight. There was only one thing left. 'The recording you made, have you deleted it?'

'Yes, of course,' she said, shooting me a look that told me she was telling the truth.

'Good, and you'll be relieved to know I got rid of all the information on Rich's computer too.'

Fiona tucked her hand into the crook of my arm. 'So, it's over.'

There was something oddly comforting about her hand. It might be over, there might be no camaraderie as such, but the link between me and this woman I'd hated, still hated, was real and probably unbreakable.

'I never got the opportunity to apologise,' she said, the words almost a whisper. 'I didn't mean to hit you quite so hard the second time, but you were confused, talking about having to get to the phone to ring for help, and I needed time to stage the robbery.'

She was lying. Her first blow had knocked me out, but only briefly. When I came to, I was confused. For a moment, I believed Rich and I had really been attacked and I needed to get help. But it was only a momentary lapse, and I had already remembered my part in our plan when I saw her lift the golf club. There was a twisted smirk on her lips, and I knew she was going to kill me.

That she hadn't manage to do so was down to luck and my thick skull. I was in a coma for forty-eight hours. When I came to, I was groggy and barely lucid. The doctors told me it was possible that I'd suffer some residual memory loss. It worked in my favour when I was interviewed by the police. My account of what had occurred that night was peppered with *I can't remember* as I tried desperately to recall what I was supposed to be saying about the sequence of events that had led to the death of my husband and his son.

Unfortunately, I wasn't able to tell them that I believed Fiona had tried to double-cross me. I wasn't even entirely sure she'd planned it. I'd had a lot of time lying in the hospital bed to give the situation some thought. Accidentally killing Phillip, a man she'd already professionally destroyed, had been the trigger. I imagined her, in our hotel room, standing over the dead body, knowing she had no choice but to go ahead with the plan. She couldn't confess and say she'd accidentally killed him, couldn't simply run away and hope I wouldn't tell the police everything. She must have been enraged, that even dead, Phillip was still causing her problems. It was that rage she harnessed to keep going with the plan to kill Rich. I'd seen it bubbling in her as she'd stood over him to check he was dead. I'd seen it glint in her eyes and should have known that she'd decided it would be better to rid herself of all the loose strings.

One blow had killed both Phillip and Rich. It must have horrified her to see me coming round and trying to get help. Had I been confused, or had I realised the danger I was in? I'm not sure.

Had she checked to see if I was alive after the second blow? Perhaps, as she'd wrenched the rings off my finger, she'd seen I was, but couldn't bring herself to strike me a third time. She'd have hoped that the injuries she'd already inflicted would see me off.

They almost had.

'Forget about it,' I said. 'And all of this. Forget it all. We'll never meet again. If we bump into each other, we're strangers, okay?'

Instead of answering, she pulled her hand back and shoved it into her pocket. 'He deserved it, didn't he?'

I heard the regret in her voice.

'Of course he did,' I said. 'He cheated on me. And he was going to leave me for you.'

She looked at me, startled. 'What?'

'Oh yes, I probably should have told you, shouldn't I? Rich told me he was in love with you. He had initially met up with you in order to get information to help Phillip, but that all changed when he thought he'd fallen in love. And just like that,' I clicked my fingers in the air, 'Phillip and I were tossed aside. A son he didn't know, and me, his wife of forty years.' It still galled me, probably always would, how Rich could simply move on, like a child in a toy shop tempted by the shiny new to leave behind the old favourite.

That he'd never get to enjoy the new gave me some satisfaction. More came from destroying the woman who was staring at me. Had she really thought she could ruin my life with no repercussions? The stupid woman knew better now. I could see disbelief vie with angry acknowledgement, rage fight with heartbreaking realisation as the sharp blade of truth sliced through her. She'd been used. Not only that, but she'd also murdered a man she loved, one who'd loved her.

She seemed suddenly older. Less beautiful. More like me. It seemed, in heartache, we all looked the same.

'You told me—' Her voice was sharp with anger and bitterness.

'I told you the truth: that Rich had been using you to get information for Phillip. You must have had your own doubts about your relationship with my husband to make you believe it was all a lie.' I could see it in her eyes, I was right, something had happened to cause her to doubt. Something Rich had done or said – him and his stupid lies. He'd never learnt.

'If he'd told me about his son—'

'You'd have forgiven him, wouldn't you?' I sniffed when I saw the answer in her eyes. Of course she would. To give the bitch some credit, I think she really did love Rich. 'Yes, you would have. He'd have left me, and I'd have had nothing.'

'And now?'

I heard the sneer in her voice.

'Now we've both lost him.' But I still had my home. I didn't have to see him walk away with her, leaving me behind like confetti littering a church yard after a wedding, slowly fading and decomposing until nothing remained. And she wasn't getting off scot-free for her part in the end of my marriage. I'd told her the truth – I had got rid of the information on Rich's computer, but not the way she thought. I'd sent it to her boss, Matt Donaldson.

I watched her walk away, that stupid pompom bobbing with every step, and knew I'd see her again. She'd soon know I'd lied, and no doubt would come looking for revenge.

I needed to be careful. She'd killed twice; I didn't want to be number three.

I stared out across the Thames and smiled. My last crazy plan to deal with a problem had worked. I simply needed to come up with another...

61

Fiona walked with her shoulders hunched, arms held rigidly by her side, gloved hands clenched. The heat of fury made her pull off her hat and fling it away.

Rich was going to leave his wife for her. He'd truly loved her. Fiona had almost had it all – the happy ever after she'd fantasised about. She brushed away the tears. If she kept thinking about what she'd lost – what she'd done – she'd go mad.

She unbuttoned her coat and walked the remaining distance to the tube station with it flapping around her. Like an avenging angel.

Fiona had killed twice. Third time was a charm.

Lydia would soon learn she'd messed with the wrong woman.

***

MORE FROM VALERIE KEOGH

Another book from Valerie Keogh, *The Sister*, is available to order now here:

https://mybook.to/TheSisterBackAd

ACKNOWLEDGEMENTS

As usual, thanks go to every member of the amazing Boldwood team, with special thanks to my editor, Emily Ruston, copy editor, Emily Reader, and proofreader, Shirley Khan. A huge thank you also to marketing guru Jenna Houston.

Thank you to everyone who buys my books, and for every reviewer and blogger who helps to spread the word.

The Wings of Hope auction was held earlier this year to raise funds for Brain Tumour Research and Birmingham Children's Hospital charity. I was delighted to help by donating the opportunity to have the winner's name used in this book. Lydia Pickering-Davis's husband made the winning bid. I hope you enjoy your character, Lydia.

As ever, thank you to my wonderful, ever-increasing family.

If anyone is curious:

'To err is human, to forgive divine.' From Alexander Pope's poem, 'An Essay on Criticism', Part II (1711).

'Heav'n has no rage, like love to hatred turn'd, nor hell a fury, like a woman scorn'd.' From the Restoration play, *The Mourning Bride* by William Congreve (1697).

'Never Wanted To Be That Girl' is the title of a song composed and sung by Carly Pearse and Ashley McBryde – if you listen to it, you can see where I got the original inspiration for this story.

I love to hear from readers. You can find me here:

Facebook: https://www.facebook.com/valeriekeoghnovels

X/Twitter: https://twitter.com/ValerieKeogh1
Instagram: https://www.instagram.com/valeriekeogh2
BookBub: https://www.bookbub.com/authors/valerie-keogh
Author Central: https://www.amazon.co.uk/Valerie-Keogh/e/B00LK0NMB8

ABOUT THE AUTHOR

Valerie Keogh is the internationally bestselling author of several psychological thrillers and crime series. She originally comes from Dublin but now lives in Wiltshire and worked as a nurse for many years.

Download your exclusive bonus content from Valerie Keogh here:

Follow Valerie on social media here:

- facebook.com/valeriekeoghnovels
- x.com/ValerieKeogh1
- instagram.com/valeriekeogh2
- bookbub.com/authors/valerie-keogh

ALSO BY VALERIE KEOGH

The Lodger

The Widow

The Trophy Wife

The Librarian

The Nurse

The Lawyer

The House Keeper

The Mistress

The Mother

The Wives

The Bookseller

The Writer

His Other Woman

The Sister

THE Murder LIST

THE MURDER LIST IS A NEWSLETTER DEDICATED TO SPINE-CHILLING FICTION AND GRIPPING PAGE-TURNERS!

SIGN UP TO MAKE SURE YOU'RE ON OUR HIT LIST FOR EXCLUSIVE DEALS, AUTHOR CONTENT, AND COMPETITIONS.

SIGN UP TO OUR NEWSLETTER

BIT.LY/THEMURDERLISTNEWS

Boldwood

Boldwood Books is an award-winning fiction publishing company seeking out the best stories from around the world.

Find out more at www.boldwoodbooks.com

Join our reader community for brilliant books, competitions and offers!

Follow us
@BoldwoodBooks
@TheBoldBookClub

Sign up to our weekly deals newsletter

https://bit.ly/BoldwoodBNewsletter